The
Great Scot

Also by Duncan A. Bruce

The Mark of the Scots
The Scottish 100

The
Great Scot

A NOVEL OF ROBERT THE BRUCE,
SCOTLAND'S LEGENDARY WARRIOR KING

Duncan A. Bruce

T·T

TRUMAN TALLEY BOOKS
ST. MARTIN'S PRESS
NEW YORK

www.stmartins.com

Design by Phil Mazzone
map by Elisa Pugliese

Library of Congress Cataloging-in-Publication Data

Bruce, Duncan A.
    The great Scot : a novel of Robert the Bruce, Scotland's legendary warrior king / Duncan A. Bruce
        p. cm.
    ISBN 0-312-32396-4
    EAN 978-0312-32396-7
    1. Robert I, King of Scots, 1274–1329—Fiction. 2. Scotland—History—Robert I, 1306–1329—Fiction. 3. Scotland—Kings and rulers—Fiction. I. Title.

PS3602.R825G74 2004
813'.6—dc22

                                                    2003070880

First Edition: August 2004

10 9 8 7 6 5 4 3 2 1

For Jenny

Contents

Contents

Part Two: The Way to Holyrood

Part Three: Rest

Prinicipal Characters

Robert Bruce, also known as Robert de Bruce, Robert the Bruce, Robert I, King of Scots, King Robert, sometime Earl of Carrick and Lord of Annandale. Freed Scotland from English rule and unified the Scottish nation. Ancestor of the present royal family.

David (Davie) Crawford, page, soldier, and later confidant of King Robert. The narrator of the book.

Sir William Wallace, Scottish hero who began the War of Independence and was captured and executed by the English. Predecessor to King Robert.

Principal Characters

Edward Bruce, King Robert's brother, sometime Earl of Carrick, eventually high king of Ireland. One of his brother's principal captains.

John Comyn (the Red Comyn), enemy of the Bruces, killed by Robert Bruce.

King Edward I, one of England's most powerful kings, who styled himself the Hammer of the Scots. Strove to subdue Scotland and steadfastly refused to acknowledge the country's independence.

King Edward II, son of Edward I. Refused to acknowledge Scotland's independence. Deposed and murdered in England.

King Edward III, son of Edward II. Acknowledged the independence of Scotland.

James Douglas, the Black Douglas or Good Sir James, depending on whether one's perspective is English or Scottish. One of King Robert's principal captains.

Thomas Randolph, Earl of Moray. King Robert's nephew and one of his principal captains.

Isabel of Fife, Countess of Buchan, Lady Isabel. A member of the Clan MacDuff, which had the hereditary right to crown the Scottish monarchs. Married to the Earl of Buchan, who was a Comyn and an enemy of the Bruces.

Principal Characters

Elizabeth de Burgh, wife and queen of King Robert. Daughter of the Earl of Ulster, who was a close friend of King Edward I.

Alexander Bruce, King Robert's brother, a Cambridge scholar killed by the English.

Thomas Bruce, King Robert's brother, killed by the English.

Nigel Bruce, King Robert's brother, killed by the English.

Mary and Christian Bruce, King Robert's sisters, captured by the English and ransomed.

Marjorie Bruce, King Robert's daughter, captured by the English and ransomed. Married Walter Stewart and eventually founded the Stewart dynasty of kings by being the mother of Robert Stewart, King Robert II, the first Stewart king. Ancestor of the present royal family.

Christiana Macruarie, Lady Christiana of the Isles. A supporter and friend of King Robert.

Lady Christian of Carrick, a friend and supporter of King Robert.

Màiri Crawford, wife of Davie Crawford.

Seumas and Iseabal (Ishbel) Crawford, children of Davie and Màiri Crawford.

Principal Characters

Bishop Lamberton of Saint Andrew's and **Bishop Wishart** of Glasgow. Clerics who bravely supported King Robert and Scottish independence.

Angus Og Macdonald, powerful Highland chief and ally of the Bruces.

Neil Campbell, ally of the Bruces. Married to Mary Bruce, King Robert's sister.

John Macdougall, John of Lorne. Highland chief who was an enemy of the Bruces.

Macdouall clan of the southwest. Enemies of the Bruces.

Bernard, Abbot of Arbroath Abbey, Chancellor of Scotland.

Philip Mowbray, Scottish knight in the service of England.

Cuthbert, an English spy in the service of Scotland.

Aymer de Valence, prominent English soldier.

Robert Clifford, prominent English soldier.

Introduction

My name is David Crawford, and I am going to tell you one of the most exciting and inspiring stories you will ever read. It is the story of the war that liberated Scotland from English control and restored Scottish independence, and of the one man who was indispensable to making that happen, Robert Bruce. It is also my own story, since my life was closely linked to his. So much was achieved by the Bruce, against such impossible odds, that the story may seem improbable. Some might say that it would not be believable even as fiction, like the fables Chaucer is now writing in England. But what I have to tell here is not fiction. My story may seem like a blown-up myth, but it is, nevertheless, the truth, and I was witness to most of its scenes.

My work is different from Chaucer's also, since the

languages we use, though related, are quite different. His speech is based on the Saxon dialects of the south of England, whereas mine is based on the old Anglian speech of northern England and southern Scotland. I think it would be clearer to call our speech Anglish and Chaucer's speech Saxonish, but common usage is already determining that our speech be called Scots and his English.

There is another language widely spoken in my country, Gaelic. This Celtic tongue is completely different from both Chaucer's and mine. Gaelic is the native language of Ireland, and the fact that many Scots speak Gaelic shows that we are partly of Irish descent. This is something important that differentiates us from the English. Also, since the Normans conquered England three centuries ago, and many Normans were subsequently invited to settle in Scotland and were given land by Scottish kings, some people in both Scotland and England, usually landed people, speak French. My first language is Scots, but I know Gaelic and French as well, so you will find all three within these pages.

The world is changing just now. There is new thinking in Italy by men such as Petrarca, Dante, and Boccaccio. These men are brilliant, ushering a new era of understanding and learning. It is as if jewels have suddenly been discovered in the darkness of a sealed room. I am writing this at my estate in the Highlands of Scotland. I am, therefore, in a remote part of a small country that is, in turn, located on the margin of this new civilisation. But I can be proud that this rebirth of learning, "*renaissance*" the French call it, has been prepared for, in part, by the works of two of my

Introduction

countrymen. The first, John Duns Scotus, also famous as Doctor Subtilis, died earlier in this century. Before Duns Scotus there was another, Michael Scot, also known as the Wizard. These Scots were renowned for their learning all over Europe.

What we have accomplished here in Scotland in my own time may have an influence on the political philosophy of the world. During the reign of King Robert I, the Bruce, Scotland became the first country to insist that the governors must have the consent of the governed, that freedom must be defended at all costs, and that oppressive governments must be replaced. I cannot know, of course, whether our ideas will be used in other places or in future generations.

I am a retired soldier and have decided to begin to write this memoir in my sixtieth year. I hope that Divine Providence will grant me the time to finish it. I was privileged to have served Robert Bruce from almost the moment he began his rise to power until his death. He was by far the most extraordinary man I ever met and I believe one of the most remarkable that I have ever heard of in history. I was with King Robert in most of his important battles and shared many of his private moments that have never been recorded previously.

DAVID CRAWFORD

ARDNABREAC, ARGYLL

MAY 16, 1352

Part One

The Road to Bannockburn

1306–1314

CHAPTER ONE

Sacrilegious Murder

My girl, Leezie Maxwell, stood in the doorway smiling at me. She looked beautiful there in the moonlight and I kissed her earnestly. Her dark eyes sparkled with mischief in the cold air. She waved good-bye to me and, still smiling, closed the door, leaving me out on the main street of the town of Dumfries. I had just turned fourteen and had come to town looking for adventure. I wanted especially to see Leezie, but also hoped that I might meet a few of the lads for a jug of ale.

I had walked the few miles to the town from my mother's croft. My mother and I were poor, but we were never hungry. We had some chickens and a cow and we grew vegetables in our little plot. And there were fish aplenty in the river nearby. The laird didn't ask us for much rent. Only three chickens at Lammas, two score eggs at Candlemas, and a stone of butter around Michaelmas. We had more milk and eggs than we could use, so we sold some at the weekly market. My father, John Crawford, I can barely remember. He was a small *feu* holder, and was killed at Falkirk in 1298, fighting alongside the great William Wallace. He had lived only thirty-seven years. My mother told me that my father had a deep hatred of the English soldiers who were occupying many of the castles in our country. One time, for no apparent reason, an English officer had slapped him so hard he fell in a filthy ditch. My father never forgot that incident, and volunteered, along with many Scots, to fight for freedom with Wallace.

It was evening when I got to Dumfries. February 10, 1306, was the date, and it shall never leave my mind. The sun had long since set and it was dark. What light there was came from a weak moon, reflected by a thin layer of fresh snow. There were lights in some of the windows, but no one was moving about on the street, so far as I could see. This was not unusual, as many folk were afraid to be outside, what with the English troops occupying the town. I stood by a stone building and drew my cloak up around my neck against the chill. And then my world changed— aye, the world of Scotland itself would change within minutes. Into the street thundered several mounted riders. In the centre of the group, I could scarcely believe it, was none other than Robert Bruce, the Earl of Carrick. He was wearing light armour and that unmistakable coat of arms of the Bruces of Annandale with its stunning reds and golds. It wasn't often a lad such as I would see so great a personage. Bruce had been one of the Guardians of Scotland, and was a claimant to the throne of the country. And Scotland needed a strong king desperately, as it had been a long twenty years since the untimely death of our great king Alexander III. For all that time the succession had been in doubt, and the English king, Edward I, was using this opportunity to try to impose his will on us. King Edward was claiming an overlordship of Scotland and his soldiers were occupying our castles. King Edward hated the Scots. He even called himself "The Hammer of the Scots," as if he was bent on crushing us. We had all heard that King Edward offered to support the Bruce's claim to the throne, but only if he would acknowledge the supremacy of England. King Edward had even promised, "*Gyff thow will hald in cheyff off me I sall do swa thow sall be king.*" But Robert Bruce had made it clear that if he were to become King of Scots his reign would be completely independent of England, and this enraged the English king. Why it should have I don't know, since our little kingdom of Scotland had been proudly existing centuries before the kingdom of England was even born.

Most of us country folk in southwest Scotland knew all about the Bruce. He was by far the most important person in the entire area, and we wished that he would become our king and lead us to freedom from the damned English, who were occupying our land and treating us like vermin. We ordinary people were choking on this rule by foreigners. We couldn't breathe without running into an English soldier. They helped themselves to whatever of ours they fancied, including our homes and our women. We wanted to live free, under our own laws. But most of the nobles, like the Bruces, were vacillating as to whether they were Scots or Englishmen. You see, most of the Scottish nobles were of Norman origin, often speaking French instead of Scots, and holding lands on both sides of the border. Most English nobles spoke French, too. In fact, the Normans were so powerful in England that the English language was dying out. The Bruces were, despite their Norman origin, of solidly Scottish noble ancestry on their maternal side. But the Earl of Carrick had not made up his mind; instead he was hedging his bets. Although he considered himself a patriotic Scot, his lands in England made him one of the richest men in that country. He was trying to keep what he had in both countries, and the pressure on him was great.

The noble party dismounted right outside the church known as Greyfriars, and Bruce went inside the chapel, leaving the others behind. I was fascinated and moved closer in the darkness so that I could better see what was happening. I didn't know then that John Comyn, called the Red Comyn, another former Guardian of Scotland, would arrive in minutes, but he did. And now I had seen two of the greatest men in Scotland one after the other. Comyn arrived with another knight, whom I later learned was his uncle, and they dismounted and gave an icy greeting to the Bruce party. It seemed obvious that these two great nobles, each with strong claim to the crown, and probably the two most powerful men in Scotland, should dislike each other. As joint Guardians there had been such a great friction between them that governing had been difficult. The Red Comyn went inside the chapel, motioning for his uncle to stay outside. To me it looked like the meeting had been prearranged and that the two great men wished to meet alone.

I couldn't resist the temptation to see all of this and moved closer to the chapel. I knew there was a side door to the sanctuary, and I entered as quietly and as quickly as I could, hiding myself behind a pillar. The inside of the chapel looked beautiful, glowing in the yellow light of the tapers on the walls. Bruce was seated in one of many wooden chairs that were arranged in ranks throughout, but he had taken his chair up to the high altar. He was sitting right there on the platform and it looked improper to me; perhaps not sacrilegious, but unseemly at least. Even seated the Bruce looked strong. He had a ruggedly handsome face, his thick, black hair set off by deep blue eyes. His frame was powerful and he looked resolute sitting there, all alone in the quiet of the chapel, when the Red Comyn entered. The stillness was broken as Comyn stalked in measured strides toward the altar, his boots echoing throughout the empty chapel and his spurs jangling. Comyn appeared arrogant as he swaggered foward, the coat on his chest adorned with the blue and gold colours of his family's arms. Bruce rose to meet him. There they were, just a few steps from me—the two former joint Guardians of the Realm of all Scotland. I was, I assure you, quite beside myself with excitement. Then these two great nobles, both strongly built, embraced and kissed—and then (it seemed to me to be a bad omen) they retreated so that they were standing more than a yard apart.

Bruce began to talk. He asked Comyn how he had been, and Comyn replied that he had been well, and asked how

Bruce's affairs were going. Bruce answered that things were going very badly indeed, and suddenly, in great agitation, he produced from underneath his coat of arms a document that he waved at Comyn. His voice was angry, and he said something in French I couldn't understand.

"What's wrong with that?" said Comyn in Scots. "Isn't that the indenture to which we agreed?"

"It is indeed," replied Bruce, who seemed to be shaking with emotion.

"I don't see your concern," Comyn said. "I have agreed to support your claim to the crown, *to mak ye king, and I sall be in your helping with ye giff me all the land that ye haiff now.* Right?"

"That's right," said the Bruce, biting the words off short, his voice breaking with anger. "Your support in exchange for all my lands."

"Then what is your problem? Oh, Robert, you don't wish to break the contract, do you?"

"Not at all," said Bruce. And then he shouted, "The problem is that our agreement states clearly that under me as king of Scots, Scotland would be as before, completely independent of England, a concept you well know is hated by the English king. We further agreed we would keep our agreement secret from King Edward. I now accuse you of violating our agreement of secrecy and of telling all to King Edward!"

"But Robert, I have breached no such secrecy. It would be dangerous for me as well as yourself."

"Your are a liar, sir! You intended to inform the English king of our arrangement, and to claim falsely that I tricked

you into signing it under duress. Further, you told King Edward that you remain loyal to him, and that I am a rebel, to be sought out and killed! Thus you will become his favourite for the post of puppet king, and then you will have all my lands as well!"

"Robert, you are mad! You cannot prove what you say!" The Red Comyn began to move his hand to his sword.

"Cannot I so prove?" asked the Bruce, now shaking with emotion. "I can prove it well. The copy of our indenture I hold in my hand is *your* copy, which my men took from *your* messenger, who was about to carry it across the border to England and King Edward. You, sir, are a traitor!"

At this point, both Comyn and Bruce were fingering their weapons and hurling insults at each other in French. As the argument got more heated Bruce pulled his dagger, a *sgian-dubh*, as the Highlanders call it, and got in the first blow. John Comyn grunted in agony and a great tide of blood welled up from his chest under his mail. He fell to the stone floor and sat in a pool of gore, his sword making a great clanging noise as it dropped from his hand. He tried to speak, making gurgling and gasping sounds. He tried to pick up his sword but couldn't. He tried to gain his feet, but fell back into the increasing mess of his own life-fluid. It was a horrible sight. I was terrified and retreated back outside to a place near the chapel door, managing to hide in the dark, where, I hoped, no one would see me. Suddenly Robert Bruce came out through the main door and said to one of his aides, whom I now know to have been Sir Roger Kirkpatrick, "I doubt I have killed the Red Comyn." Bruce said this in French, *"Je doute que j'ai tué le Comyn Rouge."*

The Great Scot

Sir Roger pulled his sword and answered in Scots that he would make sure that Comyn's life would end that night. "You doubt? *Then I mak sikker*" is how Sir Roger put it. He drew his sword, turned, and charged into the chapel.

On hearing this the other Comyn knight, the uncle, who had been relieving himself against a building across the street, finished his business and went for his sword, but one of the Bruce knights raced after him, drawing his own steel. The duel went on for only a few seconds, punctuated by the clanging of the weapons and the grunts of the knights. In the end, the Bruce swordsman won, dispatching his opponent. The fight had made a noise in the darkness, and people began to appear in the street.

In less than a minute Kirkpatrick emerged, and all of Bruce's party mounted. I heard the Bruce say in Scots, "Let us leave this place at once. When this news is out the Comyns will come back on us." They started to ride out of the town when, seeing me, they halted. "Who are you, young man?" one of the riders asked.

"I'm David Crawford, sirs," said I, taking off my cap and trembling with fear. I realised that I might be the only witness to the slaying. The Bruce asked me if I had been in the chapel, and, since my mother always told me to tell the truth, I admitted that I had seen all. At first I thought they might kill me, but the Bruce grabbed me and swung me up on his horse as if I weighed nothing more than a lapdog. "You will come with us," he said to me in Scots.

I was afraid to say anything, and we started up the road for Dumfries Castle, which was nearby. I missed my mother and knew that she would be upset I hadn't come home, but she could not possibly have imagined the company I was keeping that night. I was not to see her for quite some time. My adventure had now begun. I was riding into the night, behind the saddle, and with my arms around the waist of the most important man in Scotland.

As we rode to the castle, the whole town seemed to come awake. The streets filled at the news of the killings. But the people seemed to think the event a victory. I heard several shouts of "Up with the Bruce!" They had waited a long time for a champion to come forward, and he was widely admired, at least in my area. When our party reached the castle, the Bruce didn't waste any time. After we had all dismounted, the earl gave the reins to me and told me to stay quiet and wait. In an instant the lone guard was overcome and our knights were inside the castle, which contained a small contingent of unarmed and unprepared Englishmen. They were, of course, outraged that Bruce's arrival was interrupting their evening, but the earl made himself very clear, someone told me later, that they could either be escorted to the English border or stay in the castle while he burned it.

Bruce then met with his men and gave them instructions. He pointed to the banner high above the castle flying three leopards or lions for England; it was hard to tell which. "Make sure," he said to his men, "to take down that banner as soon as is convenient." He left several men in charge of the castle and asked me if I could ride. Of course, this is one thing I was really good at, so I said, "Yes, sir, I can indeed." Whereupon one of the English horses was made available to me, and, after I had mounted, the Bruce and I and one other horseman rode north in the dark. I could scarcely keep my breath, so great was the excitement in me. I knew I wasn't, but I felt I must be a knight!

CHAPTER TWO

The Lodge

It was too dark to ride any distance that night, and we three proceeded carefully, keeping close to the trail. Sometimes we could not even find the path. It was difficult going, and slow. I could see at times the coat of arms of the other rider, an angry-looking blue lion. I rode behind as the two knights talked during our journey, and I was able to understand that the other rider was the earl's brother, Edward Bruce. After a mile or two we turned our steeds into the forest. The trees obscured what little light there was and made it too dark to ride. We dismounted and walked the horses by their reins, using our arms to feel the route of the path. Within a few hundred yards we reached a clearing that surrounded a wooden cottage, a sort of hunting lodge, which I presumed the Bruces maintained. The earl asked me to water and feed the horses and told me that there were oats in a lean-to at the back of the building and a stream for watering. I attended to this business immediately, and when the horses had had their fill my chores were finished. I was wondering what to do next when Edward Bruce came out of the lodge and called, "Well, laddie, you can't eat your dinner out in the cold. Get in here!"

I entered the lodge as quietly as I could. There was a fire going and its warmth raised my spirits. The earl motioned for me to sit down at table and I sat, shivering. The table was rough enough, lit by two candles stuck in rude candlesticks, and the meal was some very old oatcakes and cheese, both somewhat mouldy. I noticed there were two jugs of the French wine called claret. I was given a bowl of it, and I am here to tell you that its taste opened a new world for me. I had never tasted anything stronger than ale before, and I like ale still. But the taste of this claret was something I had never expected. It was rich and earthy yet delicate, with a long sensuous after-taste. I ate some oatcakes and cheese and tried to relax, but Edward Bruce and the earl began to talk of their crime and the whole cabin became tense. They were snapping at each other.

"Robert, you look miserable. Set your mind at rest," Edward said, as he refilled the earl's bowl.

"You might also look uneasy had you just committed murder, Edward."

"Murder you call it—murder? I say an act of war against tyranny." The younger brother's voice was high-pitched and strident. He spoke rapidly.

"But it is I who did the deed, Edward. It is a dirty business, and in a holy place as well." The earl's voice was full of emotion and he spoke slowly.

"Am I not an accomplice, Robert? I am and proud of it. You have killed a turncoat, nothing more. You have wiped out a traitor. You have done a proud deed for our family and for Scotland. You will soon be king."

"Aye, you are right, Edward. But I have this sin on my conscience. It will never go away."

The Bruce brothers were silent for a while, sitting there as the soft candle-light flickered on them unsteadily, upon their fine satin coats such as I had never seen up close. Then they remembered that I was there. They were suspicious of me, and somehow they would have to deal with me. Edward Bruce looked at me sharply and began to question me. "Why were you in the chapel, Davie?" Before I could answer he continued, "Why were you in Dumfries town at all? Do you belong there?"

I was trembling, but I answered as well as I could. "I do not belong to the town, but rather to a farm a few miles away, sir. I had gone to town to have a bowl of ale with the lads, and perhaps to visit with my girl."

"Och, a girl is it? And why instead of being with your girl were you in the chapel? When I was your age, I would have preferred the girl, and no mistake."

"I was curious to see what was going on. I'm sorry, sirs. I know it is not right to listen in on others, but I was curious. I beg your forgiveness."

"Do you know, Davie, that it is dangerous to be so curious?"

"Yes, sir. I know it well. I'm very sorry."

"Who are you, Davie? Who is your father?"

"My father is dead, sir. He fell at Falkirk, fighting with Wallace."

"So he was a patriot, is that it, Davie?"

"Very definitely yes, sir, and I am, too."

"I like that answer, boy," said Edward Bruce, shaking the reddish-brown mop of unruly hair that was sticking out from under his satin bonnet. He was striking in appearance, and his piercing green eyes followed the progress of a mouldy piece of bread that he casually threw into the fire.

Thus far all these questions had been barked at me by Edward Bruce, whose inquisition, I hoped, was finished. He drained a bowl and slumped back in his chair. He seemed to be satisfied with my answers. I felt calmer then, believing that I might not be killed.

The earl could see that his brother had put me under pressure, and he looked at me kindly, but straight in my eyes. He was very good-looking, as was his brother. Both were tall and thickly set, powerfully built with heavy bones. But the earl was very dark of hair, which set off his deep blue eyes. It was colour that set apart the Bruce brothers, and voice. The earl's was rich and resonant. "Davie, tell me, what do the folk about here think of the English occupation?"

At this question the fear went out of me and I became confident. I answered boldly, "Sir, they hate it, they hate every minute of it every day. We feel we are being trampled upon. We want our freedom. In fact, sir, there are many about here who are willing to fight the English, and many who look upon you, sir, as their champion. Many men from these parts would join you should you but ask." With this I hoped I had passed some sort of test, since the earl then looked at his brother, a slight smile on his face. He said to me, "Davie, what say you that I should soon become King of Scots?"

"Sir, most of the people in these parts believe that you are the rightful King of Scots. They are hoping you will rise in the cause of our freedom. They are *expecting* you to lead them, and I would support you in the cause of Scotland to the death, as my father did before me."

Then Robert Bruce looked into his mug, his blue eyes flashing in the reflection, and said to me, "Davie, I am soon to be crowned King of Scots."

The earl waited for my reaction, but I could summon nothing to say. Immediately I realised that I had blundered into something beyond my ken. The earl *knew* he was to be made king. I realised then that there was a plan to put the Bruce on the throne—a conspiracy was probably what the English would call it. The murder of the Red Comyn was only the first part of the plan.

Bruce continued. "Davie, every king must have a page. I have *nane*. Would ye like to serve as my page?"

I thought it must be the fine wine gone to my head when the earl spoke those words. I had no idea what would follow, but I could not believe this great man was offering me such a position, lowly as it may have been. My sense of adventure overcame me and I answered, clumsily I'm afraid, that I would be honoured.

But Edward Bruce objected. "Robert," he said. "Are you sure you should be taking on a lad you've only just met?"

But Lord Robert answered quietly, "Edward, I think he will be just fine. He is good with the horses, you know. I want him. Let's have a dram on it." Edward Bruce gave a slight shrug of his shoulders, and with that the earl smiled and lifted his bowl, and his eyes seemed to command his brother to do the same. "To Davie," they both offered. The earl then told me that he had been suspicious of my behaviour in the town, but that he was no longer. He felt I was a patriot to be trusted. He liked that I understood horses, since this is a principal duty of a page, and he liked the fact that I was well-built and healthy. Then he told me he demanded my absolute loyalty to him and his cause, as well as absolute silence about anything he said. I would, in my new position, overhear many important conversations, but my lips were to be sealed about them during my lifetime.

Then the earl proposed we get some sleep, since we would have to be off at first light for Lochmaben, one of the strongholds of the Bruces. I gathered that we needed to reach it early in order to keep ahead of the wrath of the dead Red Comyn's family and allies, who might soon be upon us. I was deeply tired and soon fell asleep on the earthen floor.

CHAPTER THREE

Three Meetings

Edward Bruce woke me with a light kick in the ribs the next morning. It was still dark and the day was cold again. The fire that had warmed us in the previous evening was long since spent and the temperature in the cabin felt near freezing. I shivered as the wind blew through cracks in the wall. The earl gave me a woollen jacket to wear under my sheepskin cloak. We ate a bit of oatcake and cheese and the noble brothers told me to saddle the horses and bring them round to the front, which I was glad to do. Before we departed, Sir Edward put a small cask of the French wine in his pack and finished off the remnants of the second jug of the night before.

The snow had melted, and as we rode north again I heard Edward Bruce remark to his brother that we should pick up our pace and try to make Lochmaben long before noonday. But the earl answered that there was no use pushing man and horse too far. "We can only do what we are meant to do, Edward," he said. "This is rough terrain. Don't be so impatient, brother. We are still far ahead of our enemies." It was indeed a hard ride, all morning in the saddle. I kept looking over my shoulder to see if we were being pursued, but we saw no one but a peddler, and he was coming the other way. It was foggy when we started, and then the weather became overcast the rest of the way to Lochmaben. I had never before been invited to such a grand estate, and when it came at last into our view my heart beat faster than ever. The castle appeared to me to be very strong, much of it built of great stones, part of it actually in the loch, and the rest surrounded by a moat. Atop a parapet the red and gold colours of the Bruces of Annandale fluttered in the breeze. There was a large gravel yard in front of the castle, and once again I was bidden to feed and water the horses. All the members of the household came out across the drawbridge to greet us, including the servants. I noticed that the earl gave a small kiss to an elegant woman. I took her to be and later learned that she was indeed his second wife, Lady Elizabeth. It wasn't, it seemed to me, a very loving gesture, rather formal and dutiful. The earl then picked up a beautiful young girl of about ten years, I judged. The earl hugged her and kissed her heartily, and I realised that this was his daughter, his only child and heir, Marjorie, by his first wife. She returned the affection of her father, happy to see him. Marjorie Bruce was obviously her father's daughter, with the same striking combination of blue eyes and black hair.

Then the earl requested the attention of everyone present in the yard under the thin February sun. "You are all going to hear the news if you haven't already, so you might as well hear it from me. As you know, our position has been always that I am the rightful heir to the throne of this country. At one time the king of England recognised this right and offered me the honour of that office if I would rule under him as a sort of subordinate king. This I refused to do, as our country exists independent of his. Scotland is and always has been, and always will be, an independent kingdom. Let us all agree on that!" To this there was applause from those assembled. The earl continued, "Recently, I made a compact with the Red Comyn, who, you will know, had a claim inferior to mine, wherein I would give up property in exchange for his support of my claim and the independence of our land. Unfortunately, the Red Comyn betrayed me to the king of England, and I have therefore killed him."

At this pronouncement, the tenants, servants, and the noble ladies let out a gasp, which, because of their numbers, was clearly audible. But then the earl continued, "I believe there exists in this country great support for my right. And I believe that it is our duty to rid this country of English domination. With God's help, I shall be crowned King of Scots within a matter of days!" At this the audience let out a cheer. Bonnets were thrown in the air, and people hugged one another. Little Marjorie Bruce did a small skipping dance to express her joy.

Then the earl asked for quiet. "Now, then, there is serious business to discuss. My brother Edward and I will be riding north to gather troops and support. Therefore I am leaving my brother Nigel in complete control here." The earl gestured toward a young man of uncommon good looks. Nigel Bruce stood next to his brother, who continued, "He will dispatch some of you men to the northeast, the southeast, and the western parts of the kingdom, to announce our plans and to raise soldiers to our cause. Some of you will be leaving almost immediately. The rest of us will work here all day on these plans and assignments. In a few days Nigel will arrange to transport all our noblewomen to the north, first to attend my coronation and then to keep them out of harm's way. For mistake it not— the king of England and certain Scots barons will not take kindly to our activities. Now, let us to our tasks!"

Throughout the day, the Bruce met with various assistants and gave out orders, including directions for the preparation of a feast for the entire company. It began after dark. There was wine and ale and large amounts of victuals. A sheep was slaughtered and roasted over a spit in the great hearth. Large loaves of bannocks were baked and cut in thick portions. A piper from the west country played music and everyone danced, usually in eights, four women and four men. Some of the dances were slow, and others were quick, but everyone seemed to be having a good celebration. I knew some of the dances but was too shy to join in, so I sat in a corner and watched. Anyway, I had a lot to eat. The mutton was excellent and the bannocks were of first quality. As the party grew during the night the Bruce, his work finished for the day, took a turn at the dancing with his lady. Toward midnight he came to me and said, "Davie, say nothing about this: You are to have our three horses and one more for baggage ready to ride at first light. Fail not in this. Now get some sleep, as we have a hard day tomorrow."

I found myself a place to sleep in a hallway. The stone floor was cold in the night and a draft shook the shutters and swirled the dust on the floor. It was so uncomfortable that I could get only a little sleep and had no trouble awakening for my tasks when I thought light was beginning to show. As my lord requested, I had fed, watered, and saddled our horses even before dawn. I brought the horses around, and the earl and his brother Edward appeared. The latter handed me a bannock, which I put in my bag. We rode north in silence, the brothers Bruce and myself, as the sun rose. The birds were singing, and the early fog was lifting against the slanting sun.

After we had gone some miles a lone rider came into view in the distance wearing a blue coat of arms with three white stars. He was the first person we had seen. As the space between our parties closed, the earl halted and looked at the young horseman. He appeared to be rather short, with a strong-featured face. His black hair was shiny and long, flowing out from under his bonnet. His dark eyes sparkled with intelligence, and he smiled a confident smile, I thought. "Good morning, sirs," he said, bringing his horse to a halt only a few yards from us. Sitting straight on his steed, the young knight announced, "I am James Douglas of Douglasdale."

The earl responded, "By the look of your arms, I reckon you claim such, but know not whether you deserve them. Are you the heir of the great knight Sir William Douglas?"

"I am indeed," replied the younger. "And you, if I may be so bold, are Robert Bruce, Earl of Carrick."

"True enough," replied Bruce.

"Sir," said Douglas, "I have just returned from several years in Paris, where I was a student, during which time I learned that my valiant father was killed by the English and our lands have been forfeited to an English knight who has no claim to them whatsoever."

"Right again," replied the earl, "and a great offence to your father, whom I well knew as a true gentleman and patriotic Scot."

"May it please your lordship, I have heard this day that you are to become champion of our people and King of Scots. Is it so?"

"It is indeed," replied the lord Robert. It seemed to me that the earl was trying to stifle a wee smile.

At this James Douglas dismounted and knelt before the earl, saying, "Sir, may God grant you good speed in your quest. I hereby kneel before you in homage and promise you my undivided loyalty if you will but allow me to share your struggle, and permit me to reclaim my patrimony."

The earl responded, "I do accept your homage, and if you are even half the man your father was, I shall be quite well served. Come and join us, for we are late to ride to Glasgow."

Glasgow—so that's where we were going! I was, of course, very excited that I was going to see the city, since I had never in my life before been out of the neighbourhood of Dumfries. During the ride, Lord Robert kept up a lively conversation with James Douglas, and I noticed that his brother was very quiet, even riding at some distance from the rest of us. I got the impression that Edward Bruce was jealous of the competition for his brother's time, and upon this Douglas had intruded.

The sun had already set on our second day of travelling when we reached the town, and all four of us were tired. In the dusk I could see some of the features of its many buildings, and, most surprising, we were met as we progressed through the city streets by many townsmen waving their bonnets and shouting, "The Bruce! The Bruce!" This was, of course, exhilarating to our tired souls. It was obvious that the citizens had somehow been informed and were expecting us. As we got closer to the great cathedral, we were approached by several men on horseback. We halted and, still mounted, they introduced themselves one by one. Then one of the gentlemen said to the earl that the bishop of Glasgow was expecting him and had invited the earl and his brother to dine with him and to rest the night in his quarters. The Bruce indicated that he was pleased with the invitation, but asked if room could be made for Douglas. The ambassador replied that that would present no problem and that we should proceed to the cathedral. This was all, of course, good news to us, not only because we were so tired and hungry, but because it meant that there were many others, including perhaps the bishop, supporting the plan to put the earl on the throne.

The cathedral was the grandest building I had ever

seen, and we rode around the back to where the bishop's quarters were. By now it was dark, and Edward Bruce bade me to feed and water the horses. I was helped in this task by the bishop's servant, a young man of about my age. When we finished I walked across the courtyard to the cathedral, where I met the brothers Bruce and James Douglas. The earl motioned for me to follow him into the church, but his brother objected, perhaps because of my low rank. However, the earl said it would be all right, that I had been a witness anyway, and could probably benefit from hearing a mass in any event.

I sat with James Douglas behind the two noble brothers in the empty church, which was gloomy and lit by only a few tapers, as the last mass of the day had long since been celebrated. Presently, the old bishop of Glasgow, Robert Wishart, arrived through a side door, resplendent in his robes, which were multicoloured and sparkling with golden threads. We all stood at his entrance and James Douglas was introduced to the bishop, who already knew who the Bruce brothers were. We were surprised that he knew of James Douglas's studies in Paris and he asked the young man how he had found France, as he had studied there as a young man himself. The old bishop stood before us, smiling, and offered us a greeting, then motioned for us all to sit. Then he became rather sombre and spoke directly to the earl. "We have long known each other, Lord Carrick. And you are aware that I am, and always have been, a supporter of the independence of this country, and of your right to rule it. You also know that our country has never had an archbishop, since we are poorly served in

Rome and instructed from there that the Scottish church is to be under the archbishopric of York, which is, of course, in another country. We continue to insist, to no avail, on being governed by a Scottish archbishop, one who is of our people. Both the Scottish church and the people of Scotland are and should be allies in this quest for independence. I have suffered, as you also know, and even been imprisoned for my loyalty to this country. We have all borne the wrath of King Edward, including his occupation and rape of this country three years ago. We all mourned the barbarous death of the brave Wallace only last year. However, Robert Bruce, you have committed an act of high sacrilege, murder at a holy altar, and under these circumstances I can offer you no help. Do you repent of this ungodly act?"

The Bruce did not hesitate to answer. "I do indeed repent. I fully realise that I have committed a great sin, and I am sorry for it and will be for the rest of my days." The earl's eyes began to fill, and I could see that he was serious in what he said. "I am truly sorry for this grievous crime."

Then the bishop instructed the earl to kneel before him and absolved him of his transgression. That being accomplished, the bishop said mass and gave all four of us the communion. When he was finished, he told the Bruce that he had the support of the diocese of Glasgow and that the bishop was sure that he would gain more from other members of the clergy. The earl then replied, "Bishop, I would like to thank you, humbly, for your help. I believe it is now time for me to disclose that for several years I have kept a secret pact of mutual aid with Bishop Lamberton of Saint Andrew's. We shall all benefit, I believe, if we stand together. We shall, in the end, free Scotland of the usurper's tyranny."

"May God bless your cause, Lord Carrick," said the bishop, and his slight smile indicated to me that, perhaps, he had known of the secret pact for some time.

Then the Bruce, his brother, and James Douglas were taken into the bishop's quarters to clean their persons in preparation for supper. I went into the kitchen, where I ate with the servants, and to my surprise I was served with another bowl of French wine by a quite attractive young girl who smiled at me. Afterwards I was shown my quarters, and, despite my excitement, I fell asleep immediately, even more tired than I had been the day before.

Chapter Four

Coronation

The next weeks passed by for me as if in a swift dream. I acted as page to the earl and as a sort of servant to James Douglas and Edward Bruce. I never once opened my mouth to speak unless I was spoken to. This was the way, I believed, I should behave in such august company. But I got to speak quite a lot in spite of my self-restriction. All three noblemen were in good spirits, talking of the adventure that was sure to come and the glory they expected to win in its course. Often they would say something along these lines, and, half-joking, would ask my opinion about things. They would usually laugh when I answered, but it was in a good-humoured way and I didn't mind at all. It was a wonderful time for me. We would spend the day riding, talking to potential supporters, and raising troops. Then, at night, we would retire to a friendly castle or a peasant's lodge. The next day we would begin the adventure all over again. The countryside was now in the embrace of spring. The hillsides were turning green. The wet earth and the budding plants gave off heady fragrances. Birds were singing. I was meeting important people and drinking French wine almost every day!

Before long, we were joined by the ladies from Lochmaben and their guardians, and gradually by noblemen and -women from other parts. We attracted knights and commoners who rode or walked with us, depending on their stations. There were many young rural boys like myself, some carrying homemade weapons such as wooden spears and leather targes. There were several thousand of us now. We were an army, albeit not a disciplined one. Everyone knew that we were going to Scone for the coronation, and there was an uneasy feeling that we might be intercepted by the Comyns and their allies, or by the English lurking in Scottish castles. But day after day as we rode with more and more men committed to the earl, our force grew larger and more powerful, and there was no sign of the Comyns or of the English.

At last we arrived at Scone, the ancient seat of the Scottish monarchy. The little place was packed with nobles, commoners, and clergy, and still there was no hint of our enemies. Scone was too small to house all those attending, so hundreds of tents and lean-tos had been set up to accommodate everyone. Booths flourished with things for sale. Wine, cheese, and cloth, both cheap and dear, were featured. Fires were roasting and baking food of all kinds. Colourful pennants flew everywhere. People wore their best clothes, some of the ladies in silks and jewels. I was given a beautiful blue velvet jacket, tailored to fit, with a large collar. Musicians played continuously. The whole thing had the air of a country fair, but with a great purpose—to crown a King of Scots and to begin the war that was coming.

The coronation itself was sad in a way, as proud as we all were of it. The abbey, which had been damaged by the English, was too small to hold the entire gathering, and many had to wait outside. There hadn't been time to prepare properly, and yet despite the lack of grandeur one might have expected of such an event, there was a serious and majestic tone to it all. Of course, the famous coronation stone, the stone of destiny, the *lia fail*, was not there to make our new king, as it had made so many others over centuries. It had been stolen and taken to Westminster Abbey by King Edward I, the self-styled Hammer of the Scots. But nothing could dampen the spirits of those who attended. Many of the greatest of our country's noble families were represented. From the church, Bishop Lamberton of St. Andrew's had slipped by the English to make his appearance. And old Bishop Wishart of Glasgow, who had given the earl absolution, brought out the royal robes he had been hiding for years for use in the ceremony. He also produced a huge banner, the banner of the monarch of Scotland, all in brilliant red and gold with its angry lion rampant, that was hung from two poles behind the throne. After the ceremony everyone moved outdoors into the misty and rather warm day, but the colours of the coats of arms and all the banners brought festivity to the scene despite the meagre resources that were available and the overcast weather.

It could be argued that the coronation was illegal, since Duncan MacDuff, the earl of Fife, who had the hereditary right to place the crown on the heads of Scottish kings, was not present, being detained in England by our enemies. We were told that the earl of Fife's sister Isabel was on her way to represent the MacDuffs, but as the day grew old and she didn't appear, it was decided to crown the king without her. Robert Bruce gathered his family around him: his brothers Edward, Alexander, Thomas, and Nigel; his sisters Mary and Christian; and his wife Elizabeth, who was seated next to him. All of them were attired in the finest jewelled clothes of satin, velvet, and silk. Perhaps the most spectacular of all was his daughter, Marjorie, a smiling, vivacious little girl dressed in a beautiful red gown that complimented her black hair and deep blue eyes.

It was Bishop Lamberton who placed the thin golden circlet on the earl's head. The crowd became silent at this reverential moment in the history of what we all called the world's oldest monarchy, a moment of great emotion for the men and women who were there. King Robert held his huge ceremonial sword and smiled at the assembly. Then a *seanachaidh*, attired in the Highland manner, burst forth from the crowd, threw himself prostrate at the feet of the just-made King of Scots, and began to recite the new ruler's royal genealogy through the earls of Carrick in Gaelic: *Raibeart Mac Marsala, Nic Nèill, Mhic Dhonnachaidh, Mhic Ghillebrìde, Mhic Fhearghais,* and so forth all the way back to the kings of Ireland. Then he recited the new king's direct royal Scottish ancestry by which he claimed the throne: *Raibeart, Mac Raibeairt, Mhic Raibeairt, Mhic Iseabail, Nic Dhaibhidh,* and many more ancestors going back, once again, to Ireland. Of course I didn't remember all of this at the time, but have since got it from historians. The old man recited the musical names in the cadence of a poem, punctuating the first syllable of every ancestor's name by slapping the ground in a rhythm with his right hand. He went on for many generations; and it was an astonishing performance. There was not a sound from the crowd, which was held spellbound by the old man. It was impossible for me to concentrate, anyway, since at this glorious moment in the history of our country I was shaking with emotion and not able to keep the tears out of my eyes. I noticed that many others were as moved as was I. We had been witness to the coronation ceremony of a poor country, but a country with a patrimony second to none, and I believed that everyone there was willing to die for it. We were all, in the end, part of the same ancient heritage. We were Scots.

I don't know how many people attended the coronation of King Robert I, although I would guess that there were several thousand. The festivities that followed the event were tempered, however, by a sombre air; there were many more noblemen missing from the event than there were who attended. It was obvious that the new king had not yet won the allegiance of enough chiefs to his cause; we would have a long way to go. The Comyns and their allies, of course, were not with us, but neither were the Mac-Dougals and many other clans and families. Nevertheless, the pipers played, the people danced, and meat was roasted. As the wine flowed, I noticed that the newly made Queen Elizabeth seemed aloof from the king and the festivities, and she withdrew early from the party.

In contrast, Isabel, the sister of the earl of Fife, arrived the next day, disappointed not to have crowned the king, as was her family's right. Many were surprised that she had been there at all, since she was married to the earl of Buchan, who was not only a Comyn, closely related to the dead Red Comyn, but an ally of the hated King Edward. The Countess of Buchan was a beautiful young lady, tall and slender, with long, straight blond hair and azure eyes. Even these charms, though, were surpassed by her marvellous winsome smile. She must have had great courage to have come, and to have put her patriotism above her loyalty to her husband. But I heard it said that she was in love with the new king, and had had close relations with him before. It was obvious in her demeanour before King Robert that she adored him and would risk anything for his attention. Also, I noticed that the new king repaid her courtesies.

"Well, Isabel, welcome!" said King Robert. "What a pity you have come so late."

"Sir, I could not come faster. I have travelled several days to be here. It is my duty as a MacDuff, and I come also with great pleasure."

"Pleasure you may think it is, Isabel, but I doubt that your husband will think so."

"What my husband thinks is not my concern, sir. My concern is that I have not arrived in time to crown the King of Scots."

"Perhaps we shall find a remedy for that," answered the king.

So, partly I think because of the king's regard for the countess, but also mindful that some would say he had not been legally crowned, the entire coronation ceremony was repeated the next day, which happened to be Palm Sunday. The king held his great ceremonial sword and was in his robes again, but this time wore them open to reveal the coat of arms of the King of Scots. The great banner, identical to the king's arms, was once again mounted in its glorious red and gold. The second coronation went on, the *seanachaidh* recited his hypnotic genealogy again, but this time the golden circlet was lifted carefully and placed on the king's head by the beautiful, smiling Isabel. Some people gasped when the young countess and the new king kissed.

After this second coronation, with very few in attendance, there was no feast. Most of the throng had dispersed after the first coronation. The bishops had already left, and the king delegated his brother Nigel Bruce to take the ladies north to Kildrummy Castle, where, it was hoped, they would be safe. A baggage train was prepared for departure as early as possible the next morning. That evening the king met with his nobles far into the night at a table under the trees, discussing strategy and the available news. I waited at the table and could overhear much of what was discussed. The news was not good. King Edward was outraged at the sacrilegious death of Comyn, and was gathering knights and sending reinforcements to some of the castles he was occupying in Scotland. There was imminent danger to us and to our cause. It was like a great dark, cold cloud settling upon us.

At length the king motioned for me to come with him to the women's quarters. "I want you to see to it that Queen Elizabeth and the ladies are well-provisioned for their journey," he told me. When we arrived, he bade me stay outside to check the packs while he went inside to speak with his queen. When I had finished, I returned to my station outside the women's quarters, and I could hear the queen say, "Oh, Robert. What are you doing? Your supporters are few. I feel as if we are merely playing Kings and Queens, like small children. This must end badly. You are sending us into exile in the wilderness, and for what? You have few with you and many enemies, not least of which is the might of England itself. Are you a wise rebel? A wise rebel knows what to rebel against. King Edward offered you a kingship that you could hold under him in peace. Why not try to get him to offer it again? What would be so wrong with being united with the English? They are a good people."

The king answered, "It is too late, Elizabeth, for all that. I am no rebel, because I do not recognise King Edward's claim to be my overlord. I agree that the English are good people, and I have nothing against England, but, despite what he says, King Edward wants to subject Scotland to his own cruel tyranny. The choice has been made. We are Scots and they are English."

The queen replied, "I am not Scottish. I am Anglo-Irish and very proud of it! Robert, you are married to the daughter of the Earl of Ulster. Need I remind you that my father is King Edward's best friend?"

"Elizabeth, you are Scottish now," said the king in a quiet, patient voice. "Your father is now my enemy. I have a duty now, and a destiny. I am the King of Scots."

Then the queen said something that very much upset me, and I am sure upset the king as well. "You are a summer king, Robert," said Queen Elizabeth. "I wonder if you will be a winter king as well."

With that remark the king spoke abruptly. It was the only time I had noticed him to be flustered. He spoke very quickly, as if in a hurry to end the conversation. "Elizabeth, it is time to say good-bye. I regret having to put you through all this. I hope that we will soon meet again in better circumstances."

Then, without another word to his queen, King Robert came out and we walked back to the meeting place, where he talked again with the nobles as if nothing had occurred. Late in the evening a messenger arrived with a note for him. I received it on his behalf and handed it to him. He opened it and read it quickly, then wrote a few words and sent it off with the messenger. He turned to me and said, "Davie, I am to have a visitor in my quarters. Here is the key. Go there, and make sure everything is in good order, and await me there. No one but you is to know." Then he added, "Here, take this dirk. It's time you were armed." Of course I did as the king asked, going directly to his quarters and straightening up the place as best I could. In a little while the king's guest arrived. It was Isabel, Countess of Buchan.

CHAPTER FIVE

Disaster at Methven

You can understand, I am sure, my surprise and embarrassment as the countess entered the lodge. I think she was startled to see me as well.

"Who are you, young man?" she inquired immediately. The charming smile I had noticed earlier was gone.

"I'm David Crawford, ma'am, the king's page."

"And why are you here?"

"The king asked me to prepare this room for you, to make you comfortable, and I have done so, ma'am."

The countess seemed relieved on hearing of my official capacity, and she seated herself on a chair by the fire that I had made. She wore a long dress and a shawl against the damp chill. I had lit several candles and she looked beautiful just sitting there in their glow. The blue of her eyes matched the colour of her dress. I offered her a bowl of the

43

king's wine, which she accepted, and then I begged her to excuse me and left to take up a position outside the lodge near the door. Soon enough, though, I was tried by a drunken countryman who demanded entrance to see the king on what he called important business. I sought to reason with the man but he became belligerent, especially as I was so young. I decided to hit him a good one in the face, and down he went, out cold on the damp ground.

Just then King Robert arrived and, noticing the man splayed on his back in the contours of a crucifix, asked me what it was about. When I told him, he laughed and slapped me on the back. "Not bad, Davie, not bad." Then his mood changed and he asked me if his visitor had arrived.

"Indeed, sir, the Countess of Buchan is in the lodge, sir."

"Thank you, Davie. Please stay outside a while and guard me."

"Yes, sir," I replied, and with that the king entered the lodge and bolted the door behind him. I grew very tired and cold in the night, but I knew that I must be strong. It was quiet in the camp just then, and I thought that everyone except the king, the countess, and myself was asleep. I was a little afraid, I must admit, and whenever I heard the slightest noise I fingered the knife the king had given me, wondering if I would have the courage to use it if necessary. Once a roving sentry passed by and challenged me. I was much superior in stature to the sentry, so I looked him right in the eyes and said, "Move on to your rounds. Your king is quite safe."

The sentry hesitated a few seconds, glared at me, then

disappeared into the night. I was happy to have avoided trouble, and the rest of the night passed quietly as the cold grew bitter, and a small rain began to fall.

Early in the still-dark morning, when the moon remained high, the door opened a crack and I could hear the countess say, "Oh, Robert, I love you. Don't let me go."

The king replied, "Parting is difficult for me also, Isabel, but you must go with the other women. You are not safe here. We will talk another time." Then the door opened wide. "Davie, give your arm to the countess and see that she gets safely to her quarters. And be ready at daybreak to help the train start for the north."

I nodded to the king and walked with the beautiful lady's hand on my arm through the quiet of the small place. Her eyes were wet with tears. Her touch was soft and delicate, and she said to me, "Davie, you serve the greatest man this land has ever produced. I am not sorry for what I have done this night, although I'm sure others would think ill of me."

"Yes ma'am," I whispered just as we approached the door to her quarters.

"Thank you, Davie, for your assistance," she said as her smile returned, and then she gave me a wee kiss on the cheek and disappeared behind the door. I must tell you, as a fourteen-year-old, I almost fainted with delight. And the memory of that kiss kept me awake through the rest of the night.

Even before morning I was at work, seeing to the provisions and the packing of the train. Nigel Bruce, the king's handsome young brother, was in charge, and when it grew time to leave, he made a little speech to those who were to depart. "We are going to the north for your safety; first to Kildrummy, where I hope you all will find accommodations. We may go farther, to the Orkney Islands or even to Norway, where we would be welcome. I regret that we must put you through this ordeal, but your safety is paramount. Now let us get started."

The little group looked quite dispirited as it moved out in a cold drizzle. Most of the women had tears in their eyes, and their shawls were pulled tight as the horses slogged through the mud. I felt sure we wouldn't see them again for a long time, but my own spirits picked up as the Countess of Buchan, all but covered up in a heavy cloak, showed her lovely smile and waved me good-bye.

King Robert then called another council. He ordered the division of his forces in three parts and sent them off for a week to gather recruits and stores. He ordered that we would all meet on the seventh day at Methven, a few miles from Perth.

Spirits were high a week later when we reconvened at Methven. Several thousand men had been gathered to our cause. But the news brought by others was depressing. The English had put Aymer de Valence, the Earl of Pembroke, in charge of the war to be brought against us, and he was in the north, looking for us. We were told that he had already captured the bishops of Glasgow and St. Andrews who had been of such strong support to us—a serious blow to our cause. The lives of the bishops had been spared only because of their clerical standing. Dumfries Castle, the site of our first victory, we learned, was in English hands again. De Valence had taken Perth and was quartered there.

The king decided to attack him at Perth, and we were camped at Methven only a few miles away. When all was ready King Robert moved our troops to the town gates, demanding that the English come out and fight or surrender the castle. The reply of de Valence was to tell us to come on the morrow, and that he would then fight. De Valence was a particular enemy of ours, closely related to the English king and by marriage to the dead Comyn. Nonetheless, King Robert accepted this arrangement and we retired to Methven on high ground. Some of the men were sent to hunt provisions, and others sought sleep, gaining strength for the promised battle. Most were unarmed when the perfidious Sir Aymer, against all the rules of chivalry, came after us at night in a surprise attack.

The battle was quick, and went very badly for us. We were disorganised and the king ordered all of us to grab any weapon we could and go to it. It was my first battle and I was very frightened, but I was surprised to find that after a few minutes my fear had vanished. All I could see was a man coming to kill me, and all I could think was that I had better kill him first. I had picked up a sword from the field and managed to cut the arm off one opponent. Then I stuck another right through the chest. I was surprised at how difficult it was to withdraw the sword; I had to put one foot on the man's body to do it. I realised that I would have to win every match and kill as many as confronted me or I would not survive the night. Thus, I went at as many men as I could, and killed all. The noise of the battle was over-whelming—the clang of steel, horses whinnying, men shouting. Spears were breaking in people's chests. Men lay groaning under crippled or dead horses. The grass was wet with blood. Edward Bruce was having a fine time, baying like a maniac, his sword raining terror on the field. King Robert was calm, methodically dispatching opponents, but he had a deep gash beside his left eye and blood was running down his face.

Then a bold Scottish knight, Sir Philip Mowbray, fighting on the side of the English, seized the reins of the king's horse, yelling, "Come here and help me! I have the newly made king!"

King Robert shouted at the knight, "Mowbray, you are now a Scottish traitor! You fight not with us, so come and get your king if you can!"

Immediately the English came at King Robert, who fought them off valiantly; several of our noblemen, including Edward Bruce, Gilbert de la Haye, Neil Campbell, and James Douglas, soon formed up around him. I went immediately to join them, and if I hadn't, I'm afraid, you would not be reading this account, because almost everyone not near the king was being slaughtered or captured. There was nothing to do but retreat. The king gave the order, and all of us who could took a horse and rode out into the night in disarray. Our first battle had ended in disaster. We had lost most of our men, horses, and provisions. We heard later that King Edward, when notified of the English success against us, ordered that all prisoners be hung and drawn. But Sir Aymer, out of chivalry, could not bring himself to do this, and he spared all, including knights who agreed to fight for him in exchange for their lives. One of these was King Robert's nephew, Thomas Randolph.

When day came our men began to seek out our leaders and came to us. I, though not experienced in warfare, could see that there were only perhaps two or three hundred left, and that we were no longer so much an army as we were a band of tired, hungry refugees. Around midday the stragglers stopped arriving and, presuming that most who had survived the battle were now back with us, King Robert moved us to the south and west. The gash beside his eye was bandaged, but he seemed to be unaware of his wound.

The first thing he said to his brother was, "Edward, we can seldom beat the English in pitched battle. There are too many of them; they have too much treasure and too many weapons. We must begin a new kind of warfare, where we fight and run; hit in the night, hide in the day."

"That sounds rather cowardly, if you ask me," answered Edward Bruce.

"I did not ask you," the king replied abruptly.

That ended all conversation for most of the day. I could see that both brothers were unhappy with their brief exchange.

We moved slowly through rough terrain until we came upon the country of the shrine of Saint Fillan. This was a great experience for me. I had been raised in the Roman Catholic Church and didn't know until that day that there had been a Christian church existing all over Britain and Ireland long before the Roman church was known in some parts, and that it was still alive.

Thus in Strath Fillan our small army descended on a remnant of the ancient Celtic Church. I didn't know why we stopped there, but I supposed that King Robert wanted to make sure he had its blessing. In the Gaelic-speaking areas of our country, there was still much support for this church despite the fact that it was looked on by many as heretical. Some of the members of this church were called "Culdees" or, as they were styled in Gaelic, *céile-dé*, the servants of God. They were the spiritual descendants of Saint Columba, who had been one of the first to bring Christianity to Scotland. The Celtic church was mainly monastic and didn't have a hierarchy as does the Roman church. The abbots were hereditary, which, of course, means that the abbots married, which was not at all in line with the Catholic doctrine of clerical celibacy. The pope, for these people, was simply a figurehead, a powerful bishop perhaps, and had little if anything to do with them.

It seemed that all the people from quite a distance around had heard of our coming, and we were treated to exuberant cheering upon our arrival. They were all dressed in the Highland manner, the men with large woollen garments called plaids draped around them. Their legs from the knees down were bare. The women were in long dresses of the same material. Many of these garments had been woven in a cross-hatch pattern of several colours.

It was late afternoon and the light was growing dim. Torches flickered in a small breeze. The local people, many of whom were surnamed MacNab, were introduced to King Robert by Maurice, Abbot of Inchaffray, who was a strong supporter of our cause. The king and the abbot then marched together up the hill a short distance, with all of us following, many carrying torches, until we reached a natural stone altar on the hillside next to a stream. It all seemed mystical in the cool air and the near-darkness. Several men, called dewars, were each carrying relics of Saint Fillan. I couldn't make out what all the relics were, but I'm sure I saw a bell and what looked like some sort of walking stick that the people called the *Coigreach*. I learned later from one of our men who came from the area that the dewars were hereditary also, from generation to generation, and that the relics they guarded were centuries old.

King Robert knelt by the altar, and the abbot, Maurice, gave him his blessing. Then the abbot bade King Robert arise and he began to address the crowd in Gaelic. His speech was short, and as he spoke, two of the clansmen translated it first into Scots, and then into French. In this way, all, or at least most, would understand. The Scots version, as best I can remember, was beautiful:

"Tonight, we are honoured by the presence of Scotland's rightful *Ard Rìgh* and the brave men who follow him. For some years now our nation has been without a king, but we are no longer. The church of Saint Fillan and Saint Columba and Saint Mungo and Saint Ninian is with you, King Robert. We are the ancient church of Scotland and, while we respect the Roman establishment, no pope can take away our support for you and your cause. I hope many of our men here tonight will join you in your quest to liberate our country."

Then the abbot loudly saluted the king in three languages: "*Rìgh Raibeart! Roi Robert!* King Robert!" This was followed by strident Highland yells that I had never heard before. It was a thrilling moment, I can tell you. The local people put on a feast for us, and we drank great quantities of their ale and ate venison killed in the hunt. About fifty men enlisted in our army as well, so we were all in good spirits for several hours. When it grew late I set to fitting out the king's bed in the abbot's lodge. When I went to advise the king that his comfort was ready, I found him in a serious discussion. There was news that disloyal High-landers were preparing trouble. Despite this worrying re-port, I was able to sleep soundly.

CHAPTER SIX

Exile in the West

We rode south and west through Perthshire toward Argyll. The land was hilly and rocky, covered with trees and watered by clear streams. The birds of summer were jolly and the glens were beautiful to see, but it was difficult ground to travel over. Our aim, after suffering the catastrophe at Methven, was to get away from our enemies for a while so as to be able to regroup. We increased in strength, as others of our men who had had to abandon the field at Methven were able to find and rejoin us, giving us at least a little optimism.

But as we began to enter a narrow pass at a place called *Dail Rìgh*, "Dalry" in Scots, we suddenly found it blocked by the Macdougall clansmen of John of Lorne, who was related to the dead Comyn and was, therefore, an archenemy. As soon as they saw us, these Highlanders, wearing nothing but plaids draped loosely around their bodies, began to attack us from the front. We had little room to manoeuvre, and almost immediately others came running down from the hills above us, hitting us from both sides. The clansmen struck at our men and horses with axes, and we began to take casualties, including a wound to James Douglas.

King Robert, seeing the peril of our position, loudly commanded his brother, "Edward, start a retreat; we cannot win here."

Edward Bruce cried back, "And what of you, brother, shall I leave you alone to face this?"

"Yes, damn it all, I can handle it. I order you to retreat."

Edward Bruce snarled at these commands but dutifully turned his horse around and began to call the retreat, moving our men back in the direction we had come. This left King Robert to face these clansmen by himself.

Do you wonder what our warrior king was made of? What happened next will show you. The king himself charged at the Highlanders, daring them to come after him and our retreating men. He would charge, and then they would give way. Then he would ride back through the narrow passage to keep up with our retreat. They would follow us, and then he would charge at them again. So great was his skill and his personal aura, that none was willing to make a real challenge at him, and he was able to keep their entire squadron at bay, infuriating John of Lorne.

Whereupon Lorne sent three of his roughest men to ambush the king at a place so narrow he could not turn his horse around. On one side of the path was the water and on the other a rocky wall of stone. The three came running down the crag at the king in full confidence that they would finish him. But as the first approached, King Robert cut one of his arms off with a single stroke of his sword. The second man grabbed the king's leg, but when King Robert spurred his horse forward, the assailant caught his hand in the king's saddle and was dragged along until the king turned and split his head. The third man was also quickly dispatched. It was an awesome demonstration of his prowess and so impressed the Macdougalls, who could see all, that they lost their mood for the fight. We were able to retreat without further hindrance and rest in a secure spot for the night. We were astonished at what our leader had accomplished, so much so that we didn't even cheer. Yet our spirits were lifted in the knowledge that we were being led by such a great and valiant man.

Within days we had reached the eastern shore of Loch Lomond, which we wanted to cross straight away in order to save time. James Douglas, whose wound was healing, found an old boat, half sunk, and it was repaired so we could resume our journey. The boat could hold only three men at once. King Robert and James Douglas were rowed across first. Then throughout the evening the boat went back and forth with two passengers each time until all our men, along with their weapons and supplies, were on the western side of the loch. During this time, the king kept up the men's spirits by reading a French story aloud to them. The common men in our group were amazed that their king was sharing their fate and circumstances, and at his humanity in entertaining them despite our dire position.

As we had had almost nothing to eat for quite a few days, King Robert then took half the men and gave James Douglas the rest, and the two parties went hunting for red deer. James was a fine hunter, and it was not long before he brought back a large buck. Edward Bruce brought another, and some of our men were able to catch fish in the Loch. The camp-fire was made and the sight of the roasting venison and fish encouraged our bedraggled band. There was plenty to feed us all, and for the first time in days we all went to sleep beneath the stars with full bellies.

The next day, Sir Neil Campbell, who was from those parts, found and welcomed us, giving us provisions and the use of several galleys. Neil Campbell was King Robert's brother-in-law, married to Mary Bruce, who was now with the ladies we had sent to the north. We were fortunate that he discovered us; he was solidly on our side and able to assist us greatly. In much better spirits we sailed down the Firth of Clyde toward Kintyre, where we could find a haven at Dunaverty Castle, just a few miles from Ireland. It was September then and the weather for our journey was clear and mild. We learned along the way that the Macdougalls were close behind us, emboldened perhaps by the recruits who rallied to their cause. When he was told of this, King Robert must have been crestfallen, since our enemies were gaining strength while we were losing it. But the king said nothing to anyone, and when, at last, we arrived at Dunaverty, we were warmly welcomed by the great lord Angus Macdonald of the Isles. Angus Og, he was called, meaning Angus the Younger, and what a sight he was. A large man with a reddish beard, perhaps the tallest man I had ever seen, bareheaded, attired in the colourful Highland manner. He showed no deference to, yet great respect for, the king. Another feast was prepared, and I could see that the spirits of the king had been raised, as he had become now the friend of one of the most powerful men in the western isles. The king and Macdonald conversed in Gaelic, so that I couldn't understand what they said, but it sounded beautiful, the soft guttural sounds of the ancient tongue.

Later in the evening, as I was sitting with the men, one who spoke both Gaelic and Scots told me he believed that he had heard King Robert say to Macdonald that all Macdougall lands would be forfeited to the crown. He heard that King Robert had promised to reward Macdonald with lands in return for his loyalty when the war was over and peace established. For his part, Angus Og would furnish us with twenty galleys and the men to man them.

The next morning we were all awakened before dawn and immediately boarded the galleys to sail south. Everyone was quiet with the suspense of not knowing where we were going. The cool air brought us fully awake as we glided along in the darkness of the first light. There was no wind and the sails hung limp, so that the men had to labour at the oars, but the water was calm and the work was not arduous. The king was giving orders to the helmsman; I don't know if anyone on board knew of our destination save our leader. As we passed the Mull of Kintyre, we felt the swell of the ocean, and I began to get sick. The thrill of the voyage, however, balanced the rocking of the galley, and I was able to control my stomach.

Then the king addressed us: "You have all heard that the Macdougalls have sailed after us and that they have added strength since we faced them. We must regroup before we can fight them again. We will soon be beyond the best weather for campaigning. We are going to winter at a place our enemies will not suspect. We are going to Ireland."

To hear this word pronounced—Ireland! Well you can just imagine what I thought of that. To Ireland, the home of our ancestors who had founded our Scotland! To see the emerald isle that had been the last bastion of civilisation when Rome fell! These were enchanting ideas to a boy such as I. But then the king diminished these expectations a bit. "Our destination," he continued, "which no man knows save me and the Lord Macdonald, who has agreed to send us assistance, and those on board this galley, is Rathlin Island, not fifteen miles from our present position. We shall arrive before the end of the day. From here we shall plan the rebuilding of our forces and our return in the spring to the reconquest of our country."

After his speech, King Robert took a seat. Of a sudden, the weather became furious, with a cold rain slanting into our faces, and the galley tossed amongst the waves as if it were a cork in a rapid stream. But the wind was favourable, the sails filled, and soon we could see the darkness of Rathlin. As we drew near I wondered about the king's speech. I wondered if he really believed he could conquer Scotland and unite it. Here we were, approaching a hiding place with what was left of our army: the king's brother Edward, James Douglas, and a mixed crew of survivors, including myself. We were not an army in any sense. We faced a task that appeared to be beyond our powers. But I had not really come to know King Robert yet. He would do it. He would do things that had never been done before. Yes, he really believed what he said in his speech, and all of us knew it. We felt ourselves in the presence of one of the giants of history. He hadn't showed his genius yet, but he would.

My thoughts on the king's words gave me a little sustenance—a hope I had made the right decision back in Dumfries, a hope I would once again see my mother and Leezie Maxwell.

But as soon as we landed on Rathlin Island, we came upon some very bad news.

CHAPTER SEVEN

A Visit to the Isles

At first, our arrival at Rathlin gave us a pleasant surprise.
Two of the king's brothers, Thomas and Alexander Bruce,
were waiting on the shore to greet us. This was a surprise
to everyone in our galley, except perhaps the king himself.
It appeared that a retreat to this remote place had been
discussed much earlier, and that these two young men had
decided to prepare our way in advance. They had been successful, too. Places for us to lodge had been arranged, provisions had been obtained from the Irish mainland only a
few miles to the south, and about fifty Irish warriors had
been added to our troops.

The four Bruce brothers exchanged hearty greetings
amid much backslapping. It occurred to me that none of
us, were we to be separated for even a few days, could ever
know with any certainty that we would meet again.

Not wasting any time, the four Bruce brothers walked swiftly toward the lodge that had been prepared for their royal persons. I, of course, hurried along behind them carrying, at times dragging, the king's gear. It was heavy, but I didn't mind. I was young and a willing servant in those days. Except for me, the meeting was strictly for the family. Not even James Douglas was invited. As I began to unpack, Thomas Bruce said to the king that he wanted to talk to him privately, and he motioned towards me. But King Robert waved him away, saying, "Davie is to be trusted. You can talk in front of him. No need to worry."

So it was just me in the room, unpacking, while the brothers had their meeting. Thomas began, "Brother, we have dire news for you. The ladies have been captured, and brother Nigel is dead."

It took King Robert a few seconds to recover from this blow, but he caught his breath and asked for details. Alexander spoke: "We are informed that your queen is under house arrest somewhere in England. Your daughter Marjorie has been taken to the Tower of London. Our sister Christian is in an English convent."

"How are they treated?" asked the king.

"King Edward has given permission to his soldiers to rape all our captured women. We do not know how poorly they have been treated, but we do not fear for their lives."

King Robert took a minute or so to digest this dreadful information, then asked in a soft voice, "And what has been the fate of the Countess of Buchan?"

Alexander hesitated, and gestured helplessly for Thomas to answer. Thomas Bruce started to speak, stopped, and then finally spat out his grim report. "The Countess of Buchan," he said, "is housed in a cage, suspended from the outer walls of Berwick Castle. Our sister Mary is similarly imprisoned in a cage hung from the walls at Roxburgh. We are told that their modesty is somewhat protected by privy trips inside the walls."

There was a long pause before anyone in the room spoke. It was so quiet that I stopped my work for fear of offending. At last the king spoke. Thinking of the most handsome of all of the Bruces, he asked what fate had befallen his young brother Nigel.

Thomas answered, unhesitating, through angry tears. "Brother Nigel was dragged through the streets of Berwick, hanged, drawn, and decapitated. Many others met similar deaths."

Again there was silence in the room as everyone awaited the king's response. I felt sure the king's brothers were questioning whether their elder sibling should have decided upon this quest. Here we were, hiding with a small clutch of soldiers, fighting against the mightiest army and most resolute monarch in Christendom. Even many Scottish nobles had refused to join our enterprise. It was hard to imagine how we could prevail. King Robert was not really king of anything. He controlled no land except the small barren isle of Rathlin. I am sure King Robert realised our spirits were low. But after a few minutes passed he collected his thoughts. Then his eyes moistened and he began to speak in a resolute tone.

"Brothers, these are indeed sad notices of which you have informed me. They have infuriated me, and, I am sure, have infuriated you. But being furious will not accomplish anything without the resolution to do something. And I have resolved and hereby affirm that resolve, to win, and win we shall. We shall create a new kind of warfare, as I discussed with brother Edward several weeks ago. We cannot often fight pitched battles against the English and win. They have too much wealth, too many men, too many siege weapons, too many archers, too many mounted cavalry, too much power in general. Our new style will be to hit and run at night and to hide in the day. We will surprise our enemy. We will move constantly. We will take castles and destroy them, one at a time, until there is no place left for this great English army to hide. We shall live in the forest. The English cannot do this. We shall gather the valiant men of our nation to the task. I am certain that they will rise to support us. The Scottish people rose for Wallace, and I am sure that they will rise for me. Believe me, we shall win. We shall win for our family's right, we shall win for Scotland's right, we shall win to recover our women, we shall win to avenge the outrageous deaths of our fallen comrades, and, above all, we shall win for our own freedom. We are in the right, and may God bless our efforts, and may God damn the barbarous king of England!"

Immediately King Robert arose and strode out of the lodge, leaving us alone. His brothers, and, I may add, myself, were all taken aback by this powerful speech. I now realise it was the speech of a military genius who could plot a distant and complicated course. But at the time it seemed to be just the inspiring talk of the leader of a small band of discouraged men. For several minutes no one in the lodge spoke, but then Alexander Bruce said, "I am amazed at what I just heard. Our older brother is a great man."

Yes, that was true. Without his strong spirit our autumn and winter on Rathlin Island would have been even more difficult and depressing than they were. The weather was foul most of the time, with fog, sleet, rain, and snow some-times all in the same day. The island was bare and brown, not at all green the way Ireland is supposed to be and as Scotland is in many parts. The place is rocky, though they say there are birds on the cliffs in the summer. We didn't see many in that dark winter, except for a few ravens and falcons.

The brightest thing for me about Rathlin was that I made the friendship of Alexander Bruce, the king's young brother. Alexander took an interest in me, I suppose, because I was interested in books. He had studied at Cam-bridge in England, and had been brilliant, first among his peers as a scholar. There were on Rathlin a dozen or so books that belonged to the king and his brothers. But, in addition, we were able to borrow a few interesting works from a monastery on the mainland. We made several trips for this purpose, and I was surprised that Alexander was able to speak to the monks in Gaelic. I had not realised our language was the same as theirs. Throughout the wet and dark of the Rathlin winter, Alexander and I would sit by the fire in the lodge and read aloud in French and Latin. I had not had any formal schooling, but in Scotland in those days, even poor people had some rudiments of education.

Most of the men in my neighbourhood could read and do sums at least. I had studied a little Latin and French. Of course, Alexander was far ahead of me, but that was all to my benefit. I learned much from him in a very short time. He had a knowledge of history and geography that was fascinating. He taught me about the other countries of the world, particularly France, where he intended to go to get advanced degrees. He was even trying to get his brother, the king, to open a Scots College in Paris.

Another important benefit of that dismal winter on Rathlin Island was that James Douglas and I became friends. This was important to me in that James taught me not of things of the mind, as had Alexander, but rather of things of the body. He was strong and athletic. He liked me and taught me to use a sword, which was the most important skill I could learn for the struggle to come. Back at Methven I had just hacked away, unaware that there were certain moves that can save one's life and bring an opponent down.

James loved swordplay, and taught it laughingly. "Don't defend against me with your arm, lad! If this weren't a stick I'm holding, you would have just *lost* your arm! That's it! That's it! Now stay back, don't thrust until you're close enough to do some damage, otherwise I can come upon you! Fine, fine! Now for God's sake, Davie! Hold on to the damn sword! I'll knock it out of your hand! Your grip is too weak! That's better! But stand tall, Davie! If you hunch over you'll be losing part of your field of vision! Och, that's better, Davie. I'm teaching you all the latest methods from

France. You don't think I was wasting my time in Paris with books, I hope!"

In the last days of 1306 the king awoke me one morning and ordered me to pack our gear and get ready to sail in two hours. It was exciting, of course, but I was taken by surprise. I did as I was told, and when the sun came up King Robert, myself, and four of our men boarded a galley. The king told his brothers and James Douglas that he was off to the western isles in search of men and provisions. He challenged them to increase our body of Irish volunteers, and left Edward Bruce in charge.

We sailed northward and after several days we approached an island called Rum. It was heavily wooded, with great stands of birch trees stretching back from huge granite cliffs that fell down to the sea. Seals barked and bobbed in the water. Sea eagles cried against the wind and Manx shearwaters were returning from their winter homes. At the harbour we were met by a buxom lady standing on the shore. She was strongly built, as many Highlanders seemed to be. Her name was Christiana Macruarie of Garmoran, but was better known as Lady Christiana of the Isles. I thought her quite attractive, and so apparently did King Robert, who returned her greeting with a warm embrace. She was rather tall, with the long, bright-red hair that is often seen in those parts. She wore a long green dress that contrasted with the colourful hair running down her ample bust. Gradually I learned that she was a widow, a near relative of the king by marriage, and the heiress of an immense estate that included districts on the mainland as

well as several important islands. As the sun was low in the
sky, our men were shown their quarters with the animals,
and I accompanied the king into the lady's house. As we
entered the front room, she placed her arm around the
king's waist and said to him, "Oh, Robert. I'm so proud of
you and what you are doing. I always knew your time
would come. I'm so glad you came to see me, and I will do
anything I can to help your cause."

The king answered, "Thank you so much, Christiana. I
know that you have always been a patriot. I am come here
to raise men and supplies. I need a lot of both."

"Don't worry," she said. "You have come to the right
place. You shall have many men and much in supplies. I
will see to it myself. But now it's time for you to rest. You
must be very tired, and hungry as well."

"I am indeed both. Have you seen any English or Scottish traitors in these parts?"

"Absolutely not, Robert. Do you think that I would
allow any such thing in my lands? You are quite safe here.
There is no reason, even, to post a guard. Tomorrow we
will begin our tour of my domain to obtain support for you,
but now, Robert, the peat fire is burning, food is warming,
and wine we have in abundance."

Then King Robert addressed me. "Davie, are you done
with your unpacking? I hope so. We want to be left alone.
Christiana, can we have some food and drink for my men?"
At this our hostess produced several bannocks and two
casks of red wine for me and the lads. The king handed
them to me, and told me to go to eat and sleep with the
men, and be ready to move on the morrow. "If I am not

awake by first light, Davie, come and rouse me. Here you go now."

It was not hard to awaken from that first night's repose, since the animals were ready to go before dawn and made quite a racket. I pulled myself together and walked to the lady's lodge, startling several red deer along the way. When I reached the front door I knocked twice, rather softly, but there was no answer. Then I entered the house, walked quietly to the bedroom, and knocked again, but there was still no answer. I opened the door as quietly as I could. The king and the lady Christiana were still fast asleep in their bed. I said "Sir" almost in a whisper. This startled both the king and the lady, who pulled up the covers around herself. I don't believe she was wearing anything else.

At any rate, within an hour we were in the galley and off to another of her islands. Men were summoned, troops raised, provisions pledged. Lady Christiana was treated like a queen by the islanders. There was no doubt of her authority. It went on like that for more than a week; first among the islands and then among her mainland properties. The weather was fair for sailing. Occasionally we saw a whale or a dolphin. Every day we gathered pledges of men and provisions. The king spoke with whomever he met in Gaelic, and this increased his credibility with them as their rightful king. Every night I slept with the men and the animals, and every night the lady and the king slept together in one of her many homes. At last it all came to an end; it was time for us to go back to Rathlin. The galleys, men, and provisions that had been arranged by Lady Christiana were ready. We would return to the Irish coast in strength. The king bid good-bye to the lady Christiana one morning as we prepared the galleys for the trip back to Rathlin. She held King Robert in a tearful embrace, which I thought looked very genuine and very sad. She would be alone again, of course, and his life would be at risk again, immediately. I am sure she was worried she might never see him again. Her last words to him were, "Robert, oh, Robert. This past week has been the best of my life. Please take care of yourself. All my thoughts are with you."

The king answered, "Thank you for everything, dear Christiana." Then he turned to the men and gave the order to set sail. As our fleet got farther and farther away from land, we could still see Lady Christiana on the shore, watching us until we were out of sight.

When we returned to Rathlin with our fleet, the long winter showed signs of breaking into spring. Summer birds, puffins and guillemots, were returning and made low noises in the night. The weather moderated and everyone in our camp began to be impatient. The king's innovative strategy of small battles and destroying castles had been much discussed, and everyone had accepted it and was ready for the coming fight. But to the dismay of James Douglas and Edward Bruce, the king had chosen his younger brothers, Alexander and Thomas, to make the first sortie to the mainland. The two were most enthusiastic about their mission, and prepared for it by crossing to Ireland to recruit more volunteers.

Their expedition set sail in early February 1307 with several hundred Irish warriors in eighteen vessels supplied by Angus Og Macdonald. Their mission was to land at

Loch Ryan in Galloway on the far southwestern corner of Scotland, then to drive inland to harry the enemy in the south, which would distract them from the campaign planned by King Robert to the north. They left in the night to avoid detection, and all were in good spirits. Thomas and Alexander embraced their brother, and their galleys cast off to their destinies, the sails flapping and seagulls crying in the wind.

Several days later a lone galley sailed into Rathlin bearing a man claiming to be a spy, one Cuthbert, dressed in rags, and filthy to his beard. Immediately he was taken into the king's lodge.

"Sir," he addressed the king, holding his hat in his hands, "I have important news for you. You are in great danger. You have been betrayed to the English, and they are coming for you with many ships."

"How do you know this?" demanded the king. "Your name and speech sound English to me. Are you an Englishman, Cuthbert?"

"Indeed, I was born in England, sir, but have been married to my dear wife who is Scottish for these fifteen years. I have lived in this country all that time, sir, but still make occasional trips to England, sir, where I maintain good connections. Sir, I hope you will trust me. I have paid one of the servants of King Edward of England for this information. May I speak frankly, my lord?"

"Go on," answered King Robert, waving his hand.

"Well, sir, this servant says that King Edward rages against you day and night. He mocks you and calls you 'King Hob,' instead of 'King Robert,' as if you were a mere peasant. He is obsessed, my lord, obsessed with continuing his subjection of Scotland and with humiliating and killing you. You must leave here at once, for a large body of men and ships is already on the way."

King Robert thought carefully. This Cuthbert was not known to anyone in our group and could not be trusted at all. Yet something of his testimony rang true to the king. He said finally, "You had better be telling me the truth, Cuthbert. We are about to go to Scotland, and you will come with us. If your information proves to be true, you shall have this silver piece and the opportunity to win more. If not, I shall have your head."

Then the king looked at Edward Bruce and commanded, "Guard this man, Edward, and give him food. Make sure he doesn't escape." Then, turning to James Douglas, he said, "Make ready to sail tomorrow for Scotland, James. The hour of your destiny is come."

CHAPTER EIGHT

First Victories

James Douglas and his raiding party were preparing to sail for Scotland the next morning in galleys provided by Angus Og Macdonald. We all laboured filling the boats with provisions. The seagulls were excited by the smell of food, shrieking and flying near us as we worked. Douglas commanded several galleys and about two dozen men. The rest, about thirty galleys, some from Lady Christiana, were to depart with the king a few days hence. Douglas was resolute. His goal was to capture or at least cause harm to the English-occupied stronghold on the Isle of Arran just off the coast of the Scottish mainland. Assuming he was successful, this island or at least part of it would be secure when the galleys under King Robert arrived. Arran would then be the jumping-off point of our entire armada for the attack on the mainland only a few miles farther east. We would all land at Turnberry in Carrick, which was, coincidentally, King Robert's birthplace. In the vicinity of this stronghold of the Bruces, at the moment full of English usurpers, it was hoped we would find many who were sympathetic to our cause.

Just before we were getting ready to bid James Douglas and his fleet good-bye, King Robert ordered me aboard. I was stunned at this decision, but excited, too, to be leaving dreary Rathlin for my own country. I was hoping that my services as page to the king had not been concluded. King Robert must have sensed my concern and said to Douglas, "Take Davie with you. He will be a help, and your present task is likely harder than mine." Then he laid an arm around my shoulder and said to me, "I will see you in Arran in a few days, Davie." And this relieved me of my worry.

We pulled out into the channel on a bright day. The water was calm and smooth and we seemed to be gliding above it. The seagulls followed us, diving low and screaming in the salty air, demanding that we throw them some tidbits. The sails filled with the breeze and the men bent to their oars, singing a sad-sounding Gaelic chantey in rhythm to the creaking of the rowing.

Éirich agus tiugainn O,
Éirich agus tiugainn O.

"We must up and be away," it means. Soon we could see the Mull of Kintyre. We sailed close to it, past a small island, and then headed northeast to the Isle of Arran. I was seated next to James Douglas, who suddenly said to me, "Davie, do you know why you're here?" His dark eyes flashed.

"I do not, sir."

"Do you mind when we were fencing back on Rathlin? I thought you fought well then. I saw you at Methven, too, so I asked the king for you to come with me."

I didn't know what to make of this. We had fenced only with sticks, but it was a compliment anyway. I knew I was now a soldier as well as the king's page. I had fought my way out of trouble at Methven, and that was some credential at least. "I hope I'm good enough, sir."

Douglas laughed, "You *must* be good, young man. Have no fear. I haven't any. I love the good fight!"

I just nodded and looked out at the approaching coastline of the Isle of Arran. I will always remember James Douglas saying that—laughing at the idea of battle, scorning death. He was one of the best soldiers I have ever met, and his attitude was certainly a part of his success. He was a small man who thought himself big.

We rounded the southern coast of Arran in neardarkness and turned north to Brodick Bay on its eastern shore. The castle occupied by the English was on the bay's north side, but we wanted to avoid it for the moment. We were able to find a place just south of the castle to beach and hide our galleys. James Douglas was whispering commands now as we hid the boats carefully and quietly in the darkness. James said we should get some rest, since we would have to wait for an opportunity to strike. Suddenly, it came. Several English boats beached very near to where we were concealed. We kept so completely quiet that we could overhear their conversation, which told us that the boats were rich with provisions. Then the voices died away. Had they gone to get more help? Had they decided there was not enough light to unload the provisions? We didn't know, so we waited for a long time. Still hearing nothing, at last James decided to wait until morning, when we could get a better view of what we had to do. I don't believe many of us slept that night, so full of excitement were we.

At first light, a dozen English came out of the castle and began to unload the boats, which contained what was for us a treasure trove of swords, shields, food, and clothing. Douglas gave his signal and immediately we fell upon them, yelling and hacking, killing every man. When those in the castle heard the noise of the fight they came out, but James bravely led us against them, so that we killed almost every one of them, too. Those left in the castle closed the gates before we could enter, too terrified to offer further resistance. In a cheerful mood, James then directed us to take the enemy's galleys along with all their provisions and arms. We sailed away, in both the English galleys and our own, to a place a little distant further south, where we could beach the vessels and establish a small fort. We picked a spot a few miles south of Brodick Bay, so that when King Robert came with his fleet he would find us before stumbling upon the English. We spent the next few days building our small citadel and waiting for the arrival of the king and our main force. Our spirits were high. None of our men were dead or even seriously wounded, and what was left of the cowed English force stayed in its castle. We hunted for food and found the island to be full of deer, easily taken. All day the sounds of many different kinds of birds sang cacophonously. Eagles flew to granite peaks towering above us. Near the coastal caves, seals barked and swam.

Before the next week was out we sighted our main fleet coming up the water. James Douglas waved his blue-and-white banner with its three stars so that they could see us. King Robert was seated in a galley accompanied by about thirty others. At least he was king of this small realm! But although his domain was tiny, he saluted us with a slight wave and a broad smile. Every man's spirit was raised by his presence. When the galleys were beached, the king greeted us, and both he and his brother were astounded when Douglas told them of our success. I was quick to grab the king's gear, since I wanted no one else to even think about taking my job.

But there was no time to celebrate. The galleys had to be hidden, and, since a light rain was falling, we all had to find some shelter. I had prepared a place for the king of which I was quite proud. I had built a small lodge with a frame of tree limbs and covered it with brush, which I hoped would keep out the elements. The king sent our new spy, Cuthbert, to row across to the mainland, scout out the terrain, and determine where the enemy was. If he found conditions favourable, he was to light a fire on the shore as a signal to us. He was immediately dispatched in a galley as night was falling.

The next morning, near noon, we could see the fire signal across the water, and as night came on it appeared even brighter. So King Robert ordered everything to be readied, and when darkness fell our entire fleet, more than forty galleys, began to row across the firth to Carrick. We were very quiet as we traversed the smooth water, and when at length we reached the mainland shore we were greeted by none other than our Cuthbert. Quivering with fright, he immediately told us he had not lit the fire, was afraid of putting out an enemy blaze, and could think of nothing better than to meet us on the shore, since he knew we would follow the false signal.

King Robert immediately attacked the man, saying, "*Tratour, quhy maid thou on the fyre?*"

Cuthbert replied, "*A! schir sa God me se! I neuir maid that fyre.*"

The poor man was shaking, and the king realised he may have done the best he could. So the forgiven Cuthbert began to brief the king on the situation. He had not made the fire, because nearby Turnberry Castle was so heavily garrisoned with Englishmen that many had to sleep outside, or in houses in the village. It was dangerous for us to be in Carrick at all. I could see that the king was debating in his own mind whether to risk going on or turn away to some safer place. Everything was at stake. Our entire army was with us, just a few hundred yards up the coast from Turnberry Castle and a huge English force. It was Edward

Bruce who took the strongest stand. "Brother," he told the king, "it must be all or nothing. We have more strength here than we have commanded before. I don't want to go back to the sea. I am ready to take my chances here and now for good or ill." Then, looking at his older brother, he said, "Robert, there are foreigners in your birthplace! This castle belongs to Bruces. Let's kill them all!"

The king heard this resolute speech and asked for other opinions. James Douglas said he was ready to go, and so did several others. "Then we go," said the king, and we manned our galleys and began to slide down the beach toward the castle and town of Turnberry, as silently as we could in the darkness. The fortress was built right on the sea, and there was an unusual sea gate through which one could sail right into the castle. This entrance was, of course, guarded by a huge wood-and-iron portcullis that was closed. We avoided this approach, and instead beached our galleys at some distance from the castle and walked to the edge of the town. There we saw many men in makeshift huts. We fell upon them immediately, killing every single one. Other men quartered in the houses of the town heard the commotion and came out to fight us, many of them without shoes. They didn't have a chance, since we were much too strong for them, and they, too, were overwhelmed. As for the men in the castle, they had witnessed what had happened in the street and were too terrified to venture out to fight.

We stayed at Turnberry for several days, picking up English booty and distributing it to all our men, but also sharing some with the hard-pressed residents of the town. Each night we had a feast, lighting a fire in the main square. The English remained in the castle. Then, one night, under a plan devised by the king, we all left Turnberry for a remote spot in the hills that was well known to the Bruce brothers. Encouraged by what they had seen, some fifteen of the townsmen came with us. Around dawn we reached our new home, and the birds sang us a welcome. It had been a hard march in the night, but now we were situated on a broad hill with an excellent view of the surrounding countryside. There were caves for sleeping in; one local man told us that the great Wallace had used them at times, but I do not know if that is true.

We settled into a new life for a few weeks in these Carrick hills. The king sent out spies for information, and every day he and Edward Bruce and James Douglas would discuss what had been gathered, then debated our strategy. There was one incident I remember that stood out for me. Every morning I escorted the king into the woods out of sight of our camp so that he could answer the call of his body. This became a daily routine. But on one sunny spring morning with bees buzzing about, the king was in his usual posture when three men approached. He said to me in quiet measured words, *"Davie, yon men will slay us, and thai may! Quhat wappyn has thou?"*

I replied, *"Schir, perfay I haf a bow, bot and vrye."*

The king said, *"Gif me thame smertly,"* and of course I complied immediately.

King Robert then took the bow in his left hand and fixed the bolt with his right. He then said to the older-looking of the three, "Halt right where you are. Do not take one step farther."

But the man and what appeared to be his sons kept on coming closer, their weapons drawn, saying that they only wanted a word with the king. The king said, "Say what you will, but halt immediately, or you will regret it." But as the men continued to approach, I said to the king, "What shall I do, then, sir?" To which the king answered, "Davie, get out of the way. If I am winning, you will have plenty of weapons. If I die, run." Then, since the three approached us still more closely, the king said, "Die, traitor," drew the bolt and shot the older man in the eye, so that it penetrated his brain and he fell dead. The second man, bearing a battleaxe, came at the king, who often carried a sword hanging from a chain around his neck. The king's sword split the second man's head with one blow. The third man came at the king with a spear and lunged at him, but the king sliced off the sharp point off the spear, and then cut off the man's head. The whole skirmish had taken no more than three minutes.

"Thank God," said I, greatly relieved and in awe of such great prowess. "Sir, you have killed the traitors."

But King Robert, true to form, answered not in a vengeful way, "Davie, *thai had beyn worthy men all three, had thai nocht beyn full of tresoune.*"

King Robert and I walked back to the camp, which was in a state of excitement. Cuthbert, one of those who had been sent in search of information, had returned with news, but would speak with no one but the king himself. At once the king retired to his meagre abode, motioning for his brother

Edward and James Douglas to follow him. I went along as usual. We were all seated except for Cuthbert, and the king told him to get on with it. It seemed that the news was poor, since Cuthbert was reluctant to begin. At last he said in a low voice, "Sir, I have news of your brothers Alexander and Thomas. I regret that it is very bad news. Their expedition met with failure, sir, and they are both dead."

This last sentence was the worst that I had ever heard, and to the end of my days it will remain so. Alexander and Thomas Bruce were two of the best men I had ever met. But it was especially the death of Alexander that instantly threw my heart into the deepest grief. I had never known such a feeling before. Alexander was the most educated man I had ever known, and my mentor as well. Most of all he had been, on the long winter on Rathlin Island, my companion. Until the moment I heard of his death, I had not realised how much he had meant to me. I loved him, I suppose, and hadn't understood that men could feel such affection for another of their own sex.

King Robert was devastated, lowering his head and placing his hand to his forehead. For a few seconds no one dared say anything. Then Edward Bruce said impatiently, "All right, Cuthbert. Give us the details."

"Well, sir, they landed at Loch Ryan as planned. Everything seemed to be going well. But they were ambushed suddenly by the Macdoualls . . ."

"Macdoualls! Lowlifes! Traitors!" was the response of Edward Bruce, who punched the wall as the room fell into silence again.

Cuthbert looked around for a signal to continue, and

Douglas nodded to him. "Well, good sirs, they never had a chance. They were overwhelmed. Someone must have betrayed them. The king's brothers were captured and taken to Carlisle, where they were executed. First they were hanged, then drawn, then decapitated, and their heads were spiked on the town walls."

The room fell completely quiet again. The king never looked up. Then James Douglas said, "Have you any good news, Cuthbert?"

"Yes indeed, sir. I have received this note from one of my friends in Ireland. He confirms what I told you, that King Edward sent a party to find you at Rathlin Island."

"What is the good news of that?" shot back Sir James.

"The good news, sir, is that I was right, and that you were not there to be captured or killed. Also, I am now, I believe, entitled to that silver piece."

King Robert, somewhat recovered from the shock of the news, reached into his pocket and gave Cuthbert the promised coin. "Is there any other news, Cuthbert?"

"Only two things more, my lord. The first is that the English, angry at not finding you on Rathlin Island, are now searching for you here on the mainland. King Edward rails against you, and mocks you as King Hob. He is furious with the noblemen he has sent to capture you. He is determined to find you, sir."

Then the king asked, "And the other, Cuthbert?"

"Sir," said Cuthbert in a matter-of-fact manner, "sir, the other is that the pope in Rome has excommunicated you and all of your followers. Scotland is no longer part of Christendom."

CHAPTER NINE

The Spider's Tale

When Cuthbert left, the king spoke to Edward Bruce and James Douglas. "These are heavy blows indeed. I must have time and a space in which to think. I will take Davie here and pay a short visit to my old friend Lady Christian of Carrick. You remember her, Edward?" The brother nodded, smiled, and made a slight shrug.

The king continued, "I must clear my mind, I must rest. I am responsible for so much tragedy, I must shut this out of my head. I must regain perspective. I am sure, also, the lady will be able to give us men, arms, and provisions. Edward, you will be in complete command here. Continue your forays into the countryside, taking on recruits and supplies. You are very good at that, brother. James, I have a special task for you. Our strategy is to destroy castles so that the English will have no place to quarter troops and supplies. We have done great damage to two strongholds at Brodick and Turnberry, but we have been unable to conquer and destroy a single castle so far. I want you, James, to visit what should rightly be your own Castle Douglas, presently occupied by the English. There you will be in a familiar place with many allies in the neighbourhood. I order you to destroy your own patrimony in order to regain it. Is that clear?"

"Quite clear, King Robert," said Douglas smiling at the opportunity. "How many men will you give me?"

"Work it out with Edward here; he is now in charge. He will make sure you have enough good men to enable you to succeed. Davie, bundle our kit and let us get under way immediately."

It didn't take me long to pack and saddle two good horses, and around noon we left the camp for the estate of Christian of Carrick. It was a beautiful spring day. A quiet breeze drove the clouds across the sky, so that it was sometimes sunny and sometimes dark. The earth smelled damp and renewed. Birds argued with and praised one another. I rode just behind the king. He didn't say anything for a long while, and we were just listening in silence to the birdsongs and the rhythm of the hooves of our horses as they beat the path. My thoughts, though, were on my friend James Douglas. I wished the king had allowed me to go on the mission to destroy Castle Douglas, because the route might take me to Dumfries, where my mother and Leezie Maxwell were, and I was very homesick for both of them.

At last the king said, "Davie, what do you think?"

I immediately rode up beside him. "Think, sir? I don't know how you mean."

"Well, my leaving the men behind for a little while. Do you think they will believe me afraid, or even unbalanced?"

"No, sir. Everyone knows those words could not possibly apply to you, sir."

"Well, I hope not, Davie. I just have to clear my mind. Many people dear to me are dead. I have murdered, and in a holy place. I have a heavy responsibility. The future of my family, my friends, and my country are at stake. I have to think very carefully. We must move boldly, but our moves must be right. And I am the one who must predict, in advance, what moves will be right."

Just then we came to a clearing in the valley, and a large, attractive house appeared. Alarmed by our hoof-beats, a lovely lady stepped out the door. She was tall and slim with blue eyes and long brown hair. As we stepped down from our mounts, she ran at King Robert and hugged him, and tears began to run freely from her eyes. "Robert, oh, Robert! There was a rumour you were dead, but, thanks be to God, you are alive! Oh, Robert, we are all so proud of you. Come inside. I will give you food and drink. And I will give you men and horses and supplies. Come in! Come in!"

Believing that the two wanted to be alone, I took the horses to the back of the house, where a small clear stream ran slowly over a bed of pebbles. The horses lapped it up until I thought they had had enough. Then I tied them and went around to the front of the house to await my orders, which were quite some time in coming. I sat beneath a tree and was dozing when the king called out to me, "Davie, it's time for some food, come in."

As soon as I went in I found a seat on the floor. King Robert laughed and commanded me, "Davie, you must come to the table. You don't want people thinking that we are class-conscious in this country, do you? Davie, this is Lady Christian. Christian, this is David Crawford, my page."

Lady Christian was very kind to me, and gave me plenty to eat and a bowl of French wine to go with it. The king and the lady talked incessantly, but I felt out of place and said nothing. I felt sure that they would rather have been alone, but they both behaved very politely toward me. Then Lady Christian asked me, "David, you don't have much to say, do you?"

"No, ma'am," was the best I could manage.

"Where do you belong?" she asked.

"My mother has a small tenancy near Dumfries, ma'am."

"And your father?"

"My father's dead, ma'am. He was killed fighting with Wallace at Falkirk."

"Oh, I'm so sorry for you and your mother. But your father was a hero then, wasn't he?"

"Yes, ma'am, that he was."

"And how does your mother keep, Davie?"

"I'm afraid I don't know, ma'am. It has been more than a year since we were together."

"That's a great shame, Davie. Robert, the lad must see his mother, don't you think? David, you miss your mother, do you not?"

"Aye, ma'am," was all I could answer.

Then King Robert smiled at me and said, "Davie, I don't know why I didn't think of it before. Take your horse and ride back to camp and see James Douglas. He may find that he will have to travel near to where your mother is, in which case you will be able to see her for a short visit. Tell him I said that he should take you along, and when your duty in Douglasdale is over, come straight back here with any news."

"Thank you, sir, but begging your pardon, sir, it's very late in the day, and it will be too dark for me to return today, as I know not well this land."

"You are right, Davie. Then you will set off at first light tomorrow. You will get an adventure with James, and perhaps a reunion with your mother in the bargain, right?"

"Thank you, sir, thank you very much."

Later that afternoon, Cuthbert came with one of our men to tell us that a small force of Englishmen and Scottish traitors was in the immediate area, looking for us. Accordingly, King Robert asked Lady Christian if there was some other place nearby where he could stay. "I do not want to put you in jeopardy, Christian," he said. "Therefore I must not stay with you this night."

"There is a cave not far away where you will be safe," she said. "Come, I will take you there, before the light fails us."

We three walked through the late-afternoon chill until

we reached a cave on a hillside in the forest. King Robert and Lady Christian engaged in a lengthy embrace, which I tried to pretend I couldn't see or hear. I entered the cave and began to prepare a fire. As darkness fell, the king came inside. I presumed that Lady Christian had returned to her estate. The fire had burned down and was soon just embers, but it gave us enough light to see each other, and enough warmth to take away some of the chill. Lady Christian had furnished King Robert with several jugs of wine, and he began to drink from a wooden bowl. Soon he passed it to me, and the bowl went back and forth between us. We said nothing for a long time, perhaps several hours, but I felt close to the king, and I believe that he felt close to me. He was of the highest class and the greatest distinction, and I, well, I was really nothing but his page. I was sure he would rather be spending the night with someone else—Lady Christian, his brother Edward, or many others. But he was here with me, and I think that perhaps it was for the best, since I was someone neutral to talk to. I was a blank wall against which he could cast his thoughts. He began to speak to me as if I was an important confidant, and I believe that it was the most significant night of my life.

"Och, Davie, what do you think of all of this?" His words were somewhat slurred, since we had started on the second jug of wine and I was taking only small draughts. I didn't answer and he continued, "What have we got? What are we doing? Where are we going? Let's take stock, Davie boy. Let's take stock. Let's see. What land calls me king? I mean what is it that I rule? Not Scotland, certainly. Neither do I rule it by other names, such as *Écosse* and

Alba. Nor do I rule Carrick, where people once doffed their caps when I passed. I rule Carrick no longer, nor Annandale. I rule, instead, this cave, and there are those who would take even this away from me. Had you the inclination and a dagger, you could, in the night, usurp even this realm from me and I would rule nothing at all. What have I started, Davie? I was, not long ago, rich and well thought of in this land. My good reputation extended to England, too, where I was until recently one of that country's richest men. I had *puissance* with the English king himself, and even in Normandy, and Ireland, where I have rich and powerful relatives and friends. But now I am hunted like a wild beast. My wife, the queen, is in custody somewhere in England." At this the eyes of the king became wet with tears. "My daughter, Davie, my dear little Marjorie is imprisoned in the Tower of London. May God help them. My dear Isabel, the Countess of Buchan, is in a cage suspended from the walls of Berwick; my sister Mary is likewise detained at Roxburgh. My handsome young brothers Nigel, Alexander, and Thomas, whose careers were once so promising, are all dead, murdered in barbarous fashion by people not even good enough to bear the name of savage. Many other noble friends of mine have met similar fates. How, therefore, have I done, Davie? Have I improved the lot of my family, friends, and countrymen? Well, Davie, don't answer. We know already the answer, don't we? Do you think I deserve better, Davie; I, who came late to this struggle? Think of poor Wallace and all he endured. What a man he was; a giant of a man, a foot taller than myself. I did not help him at the beginning. Och, it's true that I took the field with him. It was just about ten years ago, and you were very young; only about six, maybe. Wallace had the people behind him, and many nobles, too. Yes, I took the field with Wallace, I even knighted him, made him Sir William, which he well deserved. But I backed off and left him and your good father and all the others to die. I had an idea that peace with King Edward, who held himself out as a friend, was possible. Look now as he reveals his true character. There is nothing to be obtained from King Edward but tyranny. Wallace cared only about Scotland, you see. I am a proud Scot, of course—always I have been. But I cared about my lands in England. I had good relationships with the English. I had standing, wealth, and power in several countries. Well, Davie, I am a pure patriotic Scot now. I now see what Wallace saw very clearly then. We are all Scots and nothing else. We have ties with the English, but we are not English. We have different ancestors and different traditions. How could I have not seen that before, when there was still time to help Wallace? Is it too late, Davie? I feel Scotland very deeply now, and I know that I am its rightful king. But are we too late? I am king of this cave only. *L'état, c'est moi!* I am the state, Davie. It is not a boast; it is the sad truth. I am the state because the state is nothing other than myself. I have tried, and so far have failed. I have nothing left but a few men and my spirit; but my spirit is going, Davie. It is not strong."

The king took a deep draught on the second jug, finished it, and began to pour the third. "Well, Davie, how can we improve this dire situation? Of course, we have our army." At this the king gave a small laugh, which he quickly stifled. "Yes, Davie, we have an army of perhaps a hundred, with perhaps a few hundred more who are ready to join us. Well, now, that's quite a few, is it not, Davie? Quite a few indeed against the power of the greatest fighting force in the world, which is, we are told, moving north to come at us. Think of them, Davie. Think of the might of the English cavalry, the best in the world. We have not, in Scotland, enough good horses to form a decent cavalry. Think of their archers, numbering in the thousands. Think of their powerful siege engines, Davie. Think of their resolute king who calls himself the Hammer of the Scots. We must admit that he is an excellent soldier, and motivated by a grand hatred of us. Well, it may be a bit too much for us, Davie. Many would say it is hopeless. Would you say we were in a hopeless situation, Davie? I the king of this cave, and you my foreign secretary? See Davie, yon spider against yon wall? Perhaps her situation could be called hopeless also. I have been watching her these last few minutes. See her there hanging by just one thread from her body. She is suspended there, swinging back and forth, trying to reach that far corner there, from which to make the first strand on her web. She has tried thrice, and failed thrice. Perhaps what she attempts cannot be done. If she cannot make the first landing, she cannot make the first strand for her web. Perhaps her situation is hopeless. What do you think, Davie? It looks hopeless to me."

The king took another draught on the wine and lay back, closing his eyes. The light from the embers danced on his tired face. I began to watch the spider as she tried and failed three more times. It did not look as if she was getting any closer to success with each try. If anything, each attempt appeared to fail by a larger margin. Then suddenly, her situation changed. She seemed to take a greater care in her effort, swinging her body with more determination, making the arc bigger, and then she was able, on the next try, to establish contact with the far corner and secure the first strand of a new web.

The king was almost asleep when I decided to speak without being spoken to for the first time since I had met him. "Sir," I began, "Yon spider's plight was not hopeless. She has secured the first strand, and is making her web." On the word "plight" my voice broke, it being that I was still in the time of the low hair. It embarrassed me and I hoped that the king didn't hear it.

At this King Robert began to rise and, blinking his eyes, looked at the spider now confidently working. "You are right, Davie, right indeed. The spider's situation was not hopeless, as it seemed to me. But we can take small comfort from this as our situation is far worse than was hers."

"Worse, sir?" I asked. "I think perhaps *her* situation was worse than ours, sir. She was probably running out of strength, and might have starved to death had she not completed her task on what was perhaps her last try."

The king sat up, his back leaning against the wall of the cave. He drank no more, but sat for a while, watching the spider build her web. For a time he said nothing. Then, quietly, he said to me, "Davie, what has passed here tonight must stay with us. I realise I must return at once to my troops. I was selfish to think I would be afforded a respite in this struggle. I should not have left. I will return with you tomorrow. Our situation is not hopeless. We are, after all, in the right. We have the advantage of being defenders of our homeland and of our freedom. The invaders will not have the same motivation. We are few in numbers, but we have enough skill and arms to win one battle; and if we win that battle, then the momentum will swing toward us in the next. The more we show our skill and our resolve, the more people will come to our cause. We shall pursue our strategy of destroying English-held castles one at a time. We are beginning with Castle Douglas, and tomorrow you will join James Douglas in that endeavour."

Suddenly I fell asleep, but it wasn't long before the early light was dawning, and the tomorrow of which the king had spoken became today. I looked for the king in vain; he had left to be with Lady Christian. I hurried out of the cave to the house where the lady was making us a fragrant breakfast of porridge and butter. The king sent me around to the stream, where I filled two pitchers with the cool, clear water. He drank one by himself as we tore into the porridge. The beautiful lady ate with us and promised King Robert that men, arms, supplies, and horses would be on the way to our camp within three days. The attitude of the king had changed. I could see the energy in his eyes, bloodshot though they were after the restless night. The determination had returned to his expression, and I could see he was excited about his prospects, and absolutely resolved to realise his destiny. He was now going to do what he had been born to do.

I left the house and busied myself with the gear and the horses so that the two could be alone. Soon the king appeared; Lady Christian stood by her door. She waved a tearful good-bye as we rode out of her courtyard.

The sun was up and the breeze was light when we headed back to the camp. The king didn't speak for a long time, and we rode in silence, our steeds kicking up earth behind us. When we were approaching the camp, King Robert addressed me. "Davie, you were a great help to me last night, and I shall not forget it."

I didn't know how to respond to this so I said, "Why, sir?"

"Why?" said the king. Then he smiled at me and said, "Davie, I am not dense, and neither are you. You know very well that you made me look at the spider's success because it might change my mood. You did it, Davie. You showed me that if a little spider could overcome adversity, I could overcome it, too."

CHAPTER TEN

Momentous Success

There was a great crowd to greet us when we rode into camp. Everyone seemed to be in good spirits at the sight of the king, who had not been expected back for at least a week. King Robert smiled as his men waved at him. He looked grand on his horse, and he uncovered his head and waved his bonnet, showing off his great mane of black hair. Everyone could see he was now ready. He dismounted and smiled broadly in greeting his brother Edward and James Douglas, who was packing for his mission. Immediately the three held a meeting at which it was decided that the king would head north. The object was to reach Campbell country, where we had allies and where we would be joined by the galleys of Angus Og Macdonald. We would then proceed up the Great Glen. Should all this be accomplished, we would be in territory where there were very few

English soldiers, and we would be in a position to conquer the Highlands. James Douglas was to continue his operation separately with six men, of which I was one.

At this point our messenger and spy Cuthbert arrived with more news. King Edward had sent letters to his commanders in Scotland raging against their inability at capturing our king. "He calls you yet 'King Hob,' sir, and he warns his commanders to get you at all costs. He himself is in the north of England, not two days' journey from here, and is preparing an attack on his own. He rants at his men that he is the Hammer of the Scots. But I see that he is very ill, and will probably not be able to make the attempt in person. Also, sir, there is a large contingent of English approaching from the east, but I perceive not whether they ken your whereabouts, sir."

This information changed our plans immediately. King Robert's move to the north would have to be postponed in order to meet the approaching threat. Our assault on Douglas Castle would have to be made from the south, since we would probably meet the enemy if we went east or northeast. We would have to head south, slip around and behind the English forces, and then go north. When we had finished our mission, we would then come west to rejoin the king in Carrick, or farther north in Campbell country should the new threat not materialise or be defeated.

We in Douglas's party left without much baggage, but each of us was carrying three swords and three dirks. It was a pleasant day, overcast with a little rain and occasional sunshine. Sir James had chosen his men from among the youngest in our army, and since he was only about twenty himself, we all considered ourselves to be daring and dauntless soldiers. The ride was easy, mostly downhill, and Sir James was in a happy mood, at last getting a chance to punish those who had stolen his patrimony. Toward dark we approached the town of Dumfries, and I was able to direct our band to my mother's place, carefully avoiding any contact with the town, which we had heard was under enemy control. At length we came to the familiar thatched cottage in a clearing in the woods. I say familiar, and yet it looked as if it were different somehow since I had left. I noticed that one of the wooden shutters was broken and hanging limply. But the colourful flowerboxes, my mother's pride, were still in their proper places.

My mother was so shocked to see me that she broke down sobbing. She hugged me so hard I could scarcely breathe. "Davie, Davie, Davie, you're alive, alive!" My comrades left us alone and tended to the horses. "Where have you been, Davie?" she asked me.

"I've been with King Robert. I'm his page. I went away with him the night he killed the Red Comyn. I had no means to let you know. I'm sorry."

She lifted her white apron above her long dress and dried her tears. Her eyes were wide. "The whole county knows you ran away with the king, Davie. You're a hero in these parts, only no one knew if you survived. Och, Davie, I'm right proud of you. He'll be a grand king, do you not think, Davie, lad? Do you really talk to him? Are you all right, Davie?"

"Yes, I'm fine, Mother. Och, aye, I talk to the king all the time. He is a great man, the greatest in Scotland, and soon we will get our freedom back."

Just then the men returned and I introduced them to her. I saved James Douglas for last, and my mother was flabbergasted that I was in such company; she made a deep curtsy. It made me think that, with the king, I was just a page, but with the youthful James I was a comrade—not an equal, but more than a page.

"We're right proud of your Davie, Mrs. Crawford. He's a good lad and brave," James Douglas said.

My mother was so taken by this statement from such a great personage that she didn't know how to respond, so she remained silent. She began to make us a dinner of bannocks, cheese, and eggs. We drank fresh milk along with it. I especially liked my mother's bannocks; none were better. Hers were cooked of whole meal and butter. She made them in a round, and then cut across them in straight lines to make triangular scones. Placed on the griddle, they puffed up beautifully. She served them with lots of salted butter. The men remarked at the quality of her cooking.

After supper she showed her guests where they would sleep and gave them blankets. When we were alone, she took me aside and whispered, "Leezie's dead, Davie. I'm sorry."

My heart seemed to have fallen into my stomach. "How, Mother?"

"The English got to her. It was when they took back the town of Dumfries. They wanted to make an example of her."

"And they killed her?"

"Aye, they killed her—and more—and worse."

I am quite sure that I have never been so angry and filled with hatred as I was at that moment. I couldn't sleep at all that night, and when the first light came I was anxious to get started on our mission. I was now more than a page. I had become a determined soldier.

In the morning, my mother gave each of us a bannock to eat and one to take along on our ride. We gave thanks to her, and she embraced me in tears.

"Are you all right, Mother?"

"Aye, I am. The English haven't bothered me yet, and if they do I have provisions hidden where they can't find them. I've put things in the forest." Her eyes welled again. "Davie, please do us proud. I am so happy with you. Fight for our freedom. But Davie, be safe, please be safe."

"I will be all right, Mother," I said. "I want *you* to be safe." I mounted my horse and as we left she waved goodbye. "Tell King Robert the people are with him, Davie."

I nodded and gave her a kiss, and the tears started again. The men thanked her once more and then we rode north from my old home bound for Douglasdale in Lanarkshire.

The morning was misty, with a light rain. We followed the valley of the River Nith for a while and then climbed higher so as to avoid being seen. At the higher elevations we encountered sleet, which stung our faces, but by the end of the day, with dark coming on, we reached a hill, and there below us we could see Douglas Castle and Douglasdale. James instructed us to make camp, but as we were just beginning the task he said, "I'm going down to see how

101

many friends we have in the neighbourhood. I'm taking Davie with me. Make everything secure by the time we return. All right, Davie, let's go."

At this James Douglas and I began on foot to walk down to the valley. It was almost dark when we reached the house of Tom Dickson, a man of considerable substance and a loyal follower of James's late father, Sir William Douglas. Dickson didn't recognise his visitor, since James had gone to France as a boy and was now returning as a man, and a man dressed in fine French clothes at that. But when James disclosed his identity, Dickson welcomed him in a most gracious manner. "My God, James. You have returned to fight, have you not? Everyone in the county has said you are with King Robert. Is it true?"

"Yes, Tom, I am proud to be associated with the greatest soldier in Christendom. But I have come here to regain my patrimony. Will you help me, Tom?"

Dickson's eyes narrowed, and without the slightest hesitation, his jaw set squarely, he said, "By God sir, I will help you, and others will as well. The English have robbed us, killed us, and raped our women. We are ready for revenge if you will but lead us to it." Then he knelt before James, and said, "I am your man, just as I was your father's. I await your command, James."

"Then arise, Tom, for we must plan. How many loyal men can you assemble quickly?"

"About a dozen, sir, whom I am sure can be trusted. What is your plan, sir?"

"I have no plan, Tom, except that I intend to destroy

Douglas Castle and kill every man in it. Is Sir Robert Clifford, that ugly usurper, resident there?"

"No, James, he who claims your property is at present in England."

"Bad luck, then; he will escape, but I must proceed anyway. I must plan an ambush and surprise the enemy. We will not be as numerous as they. We must get them out of the castle, Tom. Can you think of a way?"

"By my faith, sir, the Lord is with us. Do you know what day tomorrow is, sir? It is Palm Sunday, and even though the English are not great for churchgoing, tomorrow, all of them, or at least most of them, will be carrying palms to St. Bride's kirk, as will all of the men we can summon tonight."

"Capital," replied Sir James. "I have five men on yon hill. If you can get another dozen, plus yourself, we shall make twenty in all. With surprise, we can kill several dozen easily."

"But, Sir James," came Dickson's reply. "The English have taken most of our weapons, save those few we could hide."

"My men have extra weapons; do not fear. Can we organise the dozen men immediately?"

"Of course, James. Let me get a lantern. May I ask who attends you?"

"Certainly. This is David Crawford, King Robert's page and my trusted friend."

I don't think I have to tell you how that last remark affected me. It is true that I had become familiar with James, but I had not realised that he had thought so well of me. I resolved right then to become the most stalwart soldier in his band.

All through the early evening hours, James, Tom Dickson, and myself tramped through the damp landscape by lantern light, knocking on doors. It was the same everywhere. All were stunned at the appearance of James Douglas, and all did him homage without question. All were ready to kill our enemies on the morrow. All agreed to meet us before dawn on the hill above, carrying their own weapons, if possible. If not, they would use some of the swords and daggers we had brought.

By the time we got back on our hill, it was too late to sleep much, but I was tired and got in an hour or two. Before dawn our recruits began to arrive. It was dark and cold, but spirits were high. Every man felt he was serving not only his own interests, and not only the interests of the Douglases, but the patriotic claims of King Robert the Bruce as well. This was the first opportunity for these men to strike a blow for the freedoms that had been stolen from all Scots. It was agreed that the men would return to their homes and walk to St. Bride's for the Palm Sunday service with weapons hidden. James Douglas and his six men would wait in hiding some distance from the kirk, and then, when the service had begun and all of the English and all of Dickson's men were inside, James would sound his esteemed family's famous cry, and the slaughter would begin.

Our hearts began to pound as the sun came up on a beautiful day. It was just like my mother used to say, that Palm Sunday and Easter should be fair, and foul weather was all that could be expected or even deserved of Good Friday. From all directions, people were walking toward the kirk, but the largest contingent by far were the English coming from the castle. They looked a rather bedraggled lot. Probably they had been drinking too much of the Douglas family's wine. Few of them appeared to be armed. They were very casual in their deportment. Our men were also among the crowd moving towards St. Bride's with their weapons hidden. At last there were no more arrivals, the church doors were closed, and the service began. We followed James toward the church, and just as we reached it he let out his cry, "Douglas! Douglas!" Immediately there was mayhem inside the kirk. We opened the doors and rushed in to commit what was perhaps the most horrible carnage I have ever seen. Women were screaming, trying to take bairns and weans out of the place. The English, those who had weapons, fought bravely, but never had a chance at victory. Our men were hacking and stabbing away with a fervour I had never witnessed before. Blood and body parts were everywhere. The dying and wounded moaned unattended. Of course, it wasn't long before every single Englishman in the place had been put to death or captured. We let the women and children alone.

Then it was on to the castle, a formidable stone fortress that at its highest point was gaily flying Sir Robert Clifford's beautiful banner with its checkerboard of blue and gold and bright-red fesse. The English had left the place vulnerable, with the gates wide open; the drawbridge over the moat was down and guarded only by a cook and a porter. These two were dispatched quickly, and the prison-

ers were thrown into the wine cellar. It was then discovered that a beautiful table had been set with linen and the
Douglas family's best silver for a festive Palm Sunday dinner. Upon this news, James ordered the castle doors shut
and invited all his supporters to a feast, complete with his
best wine and the deceased chef's best creations. The idea
was that we would dine at ease, but we were too hungry
and too emotionally tied to the morning's events to be
dainty. Our men tore into the food and wine until some
had had a bit too much. James Douglas made a little
speech and drank to the valour of his supporters. Then he
directed us to take anything of value that we could carry
and to put it aside. He himself went aloft to haul down the
offensive Clifford banner. After that he ordered us to drag
the corpses of the dead from the kirk to the castle, throw
them into the cellar, and there behead all the prisoners.
We then broke open all the wine casks, threw the meal
and other provisions on top, and ignited the entire mix. As
a last gesture Douglas threw the Clifford banner on the
pyre. The whole affair was not a lovely sight, and as the
monstrous stew burned in giant flames, a great stinking
cloud soared aloft from the castle.

Most of the local men decided to come with us to join
King Robert, and bade good-bye to their homes and families, if indeed they had any families left who had survived
the harsh English rule. They were patriotic, of course, but
practical, too. If they stayed and Clifford returned, as was
certainly possible, they would have been put to death. As
we rode away, heading west uphill with our band, which
had started with seven and now numbered about fifteen,

James Douglas brought our party to a halt. He reached into his saddlebag and pulled out an old frayed Douglas banner, white and blue with three stars.

"I have been saving this for just such an occasion," he said. His dark eyes were actually merry on this grim day. He gave the banner to one of the men and bid him attach it to a spear and carry it before our small force. Then he took a last look back to the destruction we had wrought below, at the great cloud of smoke and the flames of our grisly roast. "Sir Robert Clifford," he said, smiling, "took my Douglas Castle from me, but I have taken it back, and left him with the Douglas Larder!"

II

Our little band under the command of James Douglas rode southwest for most of that day. All along our way we were joined by men, many with homemade weapons. When we told the local people of the Douglas Larder, they were encouraged that Scotland had really started on the road to freedom. We were able to gather in more recruits to our cause every day. As we passed farmhouses, stopping for water and to rest our horses and ourselves, we heard that an English force of some fifteen hundred, under the command of Aymer de Valence, the Earl of Pembroke, was moving to the west to try to capture our king. When we reached Carrick, we could find no trace of King Robert, but an old widow told us that he was with his army in the forest at Glen Trool, to the south in Galloway. Being suspicious of this information, since it indicated a change of plans, we were reluctant to believe it, but when she gave us her three sons as soldiers for our band, we acted on her advice and headed south. Sure enough, in the rough country at Glen Trool we found our army, which including our contingent now numbered about three hundred. The king and the entire group rejoiced in the tale of the Douglas Larder. It was the first of many strongholds to be destroyed, and I was proud to have taken part in it. The king's strategy of destroying castles to deny them for the use of the enemy had begun to be implemented. It was a real victory, and I could feel that the morale of our army had been lifted. We were ready to fight now, above all for our freedom.

We spent several fine days in Glen Trool. The hunting for boar and deer was excellent, and each night we were treated to a fine supper, although there was no wine or ale to be had. Our camp was pitched high above the glen and its placid blue loch. Still we did not see the English forces our informants had led us to expect. I overheard several conversations among our leaders that made me think we might leave the glen in search of our enemies, but King Robert counselled patience and ordered us to keep to the high ground.

One afternoon, an old woman climbed up to our camp, asking for alms. The king was suspicious of her behaviour and ordered her brought before him. He addressed her sternly, and almost immediately she broke down and confessed that she had been sent by the English to do reconnaissance for them. They were very near and hoped to surprise us. Upon hearing this, King Robert ordered all to arms, and himself put on armour. Then he sent the woman back to the English, ordering her to tell them we were not ready for any battle and warned her that she would be killed if she did not.

Within a half-hour they came into the glen, a grand organised army of fifteen hundred, against our ill-equipped three hundred. Yet we were confident, since King Robert had chosen his ground carefully. We were stationed far above them, and every man had a weapon and several rocks that had been gathered in the days before. When they finally saw us, they began to ride slowly up the hill, led by Aymer de Valence and Sir Robert Clifford. The king had not given us the order to fight, so that for a moment it seemed very quiet. Then James Douglas waved his blue-and-white banner with its three stars at the English, and, recognising Clifford by his coat of arms, yelled out, "Hello Clifford, you son of a bitch! How do you like your castle now?" At this our men began to laugh; they yelled vulgar remarks while the English kept coming slowly up the hill at us. King Robert suddenly let fly an arrow, striking one of our enemies in the throat. He then gave the signal for each man to roll his rocks down the hill to the great confusion of the English. Some of their knights were unhorsed, and some of their horses were knocked to the ground. Our king, seeing their disorder, gave the command, "*Apon thame, for thai ar discomfit all!*"

The battle was over in just a few minutes. We hacked

our way down the hill, and it wasn't long before their leaders could no longer keep the men organised. Soon they were in a rout, running and riding away from us in shame toward the safety of their encampment at Carlisle. We heard some days later that King Edward had raged at de Valence and Clifford and had called them cowards.

The battle at Glen Trool had gone well enough. We had withstood the attack of fifteen hundred men without taking any casualties. But the English had got away, for the most part, safely. It was really not so much a battle as it was a confrontation from which they had run away. We had not destroyed any more castles, which was our principal strategy. We had, however, survived this great threat, this battle in which we had to prevail. Many more men now joined us, realising that we had bested five times our number and were credibly a threat to the English occupier. We were able to double the size of our army in just a few weeks. However, the angry King Edward doubled the size of the English forces as well, and we were informed that now three thousand men were moving north to meet us.

Gradually we, too, began to march north. Since I was able to overhear strategy sessions, I knew that our plan was still to reach the Highlands as soon as possible. There we would encounter fewer English troops and could better pursue our grand strategy of destroying occupied castles. Before we could do that, however, we faced another challenge from the south. We were at that time encamped at Galston, where we had pacified a large area. One day an English rider approached our camp and asked for a safe passage to parley with our king. This was granted. The

English knight told our leaders that he had been sent by Aymer de Valence. The knight handed a message to the king that called us cowards and dared us to fight Valence and his army in a chivalrous manner on the tenth of May at Loudon Hill, a place nearby to our encampment. The haughtiness of the knight and of Valence's challenge angered our king. He was further goaded by his brother Edward Bruce, who said, "Robert, I cannot accept this insult. We must respond and crush these haughty men." The king, in great agitation, considered a moment, and then looked the English knight dead in the eye and said, *"Sa to thi lord that, gif I be in lif, he sall me se that day. By Loudoun Hill mete hym sall I."* And so it was set. The English knight rode away, and we began immediately to move our camp to Loudon Hill. Once again King Robert would give us the advantage by his uncanny ability to use terrain as a weapon.

We now faced a pitched battle against a superior army that we would have to win, but there was really no choice. We could not advance to the Highlands with such a strong force at our backs. It would be difficult, but if we could win, we knew that the English would be demoralised and would have to regroup, and this would give us time to reach the north. Also, if we were to prevail, our success would draw many more recruits to our cause.

Upon reaching Loudon Hill, we found the field below to be broad and bounded on either side by bogs. King Robert reasoned that the English on horses would not be able to reach us over the soft ground, and determined they would have to confront him on the firm turf, straight on.

He knew that if we defended the hard ground in the centre, that we could not be successfully attacked by a flanking movement. However, there was still too much ground for our men to defend against a huge cavalry assault. The breadth of the field would spread our men too thinly, even in the centre. The king knew we would need an additional advantage, and he devised it on the spot. He ordered three great deep ditches to be dug on each side between the hard ground and the bog, thus narrowing the field on which our men would make their stand. Not being able to go around us on the soft boggy land or through the trenches, the enemy would have to come straight at us, across the narrowed centre of the field. It turned out to be a brilliant plan.

On the morning of the tenth of May, the disciplined English army of three thousand approached our six hundred Scots on the field below Loudon Hill. It was quite a sight to see them coming at us in the early sunlight. *Thair basnetis burnyst var all brycht agane the sone; thair speris, thair pennownys and thair scheldis.* Their horses sent up a great cloud of dust, and the sound of their hooves made a noise like thunder. The beautiful multicoloured coats of arms of the English nobility added to the scene. They were coming toward us slowly, as if to taunt us, and I am sure that they expected to rout us off the field. There were so many of them that we would have lost our nerve had we not known about the secret ditches. I cannot say I was unafraid. Everyone in such circumstances knows that he may be living his last few minutes on this earth. But we were resolved, and we had confidence in the leadership of our king, his brother Edward Bruce, and of course James Douglas, who was winning fame throughout the land.

The king stood watching with the rest of us. A slight breeze had come up and the warm sun shone on his shield; on his chest was the glorious red-and-gold rampant lion coat of arms of the King of Scots. Then he addressed us. "Men, you stand here the Guardians of Scotland. This is a battle we must win. As you can all see, there are many more of them than there are of us. This should not be too discouraging, since they cannot fight in the bogs nor through the ditches and will have to meet us in the centre, where at any time they will have no more men in the front than will we. I expect every man to fight bravely, for if we lose we shall be slaves. If we win, however, there will be no more doubters in any part of Scotland that we have the will to win this war. Be especially firm when their first wave comes, for if it finds us resolute, the rest of them will be discouraged. Now let us move forward and defend the centre." Then King Robert raised his sword and yelled, "Scotland forever! *Toujours l'Écosse! Alba gu brath!*"

When the enemy saw us formed up, they charged across the width of the entire field. Immediately their horses on the flanks were caught in the bogs; those that still could moved to the already-crowded centre. This cut down their speed and caused them confusion. When the flanks of their first wave reached the trench, the surprised horses fell, some of them throwing their riders. The second wave, not understanding what was happening, entered the first ditch, falling on those who had gone before. Immediately our men attacked them, throwing spears and hacking at them with swords. Just as King Robert had planned, the bogs and the ditches forced the English to the centre, where their greater numbers were useless. Our men fought with the fervour of men defending their homeland and were able to stand their ground. The scene was terrible. Wounded men were yelling, horses were rearing up and running away. Blood was everywhere, and dust, too. The smell of death filled the air. Swords and shields were ringing and sparkling in the sun. Just as King Robert predicted, the English in the rear became discouraged by the fact that we were holding our line. Everyone could see we had killed more than a hundred or so in just a few minutes. Many in the English rear began to leave the field. Valence tried to rally his troops, but they were running away. When he saw it was no use, he himself began to retreat, whereupon our leaders urged us on even more stoutly. At this the entire English army left the field.

We had won a great victory. All Scotland soon heard of it, and men from all parts of the country came to us in great numbers. There were few doubters then. Even those still hostile to us knew we had the ability and the will to win. After we had rested awhile, savouring our victory, we began to move north, as the king had ordered. Although the English held castles there, they weren't garrisoned as well as those in the south. We expected to pick up many Highlanders to our cause as well. At last we were winning.

The Road to Bannockburn

A few weeks later, Cuthbert the messenger came to us saying that Valence had gone immediately from Loudon Hill to England, where in shame he resigned his post to King Edward. The English king, furious at the defeat, and especially that "King Hob" had not been captured, berated Valence, calling him a coward and not even a knight. King Edward, despite his delicate health, decided to lead the next expedition himself.

CHAPTER ELEVEN

Taking the Highlands

Our victory at Loudon Hill changed everything for the better. Part of our booty was the captured English supply train, which included many weapons, much food, and, most important, the wages of the English army. Spoils were the only source of money to pay the men, so this was significant. Everyone got his share. We knew the enemy was retreating to England and could not bother us for some time. King Robert therefore decided, once again, to delay our northward movement, to deal instead with the Macdoualls, our Scottish enemies who had been responsible for the death of his brothers Thomas and Alexander. I'm sure the thirst for vengeance played a part in the king's decision. I was certainly ready for it myself, since I was still crestfallen over the death of my friend Alexander.

We rode south into deepest Galloway, burning houses

we judged to be owned by sympathisers of our enemies, capturing cattle, and generally terrorising the people to the extent that many went over the border into England. We demanded tribute from some men we knew were loyal to the Macdoualls. Within a few weeks we established our order in Galloway. For the first time our patriot army was in control of a province. King Robert put James Douglas and his men in charge of the entire southwest, and the rest of us departed, at last, for the north.

As we moved toward the Clyde valley, it had become summer. The weather was fair and the news even better. Cuthbert brought us the best tidings we could have wished for: King Edward I, our archenemy, the Hammer of the Scots, was dead. The old man, still enraged at our success and at what he considered to be the incompetence of his soldiers, had mounted an attack himself, pushing his dying body along with his troops. He never made it out of England. He died, still cursing us, they say, at Burgh-on-Sands just north of Carlisle on July 7, 1307. The dying English king demanded that his tomb in Westminster Abbey be identified by the inscription *Edwardus Primus Rex, Scotorum Malleus*: King Edward I, Hammer of the Scots.

The Hammer's son, King Edward II, immediately took command of the English army and moved it into Scotland. He was not the man his father was, of course. His moves were tentative and not well thought out. He was learning to be a warrior king, and treated his invasion as a sort of field trip. He struck no blow and retreated to England by the end of August.

The Road to Bannockburn

This was, of course, great news for our weary men. Without any possible opposition from the English or the Macdoualls in the immediate days ahead, we were able to proceed northward at an easy pace. All along the way we were cheered by the people who acknowledged us as the liberating army we were. In a few months, we had turned from a rabble into soldier heroes. Feasts, usually humble, were held in the soft evenings on village greens. We were treated to food and ale. Men were now joining our army by the dozens. The people looked different; they were happy. We had cut the bonds of tyranny that had held them for so long. Their expressions bore the optimistic cast of freedom.

On one such evening King Robert took me aside from the festivities and told me to my great surprise to saddle our two horses, for we were going to visit Lady Christian of Carrick. She had arranged to meet us just outside a nearby village, in an empty farmer's cottage. When we arrived, we were greeted warmly. A fire was lit and a serving girl about my age gave us wine and some bread and butter. The fire-light danced on her shiny brown hair and she smiled at me, baring a row of white teeth.

After a few minutes, the king said he would like to be excused, and motioned to a side room that contained a bed where I could sleep. No sooner was I under the covers than the serving girl came into the room with a candle and, still smiling, began to disrobe. She was very beautiful, I thought, her body slim and taught. She lay down in the bed next to me, very boldly. I felt rather shy, but she soon helped me overcome that. After we made love I held her close and before long we were both asleep. She was gone when I awoke the next morning. I found her at the fire, making oat cakes for breakfast. The king and Lady Christian were already at table, and both smiled at me and bade me good morning. Lady Christian looked beautiful, her long brown tresses cascading down her bust, her deep blue eyes piercing. She asked me if I had indeed been able to visit my mother. When I answered that I had, she asked me, "And how did you find her keeping?" I replied that I had found her well, and Lady Christian smiled at me. I thought her a very charming person. We ate quickly and within a few minutes the king and I were on our way to rejoin our army. I waved a wistful good-bye to the serving girl without ever having learned her name.

Our army progressed northward over the next several weeks. The snow was gone from the mountaintops, and the cuckoos sang their welcome to summer. There were English all around, but for the most part they stayed clear of us. Near the River Clyde, though, we met a small de-tachment and quickly did them in. We soon entered the Highlands, where the people we encountered spoke Gaelic or, as some called it, "Irish." It sounded very beautiful to me, much softer than our Scots. I couldn't converse in it, but of course we all knew some of the old tongue. Even as far south as Dumfries, "glen" meant valley, "bal" was town, "bard" was poet, "auch" was a field, "galore" meant plenty, and so forth. We used these words and many others all the time. As Highland recruits joined us, I tried to get close to one or two of them in order to better learn and understand the tongue. I think I can say I am good at languages, perhaps because I had some French and Latin as a boy. We also had with us two men from the Low Countries, John van der Meer and George Witt, but we all called them simply John Fleming and George Fleming. Often they would speak to each other in their native Flemish, and I have never heard anything so ugly in my life. It was something like Scots, but much harsher and without our lilt. I could even pick up a word here and there, but I couldn't begin to make some of the sounds. It was good that both of them had learned to speak Scots.

We continued our march through the western Highlands, keeping to the east of the Firth of Lorn and later Loch Linnhe. We were escorted by our navy—the galleys of Angus Og Macdonald, which kept pace with us on the water. We must have seemed a formidable force, since we encountered no resistance anywhere, and we picked up volunteers almost every day. Our immediate goal was the Comyn stronghold of Inverlochy at the head of Loch Linnhe. But our old nemesis, John Macdougall of Lorne, blocked our passage. I doubt he wanted to confront us, and King Robert was anxious to get on with our northern campaign, so the two met and agreed to a truce.

Having removed this obstacle, we proceeded up the east side of Loch Linnhe. I know our lowlands are beautiful, but I was not prepared for the wild glory of the Highlands. At one point we marched through a great sweeping valley filled with streams crashing down at many places. It was a huge place, the sides of which ran up to marvellous heights far above us. It was a brooding valley, almost evil, I should say, in its aspect. One of the Highlanders told me that it is called *"Gleann Caoidh,"* or "The Valley of Weeping." As we trekked through this glen on a misty day, the name seemed apt.

A day later we arrived at Inverlochy. It had few defenders and we conquered it and reduced it to rubble in a few days. We were now at the southern end of the Great Glen, which cuts Scotland in two. Our army was certainly one of the largest, perhaps the largest that the Highlands had ever seen. We felt invincible, and I think our remaining opponents thought we were, too. We swept up the Great Glen, though "swagger" might be a better way to describe how we moved. We met almost no resistance, and when we came to Urquhart Castle on Loch Ness, our opponents had fled and all we had to do was destroy the place and carry off with us anything of value we could find.

At Loch Ness we met people who told us that there was a great monster who lived in its murky depths. People had seen it, they said, seven centuries before our time. They told us the loch was very deep and contained more water than there was in all of England and Scotland put together. I could believe that, but as hard as we all tried, none of us saw the monster.

It was now autumn and we were arriving at Inverness, where the northern end of Loch Ness empties into the Moray Firth. Once again we found the place abandoned. The men who had mocked us a year before were now afraid to meet us. They had not expected us to ever go on the offensive, and certainly not that we would be attacking with such force and speed. We took what we could in the way of provisions from Inverness and thoroughly wrecked it.

It was only a day's ride from Inverness to Nairn, and there we burned everything we found to ashes. It had all been very easy on us for some time, but we knew that harder days lay ahead. First, we found that winter comes very early in the far north. The days were only a few hours long and there was very little sunshine. It was gloomy and cold and snow covered the ground. Our men wore padded jackets and long stockings. Most wore woollen hats under their helmets. As many as could had overcoats of fur. Then King Robert became very ill. I could not say just what his malady was, but he became very weak and unable to eat much. Some days he could hardly talk, and I believe he didn't always know what was going on. His skin seemed to bleed and his eyes were sunken. His complexion turned dark. We had to carry him on a litter and this of course hurt our morale. He had taken on too much in this fateful year and a half. He had lived outdoors, gone without food, and been under more pressure than any man I have ever known. He had overcome obstacles as large as mountains. His body was giving way. His sickness was the cost of our spectacular success. Without his confidence and action, what had been accomplished could not have happened. But it had come at a heavy price.

It was up to Edward Bruce to be steadfast now, as he led us eastward to confront two powerful men who stood against us—the Earl of Buchan and the Earl of Ross. Conquer them, and we would be in control of the entire northern part of our country. There came a great change in the demeanour of Edward Bruce. Now that he was in command, he was a different person. He had been withdrawn, quietly doing his duty as an excellent soldier. But Edward was not ever happy being in second place. He wanted to be the leader of whatever he was a part of. It was difficult for him to be the brother of the king. Now that he was in command, he became happy, outspoken, and resolute in his leadership. I am sure he was born to be a leader just as his elder brother was. He had great talents and physical strength. But there was a difference between the two Bruce brothers. King Robert was calculating and patient. Edward, on the other hand, was impulsive and daring, taking risks that were not always wise.

Under Edward Bruce's leadership, our army moved generally eastward toward the sea. His spirits were so high that our morale remained strong despite the discouraging fact that we were carrying our king on a litter. Edward decided to find a strong defensive position where we could rest and perhaps find some provisions, since we were running low. He picked out a place near Huntly called Slioch. We camped there and began provisioning, but the Earl of Buchan was informed that we had come and, sensing that all was not well with us, decided to approach us for battle. There wasn't any actual battle, but for several days some of the men on both sides, mostly archers, would engage and then retreat. Meanwhile, the king's condition grew worse; he had not been able to eat for some time.

Every day the army of Buchan grew stronger, and Edward Bruce, realising we might be overwhelmed while underprovisioned, decided on one of his audacious moves. He led us all out of the place in full view of the enemy, carrying the litter of the king in the centre of our ranks. He told us all to walk or ride with a strut, to strike menacing poses, and be ready to fight, and as we did so, the army of Buchan grew confused and did nothing to us until we were well away. We settled in Strathbogie and began to reprovision.

By now Christmas had come and gone and we were in the winter of 1308. I was marking my second anniversary with the king and had reached the age of sixteen. I was no longer a boy. I was now a soldier. In Strathbogie we were able to rest and we found plenty to eat. When he thought the time was right, Edward Bruce led us back toward Old Meldrum to challenge the Comyn Earl of Buchan. During the night I attended King Robert, making him a soup of oatmeal and cabbage. He hated the taste, but I convinced him he must eat for his health. For a while he seemed no better, but then a curious thing happened. In the morning the enemy fell upon a patrol of ours, killing several stout-hearted men. When the news of this tragedy reached the king, he became agitated and immediately ordered me to bring up his horse. He told his brother to make ready for battle, for we would attack Buchan that very day.

Edward Bruce protested to his brother, "Robert, how can you think of fighting, you being so ill?" To which the king replied, *"No medicine haff couerit me as thai haf done! I sall outhir haf thaim, or thai me!"* When our men saw King Robert walking to his horse, a great roar went up. A chant began: The Bruce! The Bruce!

At once our army began to move toward Old Meldrum, where our enemies lay. King Robert rode at our head, his royal banner flying. We all felt confident, and I am certain that many in the enemy had heard that the king was gravely ill and had not expected to see him lead our charge. His presence at the head of our army was clearly disconcerting to them. Surely many of them must also have felt ashamed that they were opposing their noble king. The Earl of Buchan hated the king, as he must have known that his wife and countess, Isabel, was in love with him; he had even obtained a warrant for her arrest. I am sure King Robert hated Buchan as well, as he was legally wed to the king's love. The battle was thus a personal feud between the king and the earl as well as it was for control of the north. All in all, I believed we had a tremendous psychological advantage, and this was soon borne out.

As we approached the enemy with measured strides, they seemed to waver. When we were within a few yards of their front ranks, the king advanced a few feet ahead of the rest of us, and this was even more disturbing to the enemy. He was the greatest warrior in the world, and they well knew it. He was supposed to be sick, yet there he was. Though no contact was made, the front rank of Buchan's nobles retreated just a few feet, but all could see this little flinch, and the foot soldiers began to walk backwards, then to flee. When the nobles saw they were being abandoned, they, too, turned and ran. At this, our weary king, his role already played so well, turned to his brother and said, "All right, Edward, they are yours! Go get them!"

Whereupon our army under the command of Edward Bruce overran the fleeing troops, causing as great a slaughter as I have ever seen. But I did not take part. Instead, I helped the king back to our camp and tried to comfort him in his agony. He was pleased, I could see, beyond anything I could do, by our victory over his political and love rival. I have always wondered which, his fight for the cause or his jealousy over Buchan's wife, had the more to do with his startling recovery and appearance at the head of our army. I even flattered myself to think it may have been my cabbage soup!

After the rout of the enemy, our taking of spoils, and our tending to our very few dead and wounded, King Robert ordered his brother to waste the entire area as far as he could reach. Upon these orders, Edward Bruce cheerfully killed as many remnants of the once-powerful Comyn clan and their supporters as possible. He burned their lands; at least a dozen castles and landholdings associated with that family were methodically destroyed. The Comyns were finished once and for all, and were never again a critical factor in Scottish politics during my lifetime. It wasn't many days later when Cuthbert brought us news that at least one Comyn had slipped through. The Earl of Buchan had abandoned his estates and had fled to England. We couldn't be too disappointed to have lost him. We were now in control of all his estates and most of the northern portion of the country.

Perhaps the greatest effect of our harrying of Buchan was the inspiration it gave to the citizens of the nearby port of Aberdeen. There in midsummer the people revolted successfully against their English oppressors and forced them to flee. Thus our weakened economy was soon able to begin to recover as Scotland reopened its ancient trade with Flanders, France, Scandinavia, and Germany.

CHAPTER TWELVE

Màirì

Not long after we harried Buchan, I was awakened one morning by a general hubbub in the camp. James Douglas had returned from his campaign in the south and was surrounded by a swarm of men anxious to hear of his adventures. When I reached the circle standing about him, I could sense his great personal magnetism, the sort that is possessed by only a few people. He stood there in the morning sunlight, his straight, shiny black hair appearing as if it belonged to some beautiful animal. His face was animated; his dark eyes flashed with intelligence. He talked rapidly, as was usual for him, and made athletic gestures as he spoke. He told us how he had roared through the southwest and then had gone east into the border country. To his enemies he had become feared as the Black Douglas, a sort of devil with a sword.

James had fought in the forest of Ettrick and, having finished his business there, had decided to go north in Peebles, to a stronghouse near the confluence of the Water of Lyne and the River Tweed. When he approached the stronghold, however, he heard numerous voices, and supposing that these men were the enemy, immediately surrounded the place. His suspicion proved correct, for those inside had been sent to drive James and his men out of the country. As soon as the enemy came to realise he was surrounded by a large force, he immediately took up arms and went to battle. But Douglas was too powerful; and those English who were not killed were captured.

Our men, being well entertained by this discourse, asked for more.

"Indeed I have more," said Douglas. "I have brought King Robert a present," said he, gesturing toward three men standing beyond the circle. We had all been so entranced by Douglas's tales that we hadn't noticed them. Two of the men had drawn swords and were obviously guarding the prisoner who stood between them. He was a very handsome young man, well-built and fair. He was unarmed and not manacled, but a scowl was the most noticeable aspect of his strong face. "Come," said Douglas to the prisoner. "It is time for you to meet your king." The young captive showed no resistance and marched with his wardens behind Douglas toward King Robert's quarters. The hateful look he gave to Douglas would have terrified most men.

The assembly broke out into a low murmur as everyone tried to determine the identity of the captive, but one of our knights quickly stepped forward and said, "It is Randolph, Thomas Randolph, the king's own blood nephew, who has blackened his name fighting for the English and against us." The crowd began to surge forward, trying to follow the procession to the king, but most of them were restrained by the sentinels. In my position, of course, I was allowed to proceed.

James Douglas and I went into the king's chamber, which was a small, hastily built hut in the field. The prisoner and his guards were left outside. There were a few tapers lit but the place was gloomy. King Robert, who still had not recovered completely from his sickness, was seated on an improvised throne. He was pleasantly surprised when Douglas entered; it was the first time he had smiled in days. Douglas made a deep bow, and then the king spoke: "James, welcome! What news have you? Good news, I hope!"

"The tidings I bring are not the best, my lord. We have done well. We have destroyed several castles and killed many enemies. But I regret to say I hadn't enough men to bring the district under control. We will have to go back when we have more men."

"Well, James, that is good news. I did not expect that you would take over the entire south of the country with but a handful. Your orders were to raid and harass the enemy, and it appears that you have done that very well, and have survived in the bargain."

"Thank you, King Robert. I hope I have done our cause justice. But one thing more. I have brought you a present."

"A present?" inquired the king. "What present could you bring me?"

At this James motioned to me to bring in the prisoner and his two guards. At first the king looked at Randolph in disbelief, but soon there was a great smile on his face. "Well, well, Thomas. Welcome! My own nephew, back from the service of the king of England. What have you to say for yourself, Thomas?" Randolph said nothing, and continued to glare at his uncle. "I think at the least you owe me an apology. Here you are, one of the best knights in Christendom, and yet you choose to fight against your country and your family as well." King Robert was not smiling now. He was very serious. As Randolph remained silent, the king sat up and looked straight into his face. "Thomas, I demand an answer."

The young captive was taken aback by this, perhaps realising for the first time that he was in peril of his life. He thought for a few moments, then took a deep breath. "Very well, Uncle Robert. You well know that I was captured by the English at Methven."

"Yes, Thomas. But could you not have escaped in all this time?"

"Uncle, my life was spared on my oath that I would take up arms for England. I gave my word."

"You gave your word, Thomas, to people who gave us *their* word that they would not do battle at Methven until the morrow, and then attacked us in the night. You were not, therefore, obligated to keep your oath. Besides, any oath made under duress is worthless. You should have escaped, Thomas."

"Uncle Robert, not long ago you yourself were fighting on the side of the English."

"Thomas, I cannot listen to such a plea. I am not proud of those days, but everything was different then. There was an ambiguity about the independence of Scotland then. And we were so weak that many of us were compelled to submit to the English at times. It is now clear that the people of this country hate the English tyranny and are supporting our effort to get rid of it. That was not clear then. Also, you did not have an uncle who was king then. This is now a family affair, Thomas, and we are all royalty now. Thomas, you are clearly on the wrong side, but I will not yet call you a traitor before I hear what more you have to say."

Randolph had by this time dropped the scowl from his countenance, but still he was haughty. "Uncle, very well. You force me to say what I think. I am a knight, and the way you are fighting defies the honours of chivalry. It is cowardly. You fight not the *king of Yngland in playn fichting, rather ye ficht with slicht.*"

The king was clearly offended but tried not to show it. In a cool manner he answered, "Thomas, you do not understand several things. The first is that we are fighting for our freedom and that we have the support of the people. We will never be able to win this war by fighting by the customs of chivalry. We are a small people and would probably lose most of the time were we to fight against the might of the English in open chivalrous battles. We have chosen, therefore, to fight a different kind of war, a war of hitting and hiding, as you well know, and thanks be to God, we have been successful thus far. We are in full control of the north and, with God's help, we shall soon be able to free our entire country. I regret that our style of battle is not what you believe to be proper, but I will listen to no more of this criticism. I believe we have talked enough for one day, Thomas. You are an excellent knight, and we need you. I will not charge you with treason, as well I could. Instead, I will put you in solitary confinement, during which you will be able to reason things out, and perhaps decide to change your allegiance from the king of England to me. Good day, nephew. Guards, take this man to the cabin in the woods and watch him closely until he comes to understand the right of our cause and of our methods. Perhaps his manners will likewise improve."

This was the way of King Robert—seldom vengeful, always magnanimous. Over the next few days several of our nobles and commoners were sent to talk to Sir Thomas Randolph to explain things to him. At length he was persuaded to admit his errors and join our cause. From this sorry beginning, Thomas Randolph was to become one of our most important leaders.

II

It was now the high summer of 1308, and King Robert's health had improved greatly, perhaps from the milder climate. With the Comyns, our principal opponents in the east, now finished as a force to be reckoned with, the king decided to return to Argyll in the west to deal with the Macdougalls, who were still operating against us. The weather was much better than what we had been accustomed to in the previous winter, and it was pleasant to journey. Our army was buoyed by its successes and many new men came to join us. We were a confident lot. We knew that the chief, John Macdougall of Lorne, would hear of our coming in advance. News of such a large movement could not be kept secret. As we were now professionals in the business of war, we expected that John of Lorne would try to trap us in some way. We were therefore not surprised when, a few days before we reached it, our advance guard reported to the king that the Macdougalls were preparing to ambush us at the Pass of Brander. The pass is one of the most awesome sights in all Scotland—a tight passage between Loch Awe and Loch Etive. Travellers going from east to west through the pass must keep to a narrow trail with the river Awe on their left and an enormous mountain, *Ben Cruachan*, on their right. The mountain, which is certainly one of the highest in the country, rises steeply from the pass. It is a wild place with streams roaring down almost vertically—the perfect place for an ambush. Had we not been warned we might have been massacred, but having been apprised of the danger, we now had the advantage.

As we approached the pass, King Robert realised that our enemies would block our way ahead and that they would deploy some of their men above us on the mountain. Therefore, he ordered Sir James Douglas to take all our archers and go quietly up the mountain so as to be above and behind the Macdougall men of Lorne. When Douglas had achieved this, he was to give the signal of a bird call. When the call came, King Robert began to move his men into the pass and immediately a great volume of stones rolled down the mountain. Since we had expected this, we were able to reverse our course and dodge the volley, sustaining little damage. At the same time, Douglas and his archers began to shoot down at the backs of the men of Lorne, killing many before they even knew what was happening. King Robert then sent some of our men up the hill so that the greater part of the Macdougalls were boxed in on the mountain and suffered great slaughter. Realising they were beaten, as many of our enemies as could made for the water below, running in retreat across a bridge. After all who could had crossed it, they tried to destroy it, but our men were too quick for them and came to take the bridge so that our entire army could cross it with no opposition. There was no place for the Macdougalls to regroup, so we pursued them until they fled in all directions.

Once again we had prevailed, and over the next few weeks eliminated this disloyal clan as a factor in our war of independence. Daily our men wrought terror throughout Lorne, destroying farms and houses, taking booty, and rounding up a truly wondrous number of cattle and other animals. John Macdougall of Lorne sailed away in a galley for the comfort of England and the hospitality of King Edward II.

While our men mopped up in Lorne, King Robert again put his brother Edward in charge, and he left with me for the estate of Lady Christiana of the Isles. He was still feeling the effects of his illness. We took a galley manned by two good men. I had attained a higher position by now and was more like the king's assistant rather than just a page. I was a man now, and had grown in height, weight, and strength. In addition, I was a seasoned soldier, and completely trusted by King Robert. As we passed through the water to the rhythm of the oars, the king fell into a very deep sleep, helped along by a bottle of claret. I knew him well and realised what a great strain he had been under. He was not only fighting for himself and his men—an entire kingdom was depending on him for success. He would probably never recover the strength with which he had begun his quest. He needed some peace, and would find it with Lady Christiana.

It was growing dark as we approached her island home, and the men struggled to beach the galley. A breeze stirred the air and water lapped in the channel. The four of us walked up the gravel path and there she stood in welcome, having seen us coming from several miles away. The lady was perfectly attired in a long dress, complemented by jewels and golden bracelets. She seemed to me even more beautiful than I had remembered her. She was of medium height and amply proportioned; her hair was so red it seemed to illuminate the entire courtyard. Her smile was encouraging. The king embraced her, and she ordered her caretaker to lead our men to their quarters in one of the outer buildings. I carried the king's baggage inside and was surprised when the king said to her, "Christiana, can you find a place for Davie here in the house?"

"Of course I can, Robert. He can share Màiri's room. Davie, it's just that room by the pantry. I'm sure you will be comfortable there. Màiri is a fine young girl, and my new cook." The lady flashed her broad smile at me. "I'm sure she will welcome you."

After taking the king's baggage to his room, I took my simple kit to the little room by the pantry and knocked on the door. A young woman's voice answered, *"Có tha so?"* I guessed that meant something like "Who is here?" in Gaelic, so I answered "It's just me." The door opened and a beautiful young girl with dark eyes and hair appeared, a little stunned at first, but then smiling. I was so struck that for a moment I couldn't speak.

"You must be Màiri," I gasped.

Màiri answered, "You speak Scots. I suppose you are a *Sasunnach?*"

"I'm not sure what you mean."

"You are a Lowlander, correct?"

"Yes, I belong to Dumfries."

Her eyes were full of mischief. "We don't see many foreigners here."

I couldn't believe what she said. "I'm no foreigner. I'm a Scot, same as you."

"Och, I was only teasing. Still, our idea is that a real Scot must speak Gaelic, and you do not. What is your business here?"

"Lady Christiana says I could sleep here."

"Sleep here, in my bed? You must be dreaming, *Sasunnach.*"

"No, not dreaming. Lady Christiana told me so." Now I was doing the smiling.

"Just who are you anyway, *Sasunnach?*" Her voice had become haughty.

"I am David Crawford, page to the lord Robert, King of Scots, who is known also as the Bruce."

At this the young girl's magnificent dark eyes widened as if in disbelief. "Are you sure it is true?" she asked me.

"Indeed it is. The king has come to bide awhile here, and he will be wanting some supper, I am sure."

With this announcement Màiri became upset, forgot about me, combed her long dark hair, tied it with a ribbon, and hurried out of her quarters to the main room to await the orders of her lady. I watched her leave, and could see from behind that she was well constructed, rather tall and about my age. Myself, I was amused by the whole arrangement. Since our first visit the king had promoted me from sleeping with the men in the outer house to sleeping in the main house. I lay down on the bed to rest for a few minutes, and then decided I should put in an appearance in the large room. I was just in time; Lady Christiana and the king were about to drink the first draughts of a jug of red wine. I was offered a cup and I think that it was the first time I had ever seen such a thing. It was real silver, and the lady said it had come to her from Low Germany. I was very flattered that these two who were my elders and far above my station were treating me as if I was the king's comrade. I thought to myself, "Well, what of it? I am in fact his comrade and confidant—still a page, but also something more." Màiri was busy at the hearth. It was hard for me not to stare at her as she made deft movements while cooking.

King Robert and Lady Christiana were seated next to each other, and I was across from them at the table. We were served by Màiri, but I was glad to see that she was given the place next to me. Our supper was fresh-caught salmon, cooked with salt and butter and flavoured with onions. Also, we were served a thick, dark bannock and boiled kale chopped and tossed in butter. I noticed that King Robert didn't touch the kale, and realised that he usually ignored any vegetables. I thought the kale very good. The whole meal was delicious. All of us drank the fine red wine, and Màiri went to a cask in the pantry several times to refill the jug. The conversation was lively, and I had to remember my place and defer to the king, but I realised that he didn't want to be king this night. He wanted instead to be just an ordinary person. He was exhausted and weakened from the past two years' effort. King Robert needed to rest and relax, and I think all three of us helped him do that. He was very fond of Lady Christiana and felt comfortable with her. She put him at ease. I think, too, that he welcomed the company of Màiri and myself. After all, we were full of youth and fun that memorable evening. I told the ladies a few war stories at the king's request. Especially I talked of the heroics of my best friend and comrade, James Douglas, who, I assured everyone, had had a hundred fights and received not a mark on his face. I left out the bloodiest parts and tried to make light of war. The women were fascinated and asked for more, but I stopped before I went too far. After all, war is not a party and the outline of our battles was well known. Both women seemed to be awed just to be in our presence. Of course, the king was already a legendary figure, but perhaps a little of his aura had rubbed off on me. We were heroes.

I noticed the grace and elegance of Màiri, and I began to get a sensation in my loins and another in my belly I had never felt before, a feeling of deep longing. I noticed that Màiri, too, had changed. Her eyes had a deep shine in them, different from the way they had appeared an hour or so before. Sometimes we looked right into each other's eyes. I guess it was the wine that gave me the courage, but I put my hand under the table on top of Màiri's late in the evening. She withdrew it immediately, but I did it a second time, looking into her eyes and smiling. She was very beautiful, I thought, and the second time she let me hold her hand. Then she smiled at me.

When supper was over, Màiri began to clear the table, and I went to help her as I thought I should. She boiled some water and we cleaned the dishes together in the pantry, then rinsed them in the stream out the back of the cottage. The king and the lady sat by the hearth in the larger room, drinking a strong drink from France, but I wasn't much interested in what they were doing. I was enchanted by the grace of my fellow dishwasher. Màiri told me that she was a chieftan's daughter whose mother had died a few months previously. Her father had been out with Wallace and had been killed at Falkirk, as had my own father. Her manners were refined, not those of a cook. As I was very tired, I said to Màiri, "I really hope you don't mind my staying in your room. I promise to be on my best behaviour. I won't bite you." She said nothing and turned away from me, and I left her to finish up. I asked the king for permission to retire, which was granted with big smiles from both he and the lady.

I was sleepy from the travel, the food, and the wine, but so excited I couldn't sleep. I was praying Màiri would come to bed, and quite soon she did; carrying a candle she left on a table at the bedside. It gave a nice yellow cast to the room. I turned my head to the wall and pretended to be asleep as she undressed. The bed shuddered when she lay down, but I stayed still. She whispered, "Are you awake, David?"

"Aye, I am."

"David, the knowledge is not at me."

I turned to face her, to see her there in the faint golden light. She was exquisitely beautiful. I put a hand on her cheek and stroked her dark hair. It was then I noticed that she had let it all down, and that that was all that covered her. Her breasts fell forward in front of her. I drew her face to mine and kissed her lightly on the lips, all the while caressing one of her breasts. "Are ye afraid?" I asked.

"A little," she replied.

"Don't be, please," I answered, my heart pounding as I kissed her again.

"David, I have something I want to tell you, but I have to say it from my heart in my own language."

"And what is that?"

"*Tha gràdh agam ort.*"

"And what does it mean?" said I.

"In Scots it sounds awkward: Love is at me on thee. But it is our Highland way of saying I love thee."

The Road to Bannockburn

"Can you teach me to say it?"

"*Tha gràdh agam ort,*" she smiled at me.

"Hah graa akam orsht," I repeated, and kissed her again.

III

The next week was one of the happiest of my life. The summer days were long and mostly fair; perhaps a little fine rain in the mornings and warming up on the sunny after-noons. The king would decide on a hunt some days and we would set off in a galley with our men and sometimes a few of the local men as well. We would land at some conve-nient spot and go through the woods with our bows and arrows. There was plenty of game, especially deer—*fiadh gu leòir,* as the locals said it. Other days we would go to the streams or in the lochs, which were teeming with fish. We could have harvested great quantities of lobster and oys-ters, but the Highlanders would have none of it. *Maorach* were dirty things, they said, not fit to eat, and were rightly prohibited in Scripture. It was a wonderful time. I was young and strong and in love and close to one of the great-est men in the world. My Gaelic was improving every day. As I lay in bed at night with Màiri, she would talk to me and teach me, and on the galley or in the woods the men spoke nothing else. At suppertime we four would sit in the same seats, drinking the excellent wine and feasting on the food that had been provided mostly by our own enterprise. It was a dreamworld of course, and we all knew it couldn't last. The king could not stay with Lady Christiana. After all, he had a wife—a queen, in fact. Màiri and I would soon be separated by many miles. Who could tell if we would ever meet again? All of us were in positions that would not have been approved by the Church—neither the Roman nor the Celtic. But we were at war. Our cause was just. The king needed this respite after two years of strife and suffering. The rules of civilisation did not apply here, and none of us felt any guilt whatsoever. In fact, I think the women knew that their hospitality to the exhausted hero king and myself, his fellow soldier, was patriotic and a help to our cause.

I am sure that the king was correct in the way he ended our idyll. He didn't want our parting to be any more painful than was necessary. Thus, one foggy morning after we had all finished breakfast, he merely said, "Davie, make everything ready, and tell the men. We are leaving to rejoin the war immediately." After a few minutes our light baggage had been stowed aboard the galley. You can imagine the tearful scene, I would think, without my describing it in detail. The two women unself-consciously cried, and as I embraced Màiri I struggled to hold back tears. There was a great grief in my throat, and all I could manage to choke out was, "Good-bye." Màiri couldn't say anything. As we rode out of the courtyard, I turned my head for a last look. The two beautiful women were standing together, arms about each other. The birds were singing, unconcerned with the affairs of us poor humans. Màiri waved a wee wave at me. She looked beautiful.

CHAPTER THIRTEEN

Rescue by Sea

*A*fter two days of travel, King Robert and I and the two men joined up with our army, which was already on the move. Our mission this time was to neutralise the Earl of Ross, the only remaining power in the north who had not decided for our cause. As we arrogantly marched through the Great Glen, we were unopposed by anyone. What few people we saw cheered us on. When we approached the earl, we all knew he would not fight. There was no point. We had now a formidable fighting force, and he would have been foolish to contest against us. As we expected, he surrendered immediately and prepared for the worst. But King Robert surprised him with his usual magnanimity. He demanded and received submission, and the earl made a confession of his wrongs against the king, asked for pardon, and promised good service in the future. His behaviour after that was exemplary, and he became a loyal and important figure in support of King Robert and Scotland.

It was now November in the year 1308. The sky was a slate-grey most of the days. The mornings were foggy and a light drizzle of rain came down much of the time. A hostile wind blew in our faces. As we were in the north, there was not much daylight. We had conquered this area and there was now little to do here. It was then that King Robert conceived of an audacious plan so secret that I believe what I am now writing has never been completely revealed before. The king had sent Cuthbert on a reconnaissance in the south, but even Cuthbert did not know the true purpose of his mission. When he returned to us in the north, the king questioned him for several hours. No other person except myself was present at this interview. King Robert asked about the English garrisons and troop strength at Edinburgh and other places in the southeast that were still under English control. In particular, he asked about Roxburgh, where his sister Mary had been placed in a cage outside the castle walls.

Cuthbert answered, "Sire, your sister is still under heavy guard, but is no longer in a cage. The commander was afraid she would die of exposure and be of no exchange value, so that a few months ago she was taken inside to the dungeon, where she now rests in better circumstances than before."

At this, the king shuddered and a look of hatred crossed his face. "And what of Berwick, Cuthbert? What have you learned there?"

"My lord, Berwick is heavily garrisoned. There are a

great many English troops there. The enemy is determined to keep the town English, since they know that a great deal of Scotland's trade depends upon that port. I believe it is better guarded than any castle I saw in English hands. Also, I am sorry to report that the Countess of Buchan is still in her cage, suspended from the walls of Berwick Castle. I observed her myself not two weeks ago. They have given her blankets against the cold, but I fear for her health. She has lost much weight."

King Robert asked Cuthbert several additional questions, but I felt he wasn't really interested in any more of our spy's reports. I knew him well now, and I was certain that his mind was focused on Berwick and the countess. He dismissed Cuthbert and called for his brother Edward and James Douglas to come into his quarters. There were just the four of us in the room when he began.

"The three of you I trust more than any men. Nothing of this meeting shall be said to anyone. My plan is very simple. Edward, you are now in charge of the Scottish army, and if I die you are to be King of Scots, as I leave no male heir. I am going on a mission that is important to me personally. I will take Davie here, and James. I plan to try to rescue the Countess of Buchan from her cage at Berwick. We will scout the castle and the cage to see if it is possible, and if it is, we will do it. We will travel in the clothes of monks to disguise our identities. Davie, tonight you will go to the the monastery. You will get habits for the three of us. I want nothing fancy. Here are two silver pieces to pay for them. We leave tomorrow at dusk. Are there any questions?"

To this Edward replied, "What about our sister Mary?"

"Our informant says she is now inside Roxburgh castle, which is heavily guarded. I see no way of retrieving her short of a full siege. We have not yet the strength, not nearly, in the southeast to mount such a mission. But at Berwick the situation is different. The countess is caged outside the castle. With the cover of darkness and surprise, I think it quite possible for us to succeed. And what a blow to the prestige of the English it will be when we do!"

We left for the south the next morning. It was just the king, James, and myself on three horses, dressed as monks in plain woollen cloaks. I also led a fourth horse that carried our baggage, our weapons, and a few tools. At the outset we were concerned that we might not pass inspection as holy men, but as we rode on in the gloom, it was obvious that we were being accepted as such. People were crossing themselves as we passed. So far, at least, our disguise was working.

We were headed for the seacoast, where we could find a boat to take us to Berwick. As we controlled most of the north, we found no English to oppose us. Yet we had to remain disguised so as not to betray our mission. Should it be known that the king himself was present, there would be no more secret. We might be vulnerable to attack, or our mission compromised. The land was very hilly, some might say mountainous, so that our progress was slow. After several days of travel, however, we were within sight of the port town of Arbroath, where we had many friends, including Abbot Bernard, who had been appointed Chancellor of Scotland by the king.

It was after dark when we entered the abbey courtyard. A snow squall made me shiver. I banged with my fist on the great door and a watchman came out, rubbing the sleep out of his eyes. "We are travelling monks who need a night's rest," I began. "Could you please accommodate us?"

"I don't see how," said the watchman. "Not without the permission of the chancellor, and I don't dare to wake him at this late hour."

"But you must," I said, "for we can find no other shelter."

Then King Robert, seeing I was making no progress, stepped forward. *"Parlez-vous français?"* he asked the guard, whose face remained blank. The king, realising, as he had supposed, that the man didn't speak French, held out a silver coin to the watchman and said, "You must wake the chancellor. We are old friends. Tell him that *Robert d'Annandale est ici.*"

"I don't understand, sir."

"I know you don't understand, but the chancellor will. Just tell him *Robert d'Annandale est ici.*"

"All right," said the guard, pocketing the silver. "Roberdannandale et eecee."

"That's it," said the king. "Now go!"

Within a few minutes Chancellor Bernard was standing in front of us. He was, of course, surprised to see the king attired as a monk and instantly grasped that there was a secret nature to our visit. *"Robert d'Annandale, bienvenue,"* he began, *"Puis-je vous assister?"*

"On espère," answered the king, smiling.

With the formalities over, the chancellor ushered us into very suitable quarters in the abbey, while the watchman tended to the horses. James and I took the baggage inside. "Robert," said the chancellor in hushed Scots. "What are you about?"

At this point the king began to explain that his mission was secret, even from the chancellor himself, not because he was not trusted, but because if anything went amiss, he might be blamed if he knew. The king said he needed a good boat and crew for about a week. He would return to Arbroath at the end of the mission. He would say nothing else.

Chancellor Bernard asked when he would need it, and the king answered that he must sail on the next evening's ebb tide. We spent the night comfortably and slept long, as we were weary from our travels. The chancellor saw to it that we had a good fire in our quarters and were well supplied with food and wine. We stayed in our cell all the next day while the chancellor arranged for our transportation in a boat owned by two patriots who could be trusted. They were, he said, two of the best fishers in the port and known for their ability as sailors.

At dusk the two fishers came to collect us. William and John Graham were their names, and brothers they were. We thanked the chancellor for his hospitality and walked with the brothers to the jetty, where we stowed our baggage in their small boat. We put off from Arbroath on the tide in pitch-darkness. The Grahams were patriots indeed to be performing this mission, not knowing who they were transporting or for what purpose. The chancellor had told them nothing except that we were performing a great service for Scotland in its war for freedom.

The king introduced us to the Grahams. Pointing to James, he said, "This is Jamie. Over there in the back is Davie." Last the king said, "I am called Hob." "Jamie" and I exchanged a secret smile at the "Hob" part.

Yes, patriots were the brothers Graham indeed. They were putting out into the dark and tempestuous German Ocean not knowing where they were going. When we had cleared the port, William Graham looked at "Hob," perceiving him to be in charge, and asked him, "Hob, might I ask where we are bound?"

"Indeed, William. We are bound for Berwick, some sixty miles distant over this water. Do you know it?"

"Of course, Hob. It is Scotland's largest city and most important market. We sell our fish there from time to time. We have been there often."

William started to say something else, but hesitated. Then he said, "Hob, do you know that Berwick is in the hands of the English?"

"I know that well," answered the king.

"And you want to go there anyway?"

"I want to go very near there, William."

"Very well then, Hob. We will make for Berwick as you specify. With any luck in the weather we shall be there tomorrow night."

II

We were indeed lucky with the weather; there was no gale. But it was bitter cold on the sea, and I could not believe how rough the water had become. I had never been on the German Ocean before, and hadn't imagined what it was like. The boat went up and down on great waves, and I gradually became sick. I was embarrassed because none of the others were similarly afflicted. I tried to sleep, but couldn't manage it. I was frightened, too, as I suppose the others were. It was a difficult passage and I wondered if the brothers Graham ever got used to the challenges and dangers of being fishers.

On the next night, William informed us that we were within a few miles of Berwick. The king directed him to stop in a small cove near to the town. It was quite dark at that time and we were able to beach the boat by a great half-submerged rock. There was no one in sight and we believed we had not been observed. Then the king told us to take off our woollen clerical garb, and he opened our store of arms and tools. At this the Graham brothers' eyes widened. They had probably suspected what kind of people we were, but they knew it now. We had swords, daggers, and one bow with arrows. I slung the tool bag over my shoulder and we were ready to leave. The king then thanked the brothers and told them to wait there, make no sound, and be ready to leave on a moment's notice. He said he hoped to be back in an hour or two, and that there would be another passenger.

We walked through the cold night, shivering without our monk's habits, walking as quietly as we could. Suddenly, more quickly than we expected, we were under the walls of Berwick. It was so dark that we almost stumbled into them. The king went ahead, groping the walls and looking up, trying to find the cage. We had walked thus, one after the other, for what seemed like fifty yards when we could just make out the outline of what appeared to be a cage.

"Davie," the king whispered. "Do you think you can climb up this wall and see what is going on up there?"

"I don't know sir, but I will try," said I.

It was hard in the darkness to see the wall as anything other than a great mass. But as my eyes became accustomed to the gloom, I noted that the stones were very rough and that it would be possible to get hand- and footholds in them. I worked my way up slowly and quietly until I missed a foothold and almost fell. For a few seconds I hung by my fingers, but I was able to regain my foothold and continued to climb. When I got to the top I could see two things: the countess, or at least what appeared to be the countess, under her blankets in the cage, and a sentry walking his rounds. I knew I had been sent just to reconnoitre, but in an instant I realised I was capable of completing a large part of our mission by myself and immediately. I took my chances and worked my way around the top of the wall until I was right up to the cage. As quietly as I could I reached both my arms through the bars until my hands were inches away from the sleeping lady's face. Then, gently but very firmly, I put my hands tightly over her mouth. Of course she was startled awake and struggled, but I whispered to her, "Quiet ma'am. I am a friend." It was so dark that I had to ask her, "Are you Isabel of Buchan?"

She shook her head yes. I whispered, "You know me,

ma'am. I am Davie Crawford, the king's page. He is here.
We've come to take you away. Be very quiet and very still
and you shall escape. I am going to take my hands away
now. Will you be sure to be quiet?" The lady shook her
head yes and I released her. "Does yon sentry have the
key?" I asked. She shook her head yes again. "Then wait
here a minute. Don't move."

I climbed over the top of the wall and hid in wait until
the sentry walked back to the place where I had originally
seen him. It seemed to take forever, but he returned in a
few minutes. When he had passed me, I jumped behind
him, put my left hand over his mouth to stifle any sound,
and then cut his throat through so that the blood gushed
all over the two of us. He was dead in an instant. I wiped
my hands on his cloak and searched him. I found a ring of
keys in his pocket and went back over the top of the wall
to the cage. By now the countess was sitting up, her eyes
wide open. I began to try a key in the lock when what do I
see but James Douglas, who had climbed most of the way
up the wall, coming to find out what was keeping me. I
pulled the lady's blankets through the bars and went to
meet James. "Here," I said in a loud whisper leaning far
over the wall. "Take these blankets. Use them like a net,
and I will throw the lady down for you and the king to
catch. I've got the key. Go down, go down quickly!" I was
not used to giving orders to James Douglas, but I was worried someone might discover us, and believed that it was
the only way to get the lady down. Without hesitation Sir
James threw the blankets over his shoulder and climbed
back down the wall. I think he was stunned, but he trusted

me to make the decision. As fast as I could, I tried a key, but it wasn't even a close fit. I tried several more. I heard noises that indicated that James and I might have aroused someone with our conversations. I worked as fast as possible, going through the keys until I found the one that worked. I opened the door carefully and it creaked slightly. I gave my hand to the countess and brought her out of her horrible outdoor prison to the top of the wall. I could scarcely see the king and James below me, but I could make out that they were holding the blankets between them to catch the lady without injury. I pointed to the blankets below and asked the countess if she were ready to drop. She was, of course, terrified, but I knew, and so did she, that almost any injury, even death, would be an improvement over her daily torment. In the dark I could see her eyes. "Yes, I am ready," she whispered.

It was fortunate for our exercise that she had lost much weight, but it was still awkward for me to handle her in her weakened condition. I sat her on top of the wall, then took a look to see as best I could if the two below were ready. I held her out over the wall for a few seconds as the wind howled. "Are you ready?" I asked. "Yes," she said simply. "You must not cry out," I said, looking at her carefully. "I know," she said. "Ready?" I asked once more. "Ready," she replied. I let her go with a prayer in my heart. I heard a muffled sound that I hoped was the blankets catching her, and then in the darkness I hurried down the wall to my two comrades.

"Is she all right?" I asked.

"Yes," said the king. "Let's be gone from here immediately." Then he picked the countess up and slung her over his shoulder and we were off for the beach in the darkness. We stumbled along as quickly and as quietly as we could. James, who was leading the way, blundered into a tree and was momentarily stunned, but he got up and kept on. We could hear the sound of the waves now, and that more than any sense of direction was what guided us. I know all of us felt a sense of relief at the prospect that we would soon be safely away on the water, but as we approached the shore at the point where the large rock met the sea we suddenly felt terror instead. What a surprise we had there as three men appeared where we had left the boat—and the boat was not there! We could only retreat back from the beach to a wooded area to decide on a new course of action, hoping that the brothers had merely moved the boat and had not been discovered. James and I agreed to confront the men and see who they were. We left the king with the countess and immediately went forth as heavily armed as we could be. We slowly crept up behind the men, and when we were close we stopped to evaluate the situation. As we got near to the water its reflection provided more light and we could see better. They were passing a bottle among themselves, and they were conversing in English. It wasn't the local northern dialect, which was similar to our own Scots, but the southern speak that I had seldom heard. Worse, they were wearing swords. No doubt about it—they were English soldiers. We might kill two, but the third would cry out and bring down the entire garrison against us. James said, "Listen, Davie, I have a plan. You see how they stand; two side by side and the third opposite. We will circle around to our right. At that point we will be behind the two and opposite the one. I will kill the one with my bow and arrow, and as soon as I let it fly, we will attack the other two from behind." I nodded and we began to crawl to our right. When we had completed our move, James, not saying a word, took aim and sent the arrow straight into the one soldier's face, and he fell down dead without a sound. Immediately each of us grabbed one of the others and, muffling their mouths with our left hands, slit their throats with the knives in our right hands. In a few seconds all three were dead, and scarcely a sound had been made.

So far we had done well, but where was the boat? King Robert, who had seen enough in the darkness, ran forward with Lady Isabel cradled in his arms. She seemed to be unconscious. All of us searched up and down the beach for the boat, but in vain. We could not see her beached any-where, and we began to fear that she had been captured and that we were stuck here with an enemy garrison at our backs. Then, suddenly, she appeared. The Graham broth-ers were fifty yards out at sea and making for us. They had seen the soldiers approach and had thought it best to put out on the water, where they could not be seen, or at least not inspected. They had seen us dispatch the soldiers and then returned for us. The fisher brothers beached their boat again, and we all boarded, the king carrying Lady Isabel in his arms and laying her gently on the deck. She appeared to be in a deep sleep, and he covered her tenderly with several blankets.

What a joy it was when we were aboard and out to sea

again! A fair wind blew us to the north and all our spirits rose. The king slapped me on the back and did the same to Douglas, who was sporting a bloody gash on his forehead, a reminder of his encounter with the tree in the dark. King Robert had a huge grin on his face. I think that it was the happiest I had ever seen him. "Well done, lads!" he said. "Well done!" King Robert quickly opened a small cask of wine and passed it all around, first to James Douglas, then to myself, and then to the Graham brothers. We all ate some of the stale oat cakes we had brought with us with a great relish, so hungry we were.

William Graham was at the tiller now, and he turned to the king and said, "Pardon, Hob, but I need instructions. Shall we make for Arbroath, then?"

"Indeed you shall," said the king, "and a finer couple of sailors I've never met. Thank you for all your help. You have meant a great deal to your country on this voyage. I believe that your king will reward you well for this service."

As the sun began to rise the waves came up and a fine salt spray washed the boat. Our cloaks and everything else in the boat became soaked in salt water. The air was colder now, but I was beyond caring. We were free, our mission accomplished, and the weather be damned! Just before I went to sleep, I saw the countess stir, and King Robert attending her, looking down at her gaunt features. He offered her a cup of wine and she opened her eyes, looking at him in disbelief. "Oh, Robert, it's you. Every day I prayed you would come. I knew you would come, I just knew it."

CHAPTER FOURTEEN

The Challenge

Our passage back to Arbroath was extremely rough. I became ill again during a wailing gale. We were pelted with a devil's mixture of snow and ice coming off the grey waves, which looked like angry sea monsters trying to overturn us. Everything in the boat was soaked with brine. I knew that I could not have lasted long as a seafaring man! What a comforting sight to see the town of Arbroath again the next evening as we entered the harbour on the flow tide. It was dusk; the weather had moderated, and the quay looked empty. We helped the brothers Graham beach the boat and began to take the baggage to the abbey. The king carried Lady Isabel again in his arms. She seemed so frail that I didn't think she had long to live. The watch-man quickly opened the door for us this time, and the chancellor came immediately to greet us. Lady Isabel was given a private room and a nurse was assigned to her care. We bid the Graham brothers farewell, with many thanks, ate a hurried supper, and went to bed immediately, sleeping the deep sleep of the exhausted and weather-exposed.

When I awoke it was hours past daybreak. King Robert had left our cell and was attending the lady. He was gently holding and stroking her hand.

"Good morning, sir," I stammered. "Will you be needing me, sir?"

"Good morning, Davie. Yes, we are leaving in an hour. Make sure to have everything ready. Obtain provisions for three days." I heard him say to the lady that he must leave but that she was in excellent hands, and that he hoped for and expected a complete recovery for her.

"Oh, Robert," she sighed. "It is so painful for me that you go. Ah, but I know that you must."

"Yes, I must," said the king. "But I will send for you when you recover. I care deeply for you, Isabel."

"And I love you, Robert."

That was the last part of the conversation I heard as I left the cell and busied myself with my tasks. Within the hour we all assembled in the courtyard. The king thanked the chancellor for his hospitality and left him with a parting message. "Bernard," he began, "no one but you knows the name of the lady under your care. No one else can know. She cannot go back to her husband because he fled to England last year and died there. We have conquered his lands. Because of her patriotic act in crowning me, she is among the English the most hated woman in Scotland. If the English king knew she was here, he might send a party to kill her and you as well. No one, not even the Graham brothers, who did such good service for us, is to know the true identity of our party. We will wear this clerical garb until we rejoin our army. Thank you, Bernard, and farewell."

We rode north in the cold of deep midwinter weather. We had not noticed the turn of the year; it had become 1309. In two days we rejoined our army, and immediately King Robert called for a meeting of his most trusted commanders, his brother Edward Bruce, who was now Lord of Galloway, James Douglas, and the king's nephew, Thomas Randolph.

"It is time," the king announced, "to hold the first Scottish parliament in almost two decades. I propose to have it at St. Andrews in the middle of March. We have conquered most of the country and all of the north. We must spend some of our time from now on consolidating our victories and governing Scotland. We must begin a return to normality that has not been known for far too long. I ask you all to prepare for this significant event in our country's history. You have my full authority to act in this regard however you think best. Notify all relevant parties and make whatever arrangements are required."

The rest of that winter passed peacefully. The English made no attack on us, and King Robert was able to give furloughs to many of his soldiers so that they might visit their families. It was a time of respite for us all. It was amazing to contemplate what we had accomplished in just three years from that night when the king had swung me up on his horse in Dumfries. We had travelled a distance most thought utterly impossible. From our early days, with only a few men and our backs to the wall on Rathlin Island, we had become possessors of the greater part of our country.

The parliament was held at St. Andrews in March as scheduled, and it was a festive occasion. Booths were set up with people from many parts of Scotland selling heavy cloth from the Highlands and foods such as cheese, bannocks, and scones from local merchants. Dancers performed and musicians played lively tunes. Most of the greatest nobles in Scotland were present, many more than had attended the hurried coronation three years before. Their names ring out in the history of our country: Boyd, Stewart, Lindsay, Barclay, de la Haye, Campbell, Macdonald, Keith, and Mentieth, to name only a few. The Church was well represented also, including Chancellor Bernard of Arbroath and our constant ally, Bishop Lamberton of St. Andrews. Bishop Wishart of Glasgow was still in detention in England. The business at hand was to make sure the world knew that Robert the Bruce was the rightful King of Scots, and that Scotland was still an independent kingdom. There was to be no ambiguity whatever, and a document of loyalty was drawn up and signed by all who attended. Our independence was acknowledged in a letter from the king of France, Philippe IV, which had been sent to King Robert and addressed him as King of Scots. King Philippe acknowledged the many previous alliances between France and Scotland, and requested the aid of our country on a crusade. Our answer was polite but said in effect that we were still too occupied keeping the English at arm's length to be of any assistance. Nonetheless, the greatest power on the continent, France, had recognised our independence. And the attendance at the parliament of the highest members of the Scottish clergy showed that they cared nothing at all for the excommunication orders that the pope had placed upon us. On March 17, our Church proclaimed in a separate document that Robert Bruce was the rightful King of Scots. Our bishops were Scottish Christians first, and Roman Catholics second.

Among the many who attended the parliament was Lady Isabel. The king had instructed me to set her up in one of the best residences in the neighbourhood. She was no longer the Countess of Buchan, since her husband had died, so she was not present officially. Nevertheless, everyone deferred to her as a genuine heroine for the patriotic service to our struggle that had cost her so dearly. The lady had recovered her health by this time; she had gained some weight and, except for a few strain lines around her eyes, no doubt due to the cruelty she had endured at the hands of her English captors, she was as beautiful as ever. She and the king lived in different quarters during the parliament, but I am sure that most people knew of the relationship between them, and no one dared to question it or comment on the king's visits to the lady's accommodations. Both of them had great personal magnetism: he the best and bravest Scot, and she the bravest and one of the most beautiful Scotswomen.

I have said previously that the king was fond of two ladies, Christian of Carrick and Christiana of the Isles. He was more than fond of them. I think that King Robert loved these ladies. He had that ability with women. He liked women and enjoyed their company. I could tell, being so close to him, that despite their acute differences political and otherwise, he even had a place in his heart for his lovely queen Elizabeth, still under house arrest in England. But Lady Isabel was far more beloved by the king than the others. She was the one he thought of constantly. Had circumstances been different, he might well have made her his queen and excluded all other women from his life. Events and circumstances, however, do not give even a king everything he desires. Yet, during that parliament, the king and the lady were in constant attendance together. Their eyes glowed sometimes when they looked at each other. She often sat at his side as if she was his queen. They made us all feel better, the strongly built warrior and his beautiful lithe goddess. For myself, I could not have offered any criticism. In the last days of the parliament, Lady Isabel returned to Arbroath. I know that King Robert promised her a house, but there was not yet time for that.

It wasn't long after the parliament that King Edward II of England began sending emissaries to meet with our people concerning a settlement, but nothing ever came of these meetings. The English would not agree to recognise Scotland as a separate kingdom in exchange for peace. Those were our terms, and we would not compromise them in any way. The English king threatened to invade Scotland, but did not act on his threat. All of us close to our king heard about these meetings and laughed them off. We laughed also at the rumors that the English king was romantically involved with his favourite Gascon noble-man, Piers Gaveston, to whom he had given much power and attention, much to the consternation of the nobility of England.

After the parliament was closed, King Robert set off on a progress of his realm. The entire north and west of the country had been cleared of our enemies, both English and Scottish, so that we were able to proceed with ease. We travelled extensively through the west, giving thanks to the Highlanders, and particularly to Angus Og Macdon-ald, who had been so helpful to us in the darkest hours of the beginning of our struggle. The king spoke to the High-landers in Gaelic, and I could see how they appreciated it, both because most of them could understand nothing else and because it showed that he was one of them, their rightful king of ancient Irish descent. Many of the great Highland chiefs came from considerable distances to meet their king and to promise him their loyalty. We travelled with a suitable escort of our men, including many of our nobles displaying their colourful coats of arms. James Doug-las and Thomas Randolph were always in attendance dur-ing this time, as was Edward Bruce when he was not otherwise occupied in Galloway. Everywhere we went, our hero king was acknowledged by all the people. This was an era of good feeling in Scotland. The economy was being restored. The port of Aberdeen was open, and trading with the continent had resumed. Thanks to the protective gal-leys of Angus Macdonald, trade with Ireland proceeded as well. Through that country we were able to import arms, which somehow found their way there from France and elsewhere. The people of Scotland were united and happier than I had ever observed. There was a new confidence in the land that, despite the fact there was no formal peace, there was in fact peace, and our warrior king would protect it.

During the autumn of 1309, as we progressed through the realm, King Robert told me that we would be going to visit Lady Christiana of the Isles for a few days, and the two of us rode off from the main group. There was the fall colour on the trees, the air was cool, and the streams were clear. The day was sunny as we sauntered up to the lady's small house. I wondered—no, I prayed—that Màiri would be there with the lady. As we approached, I could hear the cries of a baby inside. The lady heard us and came out to greet us, followed by Màiri, who held a bairn in her arms. My heart beat like that of a bull as the king and I dismounted and the women came forward to greet us. Lady Christiana and the king embraced quietly. Màiri smiled at me tentatively, then said, "Good morning, David. This is your son. I have named him Seumas after your comrade James Douglas. You have said that he is your closest friend."

The king, who overheard this, roared, "Sirrah, Davie! Sirrah!" and he slapped me on my back. "Congratulations, Davie. You've done well!"

Then Lady Christiana motioned for the king to come into the house and leave the two of us alone. I came close to look at my son, my heart still pounding. I wasn't sure what babies should look like, but I thought he was beautiful. "May I hold him?" I asked. Màiri held him out to me all wrapped in a blanket. He smelled sweet and I thought suddenly that this was the happiest I had ever been. I walked around with my son, I danced with him, I had a great smile on my face that didn't go away. Then I saw beautiful Màiri smiling at me, and I walked close to her and kissed her on the lips.

Then she looked at me with those beautiful dark eyes. "Are you happy about this?"

"Yes, of course. I've never been so happy. I can't believe it. I love you, Màiri. I have thought about you every day, many times each day." At this her eyes filled with tears. "I love you, David. I have thought about you, too, but worried every day for your safety. Thank God you are alive."

"Alive, yes, and now very happy, too. But I don't understand. You named him Shaymus after James Douglas?"

"Seumas," she told me. "It is James in Gaelic. It's an excellent name, I think."

"Shaymus," I repeated. "It sounds very pretty; better than James." Still holding my son, I followed her into the house, where a celebration was already under way. The lady had already filled two jugs with her best French wine, and a leg of mutton was turning on a spit. "Davie, sit down here," the king roared with a big grin. "I can tell you, Davie, you're a man now; no doubt about it!" Then he roared again.

As Màiri nursed my son, the king grew mellow from the wine. "Davie, I've begun to think of you as my own son. You've grown from boy to man in these three years, and I have nothing but good to say about you. Thank you, I say, sitting right here in this house, for all you have done. Congratulations on your manhood, and, thinking of you as a son, I can now think of Seumas as my grandson!"

As you can imagine, I was very flattered by all of this, even discounting the influence of the wine. The good feeling went on like that for three days and nights. It was a great party for the four of us, and once again the differences in our stations were disregarded. We were all in need of what we had in that small house, and of course when it came time to part there were plenty of tears all around. I told Màiri that if she ever needed anything she could get a message to me through King Robert. We embraced. As we rode out of the courtyard to rejoin our army, I looked back, and there she was, holding my son in the blanket in her arms.

II

The next year, 1310, King Edward II launched a grand invasion of southern Scotland, proceeding from Berwick to Roxburgh and then to Biggar. He must have been greatly disappointed to find that our army, refusing to be drawn into a pitched battle, had gone to the north. The devastation wrought by his countrymen had left the area almost a wilderness, and what could be taken had been carried away by the people of the country to the safety of other parts. King Robert sent James Douglas to harass the English, and many a provision wagon was taken in the night. Eventually King Edward had to retire back to England, having accomplished nothing at all.

Of course the war had cost Scotland deeply. The English had stolen much of what was valuable over the years and impoverished our countrymen, so that we were in need of capital to continue. King Robert then decided that the English should have to pay back for the damage they had done, and we began a series of raids into northern England. At first we would go just a little over the border, but as time went by we became bolder and thrust far into northern England. By the year 1311, we had developed a routine. We would enter a Northumbrian town and demand two thousand pounds in exchange for a truce of one year. If the townsmen did not agree to pay us, we would offer them another choice: we would plunder the town and burn it. Since the English army was far to the south and afforded them no protection, and considering the alternative that our king offered, it was easiest to pay the tribute, as did town after town. So terrified were the English that the next year we had merely to send messengers to collect the tribute. Our best leader in this raiding business was my friend James Douglas. He became so infamous that the mothers of northern England sang the lullaby:

> *Hush ye, hush ye*
> *Little pet ye,*
> *The Black Douglas*
> *Shall not get ye.*

We were not barbarians in this raiding, however, and I must add that King Robert's orders were that no English person was to be harmed if the tribute was paid. So far as I could tell, none was. We had nothing against the English people. It was only their king and army that we opposed.

As a participant in these raids I, of course, shared in the booty and was becoming prosperous. Also, King Robert had recognised my services and had purchased the land my mother worked, compensating our landlord with land elsewhere. Included in the trade was a small manor house for me as well as more land. I was now a laird myself. I bought more animals and hired a man to work the place. My mother was getting old, and I was happy to have relieved her of her daily chores. I moved Màiri and Seumas to the new house and settled my mother nearby in her own place. It was a good arrangement as we all lived within a short distance. Màiri had been reluctant to leave the Highlands and become a *Sasunnach*, but I assured her that she would find the people of Dumfries to be very welcoming, and that her Highland-accented Scots was perfect and sounded better than the harshly guttural way in which we Lowlanders spoke.

After we were settled in, Màiri and I were married at the church in Dumfries. For me, it was an emotional moment, remembering that fateful night when I, only a boy, watched the Earl of Carrick begin his quest to become King Robert I. We were standing at that same murderous altar and taking vows. It seemed as if the entire town was in the church. I had become a celebrity and the place was packed. The local lad had become a laird and a confidant of the greatest Scot. Màiri and I were both quite nervous with all the commotion, but the kindly cleric was very calming. The king was suffering another of his ailments and couldn't attend my wedding, but my friend James Douglas was there, dashing as ever, with his black hair and eyes and his handsome face. Everyone knew of his exploits, and the whole town was honoured by his presence. After the service, Seumas, who was now two years old, was baptised and the "infamous" Black Douglas stood up as his godfather. It was quite an honour for me. Our irregular marriage and our son's illegitimate birth were not even issues with the people. It was a tempestuous time, not given to normality, and we had squared it all, anyway. That night we were celebrated in the town. My family and James Douglas were honoured with toast after toast by the people.

In 1312, King Robert called a parliament at Ayr, and once again it was a festive occasion. A great spontaneous fair appeared, with goods for sale and games to play. There was music day and night. The king's love, Lady Isabel, was provided with a private house and servants, and the king's visits to her were never mentioned. Parliament decided that we should invade England on a grander scale. Accordingly, more tribute was extracted from English towns. In all of this, Thomas Randolph, the king's prodigal nephew, had proved himself to be one of our best men, and was now completely reconciled to his uncle. In order to solidify our position in the north and to strengthen and extend the power of the Bruces, the king made Thomas Randolph Earl of Moray. In the same year King Haakon V of Norway recognised the independence of Scotland and our territorial disputes with his kingdom were resolved.

Throughout these several years, I was able to get much

time off between raids to visit my mother, Màiri, and Seumas at my manor. My land was productive and I became modestly rich. There wasn't much danger in soldiering at this time. We never saw an enemy army, although the English still held the southeastern corner of our country as well as a few other castles. It was just raiding and furloughs for me. King Robert was busy all the time, governing the country. He was involved less and less with actual fighting. I think his goal was to wear down the English gradually, and he was doing it. I was less and less a page and more of a soldier. Although I had no noble rank, the king thought of me almost as if he were my father, as he had indeed said before. I was a good soldier and was trusted completely. I had become, in other words, a high-ranking member of the royal court, though I had no title.

In the first week of the year 1313, as I remember it, King Robert became restless, since we had still not completely freed our country, and he decided on more direct action. We would take the fight to the enemy. The English still held the important town of Perth, and the king determined to besiege it. Perth, situated on the River Tay, was protected on three sides by a deep moat and on the fourth by the river itself. We went there with a considerable force, including many Highlanders, taking up our positions to the jeering of the Englishmen inside. We camped outside the town, making sure no supplies reached our enemies within. After several weeks of siege, seeing that the English were still well provisioned and that our Highlanders were impatient for action, the king decided on a different course. Loud enough for the enemy to hear, he gave orders to his troops. "Men, I have decided to lift this siege, since these cowards inside will not come out and fight like men. Let us leave them in their cowardice."

As we began to move away from the town, we could hear the English inside jeering us, but our men obeyed their king just the same and moved well away. When we had travelled several miles, we came to a small hill with a stream at its bottom, and King Robert ordered a halt. "Men," he said, "this is a good place to halt. We shall rest here a few days so that our enemies are convinced we are away, and then we will attack the town of Perth. Some of you who have served with us since the beginning will remember that we are now at a place called Methven. It was here, seven years ago, at the beginning of our quest, that we were defeated miserably, both by English treachery and by our own inexperience. We failed to take Perth that time. I expect that this time we will succeed!"

At once a shout went up from our men. They had followed their leader in retreat without question, but they were primed for action and now they would get it. Over the next few days our men were engaged in making rope ladders. These were constructed with heavy knots so that wooden rungs could be attached that would bear the weight of a man. At one end each of the ladders was fitted with two strong iron hooks. The ladders could then be thrown up to the top of the walls and held fast.

It was the night of January 7, I believe, when we quietly made our way back to Perth. It was very dark and our movement was not observed. We halted several hundred yards from the walls and the king ordered two men to go forward in silence to make soundings of the moat to see if there was a place where the water was shallow enough to cross. After a half hour our men came back saying that there was such a place; the water there was about four feet deep. King Robert then ordered our entire detachment to move close to that part of the moat, and we did so in the utmost silence.

It was bitterly cold and snow was beginning to fall in a swirling wind. None of us looked forward to wading through the moat, and the king sensed this. So, to keep up morale, he motioned to one of our men who was holding a rope ladder to come with him. To our astonishment, our king waded through the frigid water in full armour along with a ladder bearer. He used his spear to sound the depth of the water in front of him. At one point the water came up almost to his chest, but soon he was on the bank on the other side, and all of us followed the example of our warrior king until we were across. The men were now excited, and hurriedly threw up the ladders. The king himself was one of the first to climb to the top, and the men followed him rapidly. Of course the town was roused, people were screaming, and soldiers appeared. But they were disorganised and we had to kill very few of them. The king had warned us previously that most of the people inside were innocent Scots and should not be harmed unless they offered resistance. We took our prisoners and much booty, and then destroyed the walls and the towers of the town completely. It was a great victory, and I take great pleasure in reporting it in order to remember what an inspiring person our great king was. There was with our party a French knight whose name I have forgot. Never, though, will I forget what he said that night: *"A lord! Quhat sall we say of our lordis of France that ay with gud morsellis will bot et and drynk, quhen sic a knycht sa richt worthy as this is throu his chivalry to wyn ane wrechit hamlet!"*

III

We continued to put pressure on English-held strongholds. In the summer of that year I was with the army which under Edward Bruce besieged Stirling, perhaps the most important fortress in all Scotland. Stirling lies at the waist of the country, where at its narrowest point it is only some fifty miles across. At Stirling, one is only some twenty miles from the River Clyde, which flows west toward Ireland, and another twenty or so miles from the River Forth, which flows east to the German Ocean toward the continent of Europe. Whoever controls Stirling can interrupt trade and the movement of armies going north, south, east, and west.

It was the plan of Edward Bruce to wait for the English to run out of provisions. When this happened they would have to surrender the castle to the Scots. I have already told you that Edward Bruce was an impatient person, and headstrong as well, but he had been able to accomplish much in the war. He was one of our best soldiers and leaders, and the king had made him Earl of Carrick. So after we had besieged Stirling for several months and the English had not budged, it was easy to guess they were about to run out of provisions, though we couldn't be certain. But Edward Bruce grew more and more impatient. He was a man of action, not really fit for conducting a siege. He wanted to leave, and eventually the enemy commander, Sir Philip Mowbray, gave him reason to do so. Mowbray was, of course, a longtime enemy of ours. He was a Scot fighting for England, and will always be remembered as the mounted knight who had the reins of our king's horse in his grasp at our disastrous loss at Methven in 1306.

One morning Mowbray came out on a parapet and called for Edward to come parley. We formed a small party on horseback and moved toward the castle. I believe Edward Bruce thought the enemy wished to negotiate a surrender, but he was rudely surprised. Instead, the commander made him an offer in chivalry. If the Scots would lift their siege and withdraw from Stirling until the next Midsummer's Day, and if the English could not meanwhile mount an attack and relieve Stirling by then, then the English would surrender the castle to the Scots without a fight. As Mowbray put it, *"That gif, at midsummer tyme ane yeir it war nocht with batall reskewit, than withouten faill he suld the castell yeld quytly."*

I can still see, in my memory, Edward Bruce sitting on his horse, his armour glittering in the sun, not answering, thinking. I am sure the treachery at Methven those seven years ago was on his mind, yet this was his chance to do something on his own. This was a decision he could make without the help of his older brother. The rest of us said nothing, waiting for his decision. He must have convinced himself that the English had plenty of provisions, although we found out much later that Mowbray had been bluffing.

Edward hated the inaction of a siege. Mowbray said to him, "I offer this as a challenge of honour. Retreat like a knight and give us the chivalrous chance we ask of you."

This must have had an effect on Edward Bruce, because he answered immediately. I can still see his red hair protruding from his helmet as he said, "Agreed. We will return here next Midsummer's Day." That was all. Edward Bruce turned away on his horse and we followed him to our camp. I realised right away that the younger Bruce had probably been tricked, and that if we had waited another few weeks we might have starved the enemy into surrender. I could see, as we approached the camp of the king a few days later, that Edward was upset, fearing that he had made a mistake. But I had not realised the gravity of the error. That came when we reported the bargain to King Robert.

"Well, Edward," the king began. "I understand you have lifted the siege at Stirling and that the enemy is still in possession of the castle."

"Yes, Robert. I made a pact of honour."

The king sat up straight and looked at his brother's eyes. "You made what?"

"A pact of honour, Robert. I agreed that if they could not relieve the castle by next Midsummer's Day, they must abandon the place to us. They have not mounted a serious invasion of us in years. It will be all right. We shall have the castle without a fight or siege. I can now be useful in some other engagement."

We could all see then that the king was greatly angered. "I cannot believe that you have done this, brother."

"Done what, Robert?" Edward's face was now flushed.

"Edward, you are my brother and I love you, but you have imperilled everything we have accomplished these past years! My God, man; do you not remember that we agreed not to fight pitched battles?"

"Of course I do, Robert. But the English, since the death of King Edward I, have not made a serious attempt to invade us."

"Really, Edward? What about the invasion of three years past in 1310? Do you not remember that we withdrew our army to the north in order to avoid a pitched battle with them? This time we cannot withdraw. You have accepted the challenge, and we must all abide by it."

"But, Robert, they may not mount a campaign to relieve Stirling, and then they must surrender it to us."

At this the king leaned back in his chair and smiled, his fury partly spent. I could see he was calculating and thinking, and none of us dared say a word. Then he spoke. "Edward, you have given them reason to try for a decisive battle with us. Unless I don't know them, the English will now gather the most powerful force this island has ever seen. They know full well that we will not be able to match it. There is no possible way that we can even come close to the strength they can muster. We have not the numbers of knights, horses, archers, or common soldiers that they well possess. If they come, and I believe they will, they do not have to win the battle. They have such resources that if they lose they can regroup and try again. But we *must* win the battle if it occurs. If we should lose, they will easily overrun our country, and we will have lost our kingdom. We shall have to put everything we have into the fight. We do not have the resources to rise again. If we lose, we shall be slaves, as we were in Wallace's time. Brother, you have put us in a dire situation."

Edward Bruce looked down at the floor, now fully aware of the trouble his impetuous bargain would probably bring. "I'm sorry, Robert," he said softly, without looking up. "I apologise. If you will it, I will renounce my earldom."

Then King Robert, magnanimous as always, said simply, "Your apology is accepted. You will renounce nothing. We go forward from here."

There was a long pause in the room. It was so still that people's breathing could be heard. After a long while the king began to speak again. "We will face them, then. They have the silver and the men, but we have several advantages also. We can choose the battlefield, and we have the spirit of men defending their homeland. These things are not inconsiderable." King Robert was, in my estimation, too modest to mention another advantage we had. We had him, the inspiring Scottish warrior hero who was becoming one of the greatest military figures in all history.

"Men," our leader continued, "if this battle comes, we must win it. Let us begin to prepare for it now. We have a year. Now leave me and let me think on this."

IV

It was not two months later that our spy, Cuthbert, brought back to us the news that the English were gathering and training a huge army. King Edward II had already informed his knights that their military service would be required the following June. The news of this activity spread rapidly to all parts of Scotland, from the northern isles to the southern Lowland villages. The response was immediate. The newly free Scots began to enlist in the struggle that would determine whether they would live as slaves or as free men. Recruits began to pour into central Scotland from all parts of the country and from all ranks of society.

In the meantime, the king ordered us to try to take the castles of Roxburgh and Edinburgh, both of which are in the southeastern part of the country. These were still in enemy hands. One night in February 1314, James Douglas and his retinue, having left their horses at some distance, crawled on hands and knees toward Roxburgh, concealed in the darkness, their armour covered with black cloth. The guards, seeing this movement, thought someone had loosed the cattle in the night. But within a few minutes, the Scottish rope ladders were slung over the walls and swiftly climbed. The guards were killed. It was Shrove Tuesday, and a great celebration was taking place inside. But this turned from merrymaking to chaos when the frightening cry of "Douglas! Douglas!" rang out. The occupants of the castle were unprepared and the place was soon conquered. Most of the English soldiers were killed, but a few were able to flee. Some held out in the tower, but by the next day the Scots were in complete control. Douglas provided escorts for those who were English civilians back to their own country. Then he demolished the walls and the tower.

The Road to Bannockburn

I did not participate in the Roxburgh campaign, because I was assigned to the unit that was to take Edinburgh Castle under Thomas Randolph—who, as I have said, had been made Earl of Moray by King Robert. Young Moray had acquitted himself very well in our campaigns after having submitted to his uncle. He was, however, eager for glory and for these reasons the king chose him to capture Edinburgh, a task many thought to be impossible. If you have ever seen this fortress, perched high on solid rock, straight and sheer on the sides, you might well agree. I know that when we began our siege and I first got a good view of the place, I thought there was no way we could win, or even reach the top of the walls. The locals told us that the castle was well provisioned and that many soldiers were inside. Not seeing any way to mount an assault, Moray let it be known that he would well reward any of the locals who could show us a way. Some days later an old man named William France came to see the earl and offered his services. *"I undirtak for my service for to ken yow to clym the wall, quhar with a schort leddir may we clym to the wall up all quytly."*

The earl was, of course, sceptical of this offer, and asked William France what his qualifications were for his service. The old man answered that as a young fellow he had lived inside the castle with his father, who had served there. He added that he had been in love with a girl who lived in the town below. In order to visit her secretly at night, he had had to discover a path, and he had done so. From the top of the wall to the path, however, there was a distance of about twelve feet that had to be breached with a ladder.

"And how dangerous is your path, William?" asked the earl.

"It is indeed very dangerous, my lord. If one were to fall at some places it would be certain death. However, my lord, I know the way so well that I could guide you and your men easily, even on the darkest night, all the way to the wall."

Having no alternative, the earl agreed to follow William France's advice, and an assault on Edinburgh Castle was planned and prepared. A force of thirty of our best men was to attack the top of the castle walls. I was very proud to be one of those chosen. Once our attack diverted the defenders toward us, our main force would strike at the main door far below.

It was very dark on the night of March 14 when we walked to the bottom of the rock. Despite his age, William France climbed so well that we were amazed. He knew exactly where he was going, even in the dark. The earl was right behind him, and the rest of us followed as quietly as we could. About halfway up I took a glance below and was so frightened that I resolved not to do so again. When we came to a broad place near the summit, we stopped to catch our breaths. We heard the sentries above us laughing, and they began to roll stones down the cliff in our direction. *"Away, I se yow weill!"* one of them yelled. At first this terrified me but then I realised that in the darkness they couldn't see us. They were just pretending. We proceeded up the last segment of the path, now at a truly frightening height, threw our ladder against the wall, and ran up it as fast as we could. Before we all could reach the top, however, we were discovered, and the sentries rushed at us, crying, "*Tresoune! Tresoune!*" The few of us who had made it over the top were now engaged as we had never been before. As fast as we killed them, more came from below to meet us. Gradually, though, more of our men came up and we were able to push them back. Just then, our main force began to break down the door far below, making such a racket that the enemy, realising there were many more of us to come, began to panic, and a number of them jumped over the walls, preferring that death to death in combat. The fighting went on throughout the castle for some time, but we had the superior force and gradually the enemy gave way. Many were killed and we took the rest as prisoners. We had carried the day, and I believe that our victory over such a formidable fortress may have been unparalleled in the history of chivalry.

We stayed that night in the castle, listening to the cries and moans of the wounded and dying. The carnage was horrible. But we were seasoned soldiers and most of our men were able to get some sleep. In the morning, the earl got us some breakfast from the enemy cook, who had surrendered. Then our men and the prisoners went to work utterly destroying the walls of the castle. This occupied the better part of the day. There was a small building inside the castle called St. Margaret's Chapel, which we left alone. I noticed that there was scrawled on the wall "*Gardez-vous de Français,*" or "Beware of French." Some say that St. Margaret herself wrote this as a prophecy. If it were a prophecy, it had been fulfilled. William France had been our instrument in recovering Edinburgh Castle.

The Great Scot

Even as we did this work, townspeople who came to help us brought us news that an enormous English army was beginning to muster far to the south. We all knew they represented our greatest challenge and that we must be ready for them. It was just three months until Midsummer's Day.

CHAPTER FIFTEEN

Baттle aт тhe Bannock Burn

Lord Moray decided to spend the next two weeks in Edinburgh, reestablishing Scots law and administration over the town as best he could. I, of course, assisted him, as did a few others. When it was time for us to go, we left a detachment to hold the town, then made for Stirling. Even before we left Edinburgh, we heard stories daily about the great force that Edward II was mounting against us. There were reports of levies of men in the Midlands—over ten thousand in number there alone. We were told that there would be a regiment of the famous Welsh archers, and even men from Ireland and France joining the king of England as he came against us. There was talk that the English army might field a hundred thousand men. It was obvious that such a large force was not coming merely to relieve Stirling. As King Robert had predicted, King

Edward was coming with a force he deemed sufficient to crush us.

Riding to Stirling, Lord Moray and I came to the town of Falkirk. I knew that it was near this spot that my father was killed fighting alongside the great Wallace for the freedom of Scotland. It made me feel quite reverent toward the place, and rekindled my desire for revenge, which I hoped would come soon. Just outside Falkirk was a place called Camelon. The earl asked me if I wanted to see something historic, and of course I answered that I would. "Very well, Davie," he said. "This is Camelon, where there was a Roman fort, and over there is the wall built by the Roman emperor Antoninus Pius more than a thousand years ago." I marvelled at the enormous earthen wall, grown over now with grass and trees. On the northern side was a huge ditch, several yards across and one or two yards deep. It was a formidable barrier. The earl continued, "The Romans built the wall clear across Scotland to keep our brave ancestors, the Picts, out of their province of Britannia. It runs some fifty miles from the Forth to the Clyde. The way I see it, our ancestors were the only people who stood up to the Romans, who had conquered most of the world. Yet they couldn't subdue the Picts. In a way, the Picts defined the line between Scotland and England. It's glorious isn't it? This place marks the absolute northern limit of the Roman Empire, which defeated the world but couldn't conquer the Picts."

"Why were our ancestors called Picts?" I questioned.

"The Romans called them the picture people or the people of the designs. You can still see some of their work on standing stones to the north and east of here. But their best work was in some of the illuminated manuscripts they illustrated for the Irish monks when they came to Scotland."

"Do you mean the monks of the Celtic Church?" I asked.

"Yes, Davie. We were Christians before we were Roman Catholics."

"I learned that when we were at the shrine of Saint Fillan some years ago," I said.

The earl responded, "Yes, the Celtic Church is still alive. I know that King Robert believes in their saints with a passion. Anyway, I have seen one of those Irish manuscripts illuminated by the Picts, and they're the greatest works of manuscript art I have ever come across."

"I would guess," I said, "that the Romans thought that the Picts were savages, just as the English think we are."

"You are right, Davie. The Romans thought the Picts were barbarians who coupled in public. But mostly, I think, it was because they fought so hard and so fiercely. Not only were the Romans unable to control Pictland, but the Picts kept hammering at the wall here so that after a time the Romans had to retreat behind Hadrian's Wall down in England. Anyway, if we move in history, to the sixth century after the birth of our Lord, we find a different Camelon. After the Romans left, Camelon served as the headquarters of our illustrious ancestor, King Arthur. He was killed here at the Battle of Camelon in the year of our Lord 537. His Round Table is no longer in existence, but the round Roman temple that housed it is still to be seen. It's just a mile or two from here, and we will come to it soon."

You can imagine that all this was amazing to me. I had not realised that the earl was interested in history. He was as scholarly as King Robert's brother Alexander Bruce, who had stirred my interest in the subject back on dark Rathlin Island those years ago. Within minutes we came to the building that the earl said had housed the Round Table of King Arthur. It is a large, round, beehive-shaped building of excellent construction—just right for holding meetings around a circular table. The walls are perhaps three stories tall and built of tiers of stone blocks. The workmanship is exquisite. It is the most unusual building I have ever seen in Scotland. The width of the building at its base is perhaps eight or ten yards. It is empty now, and the Round Table is gone. The local people now call the building itself the Round Table. I walked inside the building and found it to be like a great oven, its dome open to the heavens. I thought I gained a special energy, just thinking of how our brave ancestors had contested with the Romans on this very spot. The ancient temple, which I shall call the Round Table, as do the locals, made a great and lasting impression on me. I hoped that I could visit Camelon and the Round Table of King Arthur in peaceful times.

All thoughts of history vanished when we came near to Stirling, the strongest and most important castle in Scotland, looming a hundred yards and more above its rocky base. Here we would *make* history. We were surprised at all the activity. I had never seen so many soldiers in one place. Our men were for the most part encamped in a wooded area called Torwood, which lay below the castle on the old

Roman road. They were busy building shelters for themselves and absorbed in other pursuits. In one field, some were being trained as archers. Blacksmiths were forging weapons. Implements of war made in other parts of the country were arriving daily. All Scotland knew what was at stake, and every area contributed. Many soldiers rehearsed the tactics of the *schiltron* formation that Wallace had used. In this arrangement, the men were packed together very tightly in a square, each man carrying a spear pointed outward, making the square look like a giant hedgehog. The *schiltron* had been used as a stationary defence against mounted cavalry, but it was King Robert's idea that it could be used to move forward against an enemy as well, and we would test that assumption soon.

At night small bands of trusted men went out in secret to dig pits along the Roman road. King Robert was convinced that the English must come this way to attack us, since most of the land in the neighbourhood was either forested or boggy. The pits were covered over with brush so as to be invisible, and were designed to cripple the horse of any mounted knight who came that way. Everyone seemed to be in a cheerful mood. Most of all it was very impressive that men from all parts of Scotland, even from the most remote isles, were coming to defend their liberty under our hero king. Some were speaking Scots, but we could hear also Gaelic, Norse, French, and Flemish being spoken within the space of a few yards. Many of the ordinary men came with their chiefs, who were ready to fight right alongside them. They wore diverse costumes. The Highlanders were, of course, in their long shirts covered with the heavy woollen plaids. Many of these men had put aside decades-old feuds with one another to unite and fight for their country and their gallant king. Although their ancestry and speech differed, all were ready to fight for Scotland.

Midsummer's Day was now approaching, and on June 22, 1314, our spy Cuthbert brought us the news that the English army had arrived at Falkirk, only a dozen miles southeast of our position. He was summoned into the king's quarters to address our inner circle. Reporting to the king, he seemed a bit hesitant. "Sir," he said to King Robert directly, "the English have mustered what must be the largest army in the history of Europe. There are thousands of knights, thousands of archers, and thousands of foot soldiers." I suppose that Cuthbert had been afraid to alarm us. I don't know whether or not anyone else believed him, but I was quite prepared to hear this news. "However," he said, "there are some good tidings, too. The English are very tired. They are late reaching Stirling in time for Midsummer's Day. They have had to push very hard today, more than twenty miles, and they must march again tomorrow. I think the men are discouraged and exhausted."

"Have you any news of King Edward?" asked Sir James Douglas.

"Oh, he is very confident indeed. He expects a victory. He has even promised Scottish lands to his noblemen, depending on their behaviour in the battle to come. I regret to say," the old man said, looking at Earl Thomas, "that he intends to give away your land, my lord, at the first opportunity."

"King Edward is an ass," Earl Thomas hissed. "We will show him who owns what!"

Thus the meeting ended. That evening, King Robert walked up and down among his men, making witty remarks about some of them, telling one man that his long beard made him look like a biblical patriarch, complimenting another, a stout man, on his not having missed too many meals. It was all in good fun and the men were laughing and relaxing with the most famous person any of them had ever known. I think that they were surprised that he behaved as if he were one of them. They knew he was ready to share their fate, and they knew from the legends about him already springing up that he was the greatest general in Christendom.

Our army was formed up on a hill above the valley in five divisions that had been arranged earlier by King Robert. The first was entrusted to the command of the king's nephew, Thomas Randolph, Earl of Moray. Most of his men were from the far north of the country, from on or near his lands. This unit was sent as the vanguard to the northern part of the field near St. Ninian's kirk. The second division, just south of Earl Thomas, was under the nominal command of Walter Stewart, but he was just a lad at the time. The real captain was James Douglas. Most of the men of this division were from the Douglas territory of Lanark, with men from Renfrew and the Borders as well. The third division, stationed just south of the Stewart-Douglas unit, was commanded by the king's brother, Edward. Most of his men were from the lands he had harried, Buchan and Galloway. Nearby was the reserve unit, commanded by King Robert himself. His men were made up of Highlanders, including Campbells, Lindsays, Sinclairs, Frasers, Gordons, and de la Hayes under Angus Macdonald, together with men from the Bruce heartland in the southwest: Carrick, Kyle, Cunningham, and Dumfries. The Scottish cavalry of several hundred knights was under Sir Robert Keith. It was a grand display, and I'm sure it was the greatest army ever assembled in the history of Scotland. I doubt that any nation could have surpassed our captains in leadership, courage, and experience. Their names will ring out forever.

The next morning, Sunday, June 23, came in with sunshine, and promised to be hot later on. The Scottish army heard mass and then breakfasted on bread and water, a semi-fast in honour of the day, the eve of the feast of St. John the Baptist. King Robert made a short speech to his men saying that anyone who was of faint heart had a chance to leave at that moment. But those who could hear him were eager to fight and yelled that they were ready to win or die. King Robert then directed Keith and Douglas to scout the enemy position and report back. I asked James if I could go along, and he approved my request.

We rode down the hill through the woods to a clearing from which we could see our opponents. It was such an awesome sight that none of us could say anything for some time. We just sat there on our horses, looking and listening. There they were, the might of England, still a few miles away, but marching towards us. The dust they trailed rose high in the sky. There were an immense number of men led by what seemed to be thousands of knights, all in chain mail and armour under the colourful coats of arms of the greatest families of England as well as some of those of France. Even Scotland was represented as an enemy Comyn banner stood out among the others. There were thousands more of archers and foot soldiers, and dozens of supply wagons stretching back as far as one could see. The horses' heads bobbed up and down. The bright morning sun gleamed on the polished steel of swords and pikes. Multicoloured banners flapped in the light breeze. It was an awesomely beautiful sight.

Still, none of us said anything. We simply returned with our report to King Robert. We didn't have to say anything; he could see the startled looks written on our faces. "Well, James," he said to Douglas. "You have seen a grand army, then?"

"Indeed, sir. It is even larger than what we had heard. It is gigantic. It could be one hundred thousand."

"Very well, then. We shall have to fight them no matter how great their strength. Please wipe your faces clean of the awe that is so apparent on them now, and go and tell the men that the enemy is great in number, but disorganised, and that we shall prevail this day."

With this order, we all went back to our stations. I was proud to be part of the king's brigade. We knew the English would come against us, but we had to wait what seemed like hours. At last some of them appeared under the earls of Hereford and Gloucester. They looked impressive, with their splendid arms and mighty caparisoned horses. Riding in this vanguard was Sir Henry de Bohun, who wore colourful arms and an iron helmet. He was the first to recognise King Robert; the latter had ridden out in front of his army to inspect the field, and de Bohun noticed the golden circlet of the crown our leader wore around his helmet. Seeing his chance for glory, de Bohun rode fast ahead of his brigade and lowered his spear to charge directly at our king. It happened so rapidly that we were all caught off guard and did nothing but hold our breaths. I thought that the king would retreat to be with his men, but he did not. He had chosen to duel one of the great champions of England. King Robert was seated on his small pony, about fifty yards in front of us, and he just sat there, calmly, erect, waiting for de Bohun to reach him. Then, in an instant, it was over. De Bohun was riding as fast as he could, his spear fixed straight ahead; but just at the moment when he might have killed, or at least un-horsed, our king, he was foiled. At the last instant, King Robert manoeuvred his little pony out of the way; and standing straight up in his stirrups, he raised his battleaxe high, driving it through the helmet and skull of his opponent, who fell dead instantly. So great was the blow, the axe handle broke in two.

For a moment we were all stunned into silence. Then a great roar came from the Highlanders, who impulsively began to charge toward the English. King Robert immediately called them off, since the English were retreating in confusion, some disabled in the pits we had dug on both sides of the road. Our men returned to their formations, cheering as they went. The king came with them and was quietly upbraided by his brother and others for what seemed like a foolhardy display of courage. If he had been killed, we would have been leaderless and in dire condition. But King Robert just said, "The only thing I am sorry for is that I have broken my favourite axe." Those troops who could hear what he said began to laugh nervously, and his words passed throughout our army: "Though the king has killed the great de Bohun in single combat, he is distraught at having broken his favourite axe." As the words circulated, the troops all laughed loudly at the joke, and took courage from the bravery of their king.

It was just then that we could see a great brigade of English cavalry outflanking us on the east, headed for Stirling. The king had realised that this evasive tactic was possible and had provided for it by stationing the vanguard under Thomas Randolph at the northern end of the field to prevent it. But Lord Thomas was standing next to the king, his troops not under his or any other command. The king was harsh with the earl. Looking him straight in the eye, he said, "I am afraid that a rose has fallen from your chaplet, Thomas."

The earl said nothing, mounted his horse, and galloped with a determination to his men at St. Ninian's kirk. The king motioned for me to follow him, to bring back news of what might be a battle, and I did so as fast as I could ride. When we reached the kirk, I could see the English advancing on our position. Men were shouting, ready for battle, yelling insults at the English commanders, Sir Robert Clifford and Sir Henry de Beaumont. The enemy was only yards away when Earl Thomas gave the order for his *schiltron* to move forward. And what a sight it was—hundreds of our men, packed tightly in a square, every one with a long spear pointed straight ahead of him, and the whole unit marching in unison, moving forward like a gigantic hedgehog. Every man wore a padded jacket of some sort. Some had steel helmets; others had leather headgear. The huge hedgehog moved to confront the heavy English cavalry, the pride of Europe. The English charged the *schiltron* with great confidence. When the two front lines made contact there was a terrific sound of crashing steel, but the *schiltron* held, then continued its relentless advance. The English were shocked at how well our formation had held up. Most had never seen anything like it. Heavy cavalry, they had been taught, could always triumph over foot soldiers. But the English were being repulsed, and they were astonished when the Scots struck at horses as well as riders, so that many knights were unhorsed before they could even begin to fight. The English couldn't reach our men except those on the edges of the *schiltron*, but even there they were blocked by dead and disabled horses and men as the hedgehog kept pushing them back. The enemy charged again, attacking the *schiltron* from every side, but again they were ineffective and losing ground. Our men gained confidence while our opponents were losing theirs. The English, including their leaders, were now in disorder, confused as to what to do. Contrary orders appeared to be issued. Some of their knights began to throw their weapons at the hedgehog in desperation, but this was of little benefit. The *schiltron* continued taking its deadly toll. Some of our enemies began to retreat, and seeing this, others panicked. Before long, the English were in a disorderly retreat, and the fighting stopped. Our men were exhausted by their effort, but had taken very few losses. They took off their coats and helmets and sat on the ground under the hot sun. We had won the day, and we had prevented the English from opening a route to relieve Stirling.

Many from other units came to congratulate Lord Moray and his men. The morale of our entire army had been raised greatly. We could be sure, too, that the morale on the other side had been lowered in about the same degree as ours had risen. The English had not expected their vaunted cavalry to lose. Of course, they had not attacked us with their archers, which had devastated Wallace's *schiltron* at Falkirk. Next time we would have to win over archers as well.

The fighting was finished for the day; the English had had enough, and didn't come at us again. That night all of our men were given a good meal and told to relax and be confident of victory on the morrow. King Robert held a council of war with his leaders in which options were discussed. We were facing an overwhelming enemy, probably about four times ours in size and several times that in quality. We had many fewer great horses than did the English. We had a mere handful of trained archers. We had few knights. King Robert had planned an alternate route of escape, and he now asked his subordinates whether they wanted to retreat in the night and continue another day or fight a great battle on the morrow. A hot debate ensued, with opinions expressed on both sides. Generally the leaders were in favour of battle; during the meeting, however, a sentry entered and said that Sir Alexander Seton, a Scot in the service of the English army, had asked for safe passage to report something to the king. This was granted, and Seton entered, bowing deeply. "King Robert," he began, "I beg you to take me into your service. I am disgusted with the English. They are completely demoralised after the events of today. They are tired from several days of hard marching, and are afraid you will attack them in the night. Few can sleep. They are trying to bivouac near a stream called the Bannock Burn, but they are disorganised and having trouble finding dry places to camp. King Robert, may I be drawn and quartered if I am not telling you the truth. Take my advice. In the morning, do not wait for them to attack. It will give them time to organise against you. Instead, bring the attack to them. They will be terrified to see that you do not fear battle. Believe me, King Robert, if you want to free your country, attack this dispirited camp at first light."

Seton was taken into custody and the council continued. As usual, our spy Cuthbert arrived with information, and it matched very closely with what Seton had said. At last King Robert spoke to his captains. "Men of Scotland. As you know, I have always been opposed to confronting the English in a pitched battle."

At this, Edward Bruce lowered his head and gazed at his feet. Then King Robert continued: "They are a formidable force, it is true, but we have advantages also. The first is that *we haf the richt*. We occupy the moral high ground, and may Providence protect us. We want nothing but our freedom and to be left alone. They have come here to plunder and enslave us. Their motivation is nothing but spoils, and that is not worthy. Should they lose, the spoils will go to us. *Thai haf broucht her richess in-to so gret plentee that the pouerest of us sall be bath rych and mychty. Should we lose thai sall haf of us no mercy.* This is reason alone why we must fight.

"The tothir is, *thai ar cummyn heir to seik us in our awne land.* We have chosen the field well, as we have heard to-night that many of them are bogged down in the marshes by the river. They are spending an anxious night in water, and we are high and dry in some comfort.

"The third is that *we ficht for our lyvis and for our childer and our vifis and for the fredome of our land.* I sense that there are many in the enemy who would prefer to leave for England tonight rather than risk their lives for our meagre spoils.

"Fourth, we have the element of surprise. They will not expect us to attack such a mighty force. They will calculate that we will wait for *their* advance. If at the beginning we are firm and attack with any success at all, they will be utterly demoralised. Gentlemen, I am prepared to retreat, but I think we now have an opportunity to deal them a blast that will make Scotland free forever. I think we can give them such a blow; they will lose so much treasure, and so many knights, that even if they refuse to make peace with us in the coming years they will never again have the will to gather together an army as vast as that which opposes us here and now. Gentlemen, there is great risk in this business, but I am for battle. Edward Bruce, James Douglas, Walter Stewart, Thomas Randolph, Robert Keith, Angus Macdonald: How do you say, gentlemen?"

Of course, after this emotional speech from such a wise

and beloved leader, I expected that the vote for battle would be unanimous. But the outpouring was not just a show. I found myself standing up with the rest and shouting in chorus: "Battle! Battle!"

With the decision made, it now remained for us to return to our stations. The king addressed his own brigade in Gaelic, and soon his words were brought to our entire army in various translations. Our men were optimistic. Everyone needed to sleep, but the excitement of the night kept most awake. The days were long in this season, and deep darkness never fell. The air was still and filled with the odour of a thousand camp-fires. Late in the night, the king sent for me to take him to the wood where Lady Isabel was waiting in a hut especially prepared and guarded. I dismissed the guard and took up the post myself. King Robert had brought a small cask of wine with him, and I could hear him and the lady talking far into the night. I got no sleep, of course, but even without the guard duty I would have had none. The excitement of the coming battle would not have allowed me any rest at all. The biggest and perhaps the last day of my life was soon to dawn.

II

The first light of Midsummer's Day began to colour the eastern sky. Immediately I entered the lady's lodging, as were my orders. King Robert was soundly asleep despite the import of the day, lying next to Lady Isabel, blond and beautiful as before. Although I knew he still suffered from his illness and had been exhausted by the previous day's events, letting him sleep was out of the question. I called softly to him, "King Robert, King Robert," but he didn't move. As gently as I could I touched him on the shoulder, and he awoke. "It is first light, sir."

The king sat up immediately, as if he had been awake for hours. "How is the weather," he asked me.

"It looks to me that it will be clear and hot, sir."

"Good! I hope to see those great English knights bake in their fancy armour!"

Lady Isabel was now awake, and, noticing me, she made sure to cover herself, although she was a little slow at it. She said to the king, "Robert, today is your great day. I will pray for you."

"Thank you, dear Isabel. We will do our best to justify your bravery in crowning me, for which you have paid so dearly."

The two of them embraced, without any embarrassment, right in front of me. The lady was in tears and said, "God bless you, Robert. You will save us all."

There was not time for a real good-bye. The king was alert and ready to begin his day. I helped him dress and we tramped through the wood, where he relieved himself against a tree, and then out into the nearly dark field. All the commanders were already mustered nearby, ready for the king's orders. Bernard, the abbot of Arbroath, was saying the mass for us, and priests went to our other divisions as well. An assistant to the abbot carried the sacred *Brecbennoch*, a metal box of beautiful design containing the relics of Saint Columba. Also the dewars from Strath

Fillan as well as the abbot of Inchaffray brought their relics. It was an important event for both the Roman church and the older Celtic one, which seldom agreed on anything and were mutually suspicious. But their clergy were very polite to one another on this most auspicious day. The leaders of both denominations blessed King Robert and his men, and all prayed for a Scottish victory.

Without much ceremony, the king called upon Edward Bruce, James Douglas, and Walter Stewart to move forward towards him. When they were beside him he asked them to kneel, and then he knighted them, tapping each on the shoulder with the broad side of his sword, saying, "Arise, Sir Edward. Arise, Sir James. Arise, Sir Walter." It was a great moment for me, since Sir James was my great friend. He smiled broadly, but young Stewart was reduced to tears. We all congratulated them, of course. I think this simple moment may have relaxed us all and made us better soldiers.

Our men then formed up in their divisions. Sir Edward Bruce was given the honour of leading the army, commanding the Scottish right. On his left was the division led by Thomas Randolph, Earl of Moray, and farther left was the division led by Douglas and Stewart. The king's division was in reserve, as was our light cavalry commanded by Sir Robert Keith. Everyone had a Spartan breakfast. Meanwhile, the king addressed them. He spoke to this vast audience with long silences between his phrases, so that his words could be relayed to the more distant troops and translated into our several languages during the pauses. "Men of Scotland. Today we can make history. If we are fearful, we will lose this fight, and we and our wives and our children will wear the chains of slavery forever. But if we are valourous, if we fight with discipline and honour, we shall be free and rich in the bargain. We are in the right, and God will help us. Let us do or die!" With that the king drew his sword and gave the forward motion to his brother, Sir Edward, to begin the attack as the sun rose.

Since I remained with the king in the reserve division on our hill, I had an excellent view of what happened next. The sun had risen behind us and I could see clearly what we were facing to the southeast. There it was below us: the might of England, a vast, awesome military machine brilliantly illuminated by the slanting low rays of the morning sun. My breath was taken away by the sight; hundreds of beautiful multicoloured pennants and banners in profusion, handsome coats of arms, great horses, and, above all, steel—steel of pikes and swords and armour reflecting in the dazzling light. The sight of so many thousands of soldiers was sobering. I am sure not a man among us did not wonder if he would see the end of that day. My mouth was dry and my heart was pounding. I hoped that I would survive to see Màiri and Seumas again. But somehow I knew, that, live or die, when the time came I would acquit myself well. There would be no coward's grave for me.

Sir Edward Bruce's division marched first, followed in echelon some yards behind and to his left by Moray's, and then further behind and to the left by Douglas's. All had banners flying. They were so many fewer than their opponents and so poorly equipped that I was proud of them, proud of their courage. Most wore ugly leather helmets and short padded jackets. Their legs were bare, their footwear of light leather. Their armour, if they had any, was usually rusty. Yet they marched, dignified and resolute, against their formidable foe. They had no cavalry, but still they marched steadily toward the English.

As usual our spy Cuthbert had gone behind the English lines. How he was able to do it as often as he did I never found out, but I do know that King Robert paid him handsomely in silver for his information, and he must have spread it around generously to the English soldiers by way of bribes. At any rate, what I am about to tell you now I did not learn until sometime later. Cuthbert was able to describe two conversations between King Edward II and Sir Ingram d'Umphraville, a turncoat Scot who ranked high in the English army. These snippets were very revealing as to what happened later in the battle. The first conversation shows that King Edward, on seeing our advance, was stunned by it. *"Will yon Scottis ficht?"* he asked his knight in disbelief, so confident had he been that we would await *his* attack. "Yes indeed they will, sir. *Agane the gret mycht of yngland in plane hard field to gif battale."* Sir Edward Bruce's division was then perhaps a hundred yards in front of the English cavalry when the Scots suddenly halted and knelt as if in prayer. King Edward said excitedly to Umphraville, "See, *yon folk knelis till ask mercy."* The knight responded, *"Thai ask mercy, bot nocht at yow. For thair trespass to god thai cry. I tell yow a thing sekirly, that yon men will win all or de."* Whereupon King Edward, with an ugly expression on his face, replied, "Then be it so. *We sall it se but delaying.*"

From high on the hill I could see our men kneel, then rise. I heard the English trumpets sound the attack, and immediately the English cavalry charged against the position of Sir Edward Bruce. I was surprised, because their movement did not seem organised. First, some came and then others, rather than in a general charge. Sir Edward's division formed into the *schiltron*, and then, very slowly, the gigantic hedgehog moved steadily and bravely forward against the charging cavalry. The result was the same as it had been the day before. We could hear the clashing of the steel, but the English made no headway. Horses and riders were felled and trampled, some horses stampeded, and all was confusion for the English, yet the hedgehog of Sir Edward Bruce continued to move forward like a great angry beast. The Earl of Moray, his red-and-white banner waving in the breeze, moved his men in line with Sir Edward's just to their left and attacked the English cavalry on its flank. Then the Douglas-Stewart division came into line to Moray's left, and slowly but relentlessly the English cavalry was pushed back. Many scions of the most famous English families were dead on the ground, their beautiful coats of arms trampled by horses on the gore-covered field.

The entire English army was now penned in between the Bannock Burn and the Pelstream Burn. Their brilliant archers could not shoot without hitting their own men. The English foot was useless behind the cavalry, with no room to manoeuvre. And still our hedgehogs moved forward.

To watch all this was exciting, but victory was not to come so easily as we might then have thought. The English sent their archers away from the line of battle so that they were actually behind our men. They let loose a volley and then another, which were particularly devastating to the division of Sir James Douglas, as they had been to Wallace at Falkirk. The archers were what the English needed to win the battle. It was a terrifying thought that they were so effective, as we could well see. Of course, King Robert saw this threat, but his greatness as a general showed here, and, like all brilliant commanders, he could see all possible moves and determine which one was most effective for the situation at hand. Calmly and without any hesitation he ordered our light cavalry under Sir Robert Keith, the Earl Marshal of Scotland, to attack the archers. This they did, charging the bowmen with great relish. Our cavalry were well armoured and carried spears. They came at the archers at a gallop and killed many; the rest fled behind the English lines.

Meanwhile, although the English foot soldiers were still penned in, their cavalry was beginning to hold against the *schiltrons*. The clanging of steel could be heard clearly, as could the moans of the dying and the whinnying of wounded horses. There was so much blood on the field that it gathered in puddles. It appeared to me, right then, that the English might rally. There were still many of them who had not even joined in the fight, and our men were wilting in the heat. But the king, of course, knew better than I about such matters. I saw a great smile come on his face. He knew then, as I did not, that our defeat of the archers had decided the battle, that we had passed a crisis, and that bold action now would win the day. Just at that point Angus Macdonald came into the king's presence and, standing next to him, said, "King Robert, I have brought here men from the Scottish Highlands and from Ireland. They are not used to standing by as spectators to a fight. I know not if I can contain them any longer." King Robert continued to smile, and said, "Your time has just come, Angus. Do you think your men would like to join Douglas on the left, as he has lost quite a few men to those archers?"

"Yes, *Ard Righ!*" was Macdonald's answer, delivered with a grin. "Very well then, Angus," said the king, "take your Gaels and proceed, and Angus, my hope is constant in thee." The tall Isle man waved his men to come forward, and soon the air was filled with the shouts and screams of angry Celts, running down the hill toward Douglas and his men, bareheaded, their long hair streaming in the breeze. This must have further demoralised the English who could see it, and it all would soon get worse as the Highlanders hacked at the enemy with the vigour of fresh troops. Then King Robert said to the remainder of his own division, "Men, we are clearly winning this battle. We are now going to move into the line. A little more pressure and they will give up. Make sure that you fight with honour and passion. Follow me and the day is ours." We rode with our men down the hill and entered the line to the right of Sir Edward Bruce. Our *schiltron* was fresh, our men eager for glory. I was able to contribute to this effort as we were on the right and our flank was partially exposed. But as fast as they came at us, we were able to cut down these tired and disheartened warriors. The giant hedgehog moved forward, and forward again. Our entire line was freshened by the new troops, and as we advanced against the faltering English, standing on marshy ground as they were, and trapped by two streams, it became clear to all that we were winning. The men began to chant, *"On thame! On thame! Thai faill! Thai faill!"*

Just then our camp followers, seeing victory coming close, decided spontaneously to play an extraordinary role in the events of the day. I have not mentioned them before, as they were heretofore none of my concern, but I must tell you they were camped on a hill behind us, at a considerable distance, and they were there in the thousands. There were probably as many of them as there were of us soldiers. There were bakers, blacksmiths, petty merchants, wives, prostitutes, servants, musicians, and even some self-armed would-be soldiers who had arrived too late to be trained for the *schiltrons*. I have even heard it said that there were several mounted Knights Templars among them who had been protected by King Robert and Angus of the Isles since they had fled France seven years before—excommunicated knights seeking refuge in our excommunicated country. At any rate, these denizens on the hill, waving colourful homemade banners on sticks, began to yell and run toward the battle, coming up behind our lines, most of them, no doubt, seeking the plunder that would become available should we be victorious. As I have said, their numbers were in the thousands, and the English, in the confusion of battle, had no time to study their composition. Seeing the sun glint on their few weapons, and perhaps on an occasional Templar crossed shield, our enemies must have thought that they were seeing an entire new reserve of soldiers, far greater than any they had so far confronted.

The effect of this charge was immediate. While most of the English were fighting valiantly and only a few had fled, the sight of what appeared to be a large reserve charging unnerved even some of the bravest, and the English began to lose heart and a few retreated. Two great English knights, one of whom was our old enemy Aymer de Valence, realised that the battle might soon be lost, and led King Edward off the field. When it was seen that his tall standard was leaving, most of the English fled or tried to flee the battle. Not many could. Our *schiltrons* broke and we began to fall upon the panic-stricken English with murderous intent, punctuated by the war cries of our men. The gorge of the Bannock Burn soon filled with so many bodies that it was possible to walk across it dry shod. At this point King Robert called to me, "Davie, take six men and guard yonder wagon with the three gold lions painted on it. I believe that contains King Edward's personal treasure that he has left behind." I did as I was ordered, and that was the end of the battle for me.

It was just as well. What I had seen was horrible, and the carnage became even more so. Many English soldiers tried to make for the River Forth as a means of escape, but thousands were drowned in its waters. I stood guard for about a half-hour before King Robert came by with Sir James Douglas. They were saying that King Edward had sought the safety of Stirling Castle, but was refused admission by the commander, Mowbray, bound by his chivalrous bargain with Sir Edward Bruce under which he had agreed not to surrender it unless it was relieved. With this new defeat, our enemy monarch with his retinue of five hundred knights rode around the castle, reversed course, and slipped by the battlefield, making for Dunbar on our east coast, where there were ships waiting to assist him in making his escape. James Douglas was for pursuing, but King Robert would give him only fifty mounted men. The battle was not completely over, and the king was taking no chances. He wanted a full army just in case some English might rally. I was chosen one of the fifty and we all made for the coast. On the way we passed King Arthur's Round Table, and I couldn't help thinking how proud our ancient hero would have been if he had seen how we had acquitted ourselves that day.

Of course it would have been marvellous for us to have captured King Edward. The ransom would have been more money than there was in all of Scotland. It would also have guaranteed us a recognised independence and permanent peace. But when we found the escaping party near Linlithgow, it was obvious that there were far too many of them for us to take on. Sir James dismissed me and several others as we wouldn't be needed, and so we might return to the battlefield and be of service to King Robert. Sir James, of course, pursued King Edward and his retinue all the way to Dunbar, dealing sternly with any of them who dared to confront him or any who had strayed from the pack. He followed them so closely, it was said later, that the English did not have time to stop, even to make water!

III

When I returned the battlefield was much calmer. Fighting continued sporadically, but it would soon be over. The howls and cries of the wounded were the main sounds now. There was blood everywhere, and dead bodies by the thousands. The field stank in the heat of the warm sun. I found King Robert in the middle of it all. His boots were soaked in bloody mud, and he was surrounded by some of his Highlanders and Carrick men.

He was no longer just a general. He was now playing the part of the head of a commissary involving thousands of people. Of course, he couldn't control everything. Our men were entitled to spoils, and they went ahead in this activity with a vigour. Many were made rich on the spot, since the English had abandoned enormous amounts of treasure. Many of the English nobles had carried gold and silver coins, ornaments, and utensils, and these were taken. Dead knights were stripped naked, their fine arms, spurs, clothes, and armour appropriated. Hundreds of fine horses were collected, and cattle, sheep, and pigs, too. Thousand of swords, maces, spears, and longbows were to be had everywhere. Grain and wine were in abundance. I doubt there was a household in Scotland that didn't benefit in some way from these spoils. For my part, King Robert handed me a bag of English gold coins. I had never seen so much money.

There were dozens, perhaps hundreds, of captured supply carriages, and these were put in a circle near King Robert and were well guarded. These contained King Edward's personal items as well as the pay wagons for the entire English army. It was probably the most wealth ever assembled in one spot in the history of Scotland. Our king now had the wherewithal to begin to rebuild our impoverished country.

Late in the day the governor of Stirling Castle arrived and asked for an audience with the king, which was granted. Sir Philip Mowbray entered into the king's presence and fell on his knees. "Sir," he began. "You have won the castle by the laws of chivalry, since King Edward's forces were not able to relieve it by Midsummer's Day as required. I would like to present to you the keys to the castle." He held out the keys in his right hand.

The king responded, "I believe it is my brother, the Earl of Carrick, Sir Edward Bruce, with whom you are well acquainted, who has the right to accept those keys."

"You are right, my lord. It was with Sir Edward that I arranged the challenge that has today brought you victory."

"I believe," said King Robert, "that you should not claim any credit for this victory, Sir Philip, as you had hoped for a different outcome, and that your challenge, clever as it was on your part, was accepted by my brother, who had not the experience necessary in these matters."

"May I then apologise to your brother, sir?"

"You may, and may I add that anyone who saw his strong attack that began this battle today, and who watched him fight valiantly and steadfastly through it all, will find him deserving of an apology."

At this, the king motioned for Sir Edward Bruce, who could not contain his emotions nor erase his broad grin, to come forward to receive the keys and the apology. After this the Bruce said to Mowbray, still on his knees, "How do you find our present situation, Sir Philip? Would you join us now?"

"It would be my greatest honour, sir, to serve the rightful King of Scots."

"And do you agree to swear loyalty to me and to hold your lands in Scotland alone, and reject any now owned for service to the King of England?"

"I do so swear, sir."

"Then arise, Sir Philip, and go in peace, and welcome to the service of the kingdom of Scotland."

This transaction was the first of many. From that point on, Scottish noblemen holding lands in both England and Scotland would have to renounce their English lands or leave Scotland. There would be no more dual loyalties permitted by the King of Scots.

Later Sir Edward Bruce proved himself in another way, as he had rounded up several highly placed prisoners, including the Earl of Hereford. For the safe return of these important men the Bruce demanded the return of his wife, Queen Elizabeth, his daughter Marjorie, his sisters Christian and Mary, and the ancient Bishop of Glasgow, our old ally Robert Wishart, who had gone blind. All were subsequently returned by the English, who were surprised at the civil treatment afforded their own imprisoned country-men. Some who had been friends to King Robert were let go without ransom. The body of the Earl of Gloucester was attended personally by the Bruce, and the bodies of several English noblemen were given separate burials, while the common soldiers were buried together in their thousands in an enormous grave. I wouldn't be surprised if the field on top of that grave is not accursed in some strange way.

We had accomplished much. In my eight years with King Robert I had gone from boy to man, from page to sol-dier, from youth to father. We who had started with almost no men had grown to a respected and victorious army. We who had controlled not one acre of Scotland now ruled almost the entire country. King Robert, previously recog-nised as king by but a few, was now universally acknowl-edged in Scotland and in some European countries. Even more, he was being acclaimed as a military genius and as one of the greatest soldiers who ever lived.

There was more to be done, but we had achieved much. The decisive days in June 1314 were not the end of our quest, but that battle at the Bannock Burn, which should never have been fought, was the one that meant the most. Had we lost, I truly believe that Scotland would have ceased to exist. We would have been crushed and totally occupied by the English. Never could we have recovered our independence. I believe that Scotland will not forget what we did that Midsummer's Day. I shall never forget the bravery, the hot sun, the cries of the dying, the stench of the blood-soaked field, the ring of clashing steel, the beauty of the coats of arms and pennants, the enraged horses, and the relentlessly forward-moving *schiltrons*. I cannot go to sleep at night without reliving these memories, and above all the memory of the cool, brilliant leadership of King Robert the Bruce, the victor at the Bannock Burn.

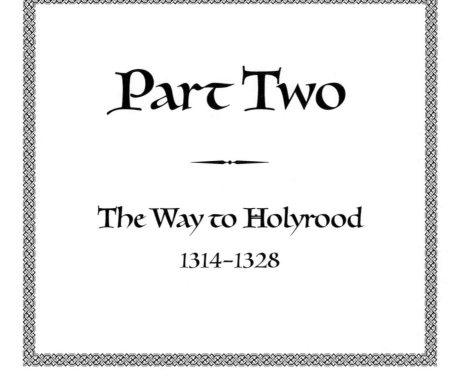

Part Two

The Way to Holyrood

1314–1328

CHAPTER SIXTEEN

Imperial Aspirations

The sun's slanting rays began to mark the end of that momentous day. The battlefield was quite still then except for the moans of the dying, the maimed, and the trampled. These were the losers, most of them ordinary Englishmen. On the higher ground above the field, Scottish musicians, among the winners, were playing lively music, rather incongruously, I thought. Soldiers and women were dancing. There were dozens of fires cooking fine English beef, and everyone was drinking good French wine, courtesy of King Edward II. Some men, more serious, were trying to attend to the wounded. The dying were left to die. Everywhere was the stench of the blood and the bodies.

The surviving English had fled in many directions, but in general toward the south. What else could they do? We had all their provisions under guard. They had lost thousands of soldiers. They would not be back, nay, they could not return soon now. We had won. It was sinking in. We had won a battle we should never have agreed to fight, but we had gained a great victory. It was over.

I noticed Lady Isabel, the former Countess of Buchan, walking toward King Robert, dressed in a gown of fine blue velvet that was quite worn. Even dishevelled she looked lovely, her long blond hair set against the colour of the gown that matched her eyes. The king was surprised to see her, since he had expected her to remain in the hut back up on the hill. The king addressed his lady. "Isabel, what are you doing here? You are supposed to be awaiting me above."

She embraced the king. "Nonsense, Robert. I came down to the field with the small folk. Do you think I would have missed the greatest show in the history of our country? Robert, congratulations, you have saved Scotland. I'm so proud of you and all your men. I'm so happy." She passed him a jug. "Here, have a celebratory drink."

The king grinned at his plucky lady, raised the jug, and gave the Gaelic toast to good health, *slàinte mhath!* He took a swig and passed it to me. Soon more of King Edward's wine was being consumed all around. The wine tasted especially good, in that we had won it as justified plunder.

Someone raised a jug derisively. "Here's to King Edward!" We all had a good laugh at that. We were feeling the glow of victory and the security of the knowledge that we would not have to fight again, at least for a while. Yet there was much to do. Our success had to be consolidated. Thomas Randolph, the Earl of Moray, was put in charge of the prisoner exchange. Sir James Douglas was given the duty of demobilising most of the army with generous payments to each man. Sir Edward Bruce had the responsibility of protecting and distributing the enormous spoils of the battle. These were complicated undertakings.

Having secured these arrangements with his best lieutenants, the king was now ready to end his day. He turned to me and said, "Davie, get our horses and one for the lady, and we shall be on our way." I did as I was told and returned with the horses, freshly saddled. I rode up the hill behind the lady and the king, but I heard nothing. Perhaps they were both too tired to talk. I noticed that King Robert's eyes were sunken, and despite the thrill of his greatest day, he appeared to be depressed. He would turn forty within a few weeks, but he looked much older than his years. Just before we reached the hut the king said to the lady in a low voice, "The queen will be ransomed. She will be returning."

Lady Isabel answered only, "Yes." Nothing more was said between them as they entered the hut. I arranged for the guard to be changed, and stationed myself outside, with orders given to wake me at the slightest provocation.

Before dawn the king woke me. "Davie, I have important business for you. I want you to take Lady Isabel to lodgings I have arranged for her with Sir Neil Campbell in his country. She will have a fine manor in the west, and a servant awaits her. You will take two strong men with you. You will choose them with Sir James Douglas. I am sending along four bags of silver pieces in this saddlebag. You will leave one with Lady Isabel. You will take one each to Lady Christian of Carrick and Lady Christiana of the Isles. The fourth bag is for you, for your valiant and trusted service to me. I know that you are tired and would like to go home to see your family, but you are the best man for this job. You know the ladies, you know where they live and how to get there, and I can trust you to carry out this assignment. You are allocated a half-year to do this. After you have disposed of the three ladies, you will dismiss your men. You should then have plenty of time to see your family. You will report back to me in January."

"I will do all as you wish, sir, but why are you giving more silver to me? You have compensated me well already."

King Robert looked at me and smiled. His face was no longer haggard. It came alive and his blue eyes sparkled and he rested his heavy hand on my shoulder. "Davie, Davie," he said. "Don't you yet know who you are to me, for all you have done for our cause? Take the money. I am still much in your debt. Get on now, Davie, and don't forget to thank the ladies for all the help they have given me. Also, tell them how fondly I think of them, and that they may solicit me for aid should they need it."

The king and I embraced, and without a word I left him there. Our lives had changed forever. Immediately I went to see Sir James Douglas and asked him if I could have five good horses, including one for baggage, and the two Flemings, John and George, for my mission. They were great soldiers, and I knew they had survived the battle because they had been in our division and I had seen them in the fight from first to last. Sir James gave me the order for the provisions necessary, and then we embraced and smiled. He was my best friend and I would miss him. He looked at me and said, grinning, "Quite a show yesterday, Davie. Quite a day." I nodded and bade him good-bye on the quieted field, which only the day before had seen so much activity. It seemed odd that the great tensions of the previous day had vanished and we were now relaxed. I waved a smile at Sir James and then I was off on my progress throughout the west.

The weather was fine throughout the journey, and while the Flemings conversed in their impenetrable tongue and Lady Isabel was lost in her own thoughts and spoke very little, I had plenty of time to think. I had spent eight years with King Robert on an incredible adventure. I was now a man and a veteran soldier. All across our journey to the west the people we encountered treated us like heroes. Everywhere we received the hospitality of shelter, food, and drink in exchange for our tales of adventure delivered at a fireside. Of course, we relied upon the local people to give us directions. Most of those we encountered had never met anyone from the Low Countries, so the Flemings were an added attraction. They were both eager to discuss their native land just across the German Sea. They spoke of a rich country with great ports and manufactories, much more prosperous than our little Scotland. But Scotland showed herself well on our journey, through her friendly and honest people and her magnificent scenery. The land of the Flemings was, they told us, very flat. That seemed to be very boring compared to our country. On our tour of the west we passed constantly through beautiful brooding glens with streams rushing down from green heights, heavy forests, and wild blue lochs.

After a time the Flemings got tired of speaking to me in their rather poor Scots, and I knew no Flemish. We decided therefore to speak in French—not their first language, but one in which they were fluent. This was a great benefit to my use of French. We conversed for hours each day throughout our sojourn in the west.

As we neared the lands of Sir Neil Campbell in Argyll, the lady began to talk with me.

"Davie."

"Yes, ma'am."

"There's no need to call me ma'am. We have known each other well these eight years. Besides, with my husband dead, I am no longer a countess. Just say Isabel, please."

"You have been very quiet for days, Isabel. I am sorry for the great pain you must be keeping."

"Yes, sadness is what it is, not really pain. It is deep within me, and I can see no relief. He is gone from me forever. He is the king, and he has a queen. The country needs a male heir. I understand it all quite well. It is all so logical, and yet life is not quite so logical, is it? What is logic compared with feelings?" She sighed and smiled at me bravely. "Ah, well, Davie, I must suffer in silence. There is no use of discussing it, really. In one's life there is only space for one true love. Robert Bruce has been mine. We have known each other since we were children. As a young maiden I had hoped that he would be my husband, but politics interfered, and he was wed to another. I was married off to Buchan. It was all politics and power, once again logic triumphing over feelings. If women ruled instead of men, there would be more importance placed on feelings and less on logic, I'll warrant."

The lady looked beautiful even though we had been riding for days and living off the rough country. She had the same faded blue velvet gown that had become even worse-looking as the days went by. We had travelled though every weather, experiencing at turns wind, rain, heat, cool, and sunshine. She was dishevelled, and yet neither her beauty nor her serene disposition could be masked. I said to her, "Isabel, there is nothing I can say any more than 'I am sorry.' I truly mean it and I feel sad for you as I say it."

"Thank you, Davie. You are my friend, and I will miss you, too."

At last we reached the cottage Sir Neil had made available. It was fine and strong and had a view across a small loch, or a *lochan*, as they are called in the Gaelic. The servant woman introduced herself to her new mistress, addressing her in the ancient tongue, which was, I assumed, the only one she knew. She helped the lady with her baggage, which was small indeed. There was a peat fire going in the hearth and something cooking in a pot. As the servant busied herself I was able to find a small place in one of the walls and I hid the bag of silver pieces there. When I had the chance I told the lady that I had hidden some money in the wall, and showed her where.

"It's a present from King Robert," I told her. "He wants you to have it. If you ever have need of anything whatever, you are to send word to him and your needs will be met."

Lady Isabel looked at me with tears in her eyes. "So,"

she said. "I'm to be a comfortable exile. It's better than being an *uncomfortable* exile. I see no other solution, but I still have hope, Davie, that someday, somehow, everything will change and I will be with Robert again."

I felt very badly, of course, to see such a good and noble friend in such distress, but there was nothing I could do. We walked outside and I prepared to go, leaving her with one of the horses. There were birds singing in the trees and fish jumping in the loch. It was a beautiful day to continue the journey, but even I had tears in my eyes when we parted. She looked beautiful in her shabby gown. She embraced me and gave me that small kiss, the same one that had so excited me all those years before. Then the Flemings and I rode away, westward again. A long time would elapse before Isabel and I would meet again.

Days later we arrived at the shore across from the main home of Lady Christiana Macruarie, Christiana of the Isles. The people had been very hospitable all along the way, and here they agreed to give us a lift to the island on a boat. We left the horses and crossed in a brisk wind. When we came into the cove, I recognised it immediately. Nothing had changed in all those five years since I had visited this place, except the lady awaiting us in the courtyard. She stood there, tall and proud as ever, her red hair now tinged with a bit of silver. When she recognised me, she smiled and walked toward me and gave me an embrace.

"Davie, it's you. Oh, Davie, come inside and tell me about the great battle at Stirling. I have heard that the war is over. Is it true?"

"I hope so, Lady Christiana. We are all tired of the

fighting. I am sure King Robert will want to try to negotiate a peace. The English army was utterly defeated, with thousands of casualties."

"And what of Màiri, and Seumas?" she asked.

"Màiri and I were married several years ago, but I have heard nothing of her for some time. I am on my way home now, after this visit to you." In this manner I avoided mentioning Lady Christian of Carrick, who was really our next stop. At least I hadn't lied. The Flemings were busy with the boat so that I used the opportunity to deliver the bag of silver pieces. The proud lady was upset and refused it.

"I'll not take any payment for the aid I gave to the Scottish army or the king. It was my duty and I want nothing."

"But Lady Christiana, practically everyone in Scotland has benefited from the spoils left by the English army. The king very much wants you to have a share, and will be disappointed at both of us if you do not. Please take the bag. You deserve it. Look at it as a reimbursement for your expenses direct from King Edward!"

With that, the large woman gave a small laugh and took the silver. "You're very convincing, Davie. Now, what news is there of Queen Elizabeth? Is she yet alive?"

"We are told she is."

"And will she be ransomed?"

I knew my answer would be unsatisfactory. "I believe she will."

"Yes, of course she will. She will be the first. Yes, the nation needs a male heir." She looked resigned, and I said nothing, studying my boots.

Then I said, "The king directs me to tell you that he

remembers you with great fondness. He thinks of you often, and thanks you for your most valuable help in our fight for freedom. Further, the king asks me to tell you that should you ever have any problem which he might solve, that you are invited to send to him for aid."

The lady made no answer for a moment to this, then said, "King Robert is the greatest Scot. It has been my honour to serve him." She paused again and sighed, "Well, Davie, will you stay awhile?"

"There is nothing I would like better, my lady, but we must be off while there is still light. I am hoping to trade you the four horses I left on the other shore for a boat that will hold my two men and myself."

"I accept the trade, Davie, but I am getting the better of it, I believe. Would the boat you came across in suit you? You may have it if you like."

"That boat will do us fine. My two companions are shaping it up as we talk here. I would appreciate it if you would give us a jug of water and some food for our journey to the south."

"That you shall have immediately, Davie." She slapped her palms together and gave orders to her servant. We walked to the shore and I introduced her to the Flemings and told them to get the provisions from the servant in the house. Within a short time we were on our way. The lady walked with us down to the shore, and I perceived her breathing to be difficult. I wondered if I should ask if there was something wrong, but decided against it. I didn't want to wound this stalwart woman's pride. The Flemings loaded the boat and made ready to cast off. Lady Christiana took both of my hands in hers, and then we embraced. She smiled a broad brave smile, and then said, "Remember me and this fine day, Davie, and please give my good wishes to the king." We said nothing further and I boarded the boat. The sail soon filled and we were out on the water. The lady waved at us again, and then she was out of sight.

We sailed that way for days through alternating sun and rain. There was almost always plenty of wind, and nothing to do but take turns steering our vessel down through the Sound of Mull, into the Firth of Lorn, and down into the Sound of Jura, being careful to avoid the dreaded whirlpool of Corryvreckan. At last we reached the Mull of Kintyre and turned toward the mainland. When we reached Carrick we beached the boat and set out on foot for the realm of Lady Christian of Carrick. There was no one about, so we couldn't trade the boat for horses, and even if there had been someone to trade with, I was sure the vessel was not worth the price of three steeds. After a hike of several days we reached the estate of Lady Christian one midmorning. It had been a rough march through lonely country under an almost constant drizzle. The lady's welcoming smile brightened our spirits. She looked lovely, her long hair still a deep chestnut colour.

"I have heard of a great battle at Stirling," she said embracing me. "Is it true Davie, that we have won?"

"It is indeed true, my lady. Scotland won a truly great victory near a stream called the Bannock Burn, which lies below Stirling. Most of the English troops have already left our country. Scotland is free now."

"God be praised! And the king, how fares he, Davie?"

"The king is fine, my lady. His illness has subsided and he is in good spirits."

Then came the question I next expected. "The queen, Davie; is there any news of Queen Elizabeth?"

"There is, my lady. She has survived the war and her captivity, and we expect that she will be exchanged for some captured English lords."

"Yes, of course." I could tell that she was trying to show no emotion at this. "Well, Davie, come inside and we will have some supper."

Since we had had very little to eat in the previous days, I accepted this invitation, and introduced John and George to her as my companions. I could see that her estate was somewhat derelict from the hardness of the war years. When I gave her the bag of silver pieces and told her they were a gift from King Robert, she took it quickly, holding it to her chest and bursting into tears. "I didn't expect this," she said. "I wasn't sure the king would remember me in this way. Help right now is very important to me. It will relieve my burdens greatly."

"The king sends his best regards, my lady, and says that if you are in want for anything that you should send a messenger to him and you will be rewarded. He asked me to tell you specifically that your help during the war was of great help to his cause, and that you are always in his thoughts."

The lady gave us a supper of fish and wine and asked me

if we could stay. I declined of course because it was past midday, with plenty of light left, and I was anxious to see my family, still several days' march away. There was another tearful embrace with Lady Christian. She asked about my mother, and I told her I was going to see her and my wife and child. I thought of her fondly since she had treated me so well at our previous meetings. I would always remember her kindness.

"Please send my best regards to King Robert, Davie, and thank him for the present he sent me. Thanks to you also for bringing it." Her eyes were wet again as I waved good-bye, and the three of us started off toward the east. There was a village nearby and there we stopped to ask directions. The Flemings were going back north to Stirling and I was going to the east to my place near Dumfries. We bid good-bye there in that hamlet. They were really good men, John and George, and I am sure that the king had rewarded them well. Who could tell if we would meet again? I thanked them and we went our separate ways. I travelled in rough country until I reached the valley of the River Nith, which took me home.

I arrived at my little estate of an evening just as it was becoming dark. The warm day had given way to a cool close, and a light rain was falling. My mother and my wife were sitting outside, and I ran at them with a great joy. I had not seen them in almost two years, and the thing I noticed first was another child, a small golden-haired girl. The women were in tears and I was a bit choked up myself, so that at first none of us said anything. I just hugged my mother and my wife. My son, Seumas, now about five years old, didn't recognise me and he seemed very wary. "Hello, Seumas," I began, but he turned and ran away. "Who is this, Màiri?" I asked, pointing to the little girl.

"This is your daughter, Iseabal," my wife answered. The way she pronounced it sounded like "Ishbel." "I have named her after your friend, the former Countess of Buchan. She has just started toward walking."

I smiled at my wife's Gaelic-idiom Scots, and also at her beauty, still dazzling in her motherhood. *A Mhàiri mo ghaol!* "Mary, my love," she had taught me to say. I picked up Iseabal and held her in my arms. "Ishbel," I said softly, and I would ever after call her that. She did not seem afraid of me at first, but soon began to cry, and I handed her back to her mother. What a homecoming! My son didn't know me, and my daughter was afraid of me! Och, aye, we would have to change that! There would be time to settle in a bit now and I would get to know them. I had several months before I had to return to duty. I gave the bag with the silver pieces to the ladies and their eyes lit up like stars on a dark night. I am sure they had never seen so much money in their entire lives combined. I didn't even show them the other moneybag I carried. We were rich, all right, and no one was dead, maimed, or ill. It was quite an achievement in those times, I assure you.

The next months were among the best of my life. I got to know my children, who were now bilingual, speaking in Scots to my mother and me and in the Gaelic to my wife. I didn't have to do anything, but after the first week I began to busy myself with the place. I fixed several breaks in our stone dykes and built a one-room extension on the house. I found a new tenant to manage things and to look after my family when I should be gone. I took Seumas to the stream for fishing and he was amused with what we caught. I even helped him take a few for himself. Ishbel began to like me and I hugged her many times each day—Seumas, too. Màiri and I took Ishbel to the church in Dumfries to be baptized. It was incredible for me to think of that lad of fourteen, hiding behind a pillar on that fateful night eight years before, and now to be standing there at that same altar. I could see the whole scene vividly, as if it had happened the day before. I could see the Earl of Carrick sitting and waiting for the Red Comyn, hear the clash of steel, and see the river of blood. The Earl of Carrick was now King Robert and the lad was now his trusted confidant. It was strange indeed.

The period with my family was an ideal time in my life, but it was, of course, troubled by the thought that there would be more fighting, and I would have to go. The women were worried about my safety, so I pretended not to be concerned that war would soon erupt again. I knew, though, that since we hadn't captured King Edward, most probably he would not recognise our independence and we would have to do battle again. I knew also that King Robert would never rest until Scotland was free, and that I was committed to do anything he asked of me.

I bought a horse from a neighbour and, when the weather grew cold, I prepared to leave. When the day came, there were all the usual tears. Even the children, who had become used to me, wailed. I kissed them and my mother. Last, I kissed my beautiful wife. *"A Mhàiri mo ghaol!"* was all I could manage to whisper past the crook in my throat. Quickly I mounted the horse and rode for Stirling.

II

When I arrived at Stirling, I found the place busy and excited. King Robert had called a parliament at nearby Cambuskenneth Abbey, and it seemed as if all Scotland was going to be in attendance. It was November now, and the skies were mostly grey, but there was exuberance everywhere among all of the people, high and low. There was a great festival in the streets, with musicians playing and jugglers performing. There was even a man putting on a show with a dancing black bear.

The parliament opened and I was given a seat in the audience. Queen Elizabeth, rescued by ransom, sat next to the king on his throne. She looked quite regal, but there was some aging around her eyes after eight years of captivity. Sitting on the other side of the king and queen were Sir Neil Campbell and his wife, the king's sister, Mary, also retrieved from her English captors. The king's daughter, Marjorie Bruce, newly released from English captivity, was no longer the dear little girl I had seen at Lochmaben those years ago. She was now a woman and, I am sorry to say, looked older than her years. The long imprisonment in England had stolen her youth. How awful, I thought, to have spent all one's growing years without friends, schooling, and, most of all, freedom. Marjorie had been promised by King Robert to Sir Walter Stewart, and I hoped, at least, that this union would be happy for her.

All around the royal couple were the nobles of the country. Unlike the coronation, when many had been absent, now almost everyone of importance had arrived, dressed in their tabards with their colourful armourial bearings. Not a few who had been on the English side had been summoned and were concerned to learn of their fate. But King Robert welcomed them all, saying that they would be restored to their lands on two conditions. The first was that they maintain absolute loyalty to him. The second was that if they had any lands in England they must surrender them or forfeit their Scottish lands and leave the country. All agreed to these conditions, and they were enacted into law. This gesture toward reconciliation was typical of King Robert. I had seen it before; it was his way. The king then made the Baron of Erroll, Gilbert de la Haye, Lord High Constable of Scotland, to be forever the hereditary right of his family.

When all other business had been acted upon the king addressed the parliament. "My lords, ladies, and gentlemen of the Kingdom of Scotland. We have reached a new stage in our country's history. Except in a few places the usurpers have fled. We are in control of our ancient nation again, thanks to the valour and discipline of our sons and daughters. The Scottish nation has proved itself worthy of the august destiny to which it was called!" This brought forth great applause from all of those assembled. Then King Robert raised his hand for silence and continued, "You are all here, my friends, representing all of the people of Scotland." Then the king's blue eyes darted about the assembly and a small smile came to his mouth. Quietly he said, "May I ask your consent to proclaim, *L'état c'est moi?*" "I am the state," the king had spoken in French. At this there was what was perhaps the most resounding applause I have ever heard. Everyone stood up and a piper began to play. Yes, he *was* the state. He was their king. The people roared their approval of this great leader. Many were moved to tears. The Highlanders in attendance, in particular, shrieked their peculiar sounds. There was no doubt among any that day that Scotland had found her rightful king.

Then King Robert held up his hand for quiet again. "We have accomplished much, and will build on it, but I fear that we are not finished with King Edward II. As you may know, we captured the great seal of England on the field at the Bannock Burn last summer. You may not know that I returned it to King Edward in the hopes that it would spur him to recognise our independence and promote amity between our two countries. The King of England, however, has spurned our offer of peace and, our agents tell us, he is preparing to make war against us again. Since we cannot obtain our freedom from him by peaceful means, therefore, we shall have to obtain it from him by warfare."

The king then said that his principal lieutenants, Thomas Randolph, the Earl of Moray, Sir James Douglas, and his brother Sir Edward Bruce, the Earl of Carrick, would be in charge of making war against England, and were looking for volunteers immediately. In fact, the fighting had already begun. During my absence, Sir Edward Bruce and Sir James Douglas had attacked the north of England, collecting tribute and taking property in Northumberland, Cumberland, Durham, and Yorkshire.

In November King Robert himself led the next expedition, and I was part of it. We thrust into Tynedale, finding the people completely unprotected by their government. They made no resistance to us whatsoever, immediately agreeing to pay us the blackmail to which both we and they had been so long accustomed. The king was feeling well, and seemed to be at least temporarily recovered from his sickness. In the summer of the year 1315, I volunteered for an expedition to Durham led by my friend Sir James Douglas and Thomas Randolph. We returned with much booty and to great acclaim, but the king could see that our raids, while profitable to us, were of no value in changing the thinking of the English parliament or its king. They were based in the south, where there was great prosperity. The English court didn't care about the ruination of their northern shires. Our raids would not help us gain recognition of our independence from the English. We would have to do something more. King Robert then decided to put more pressure on our enemy. If he could arrange it, he would force the English to fight us on another front. He decided, therefore, to offer Ireland the assistance of a Scottish army headed by his brother, Sir Edward Bruce.

When I first heard of this scheme, I thought ill of it. But there was a council held with all the important men present, and I was there. It was brought out that Ireland was being oppressed by England just as Scotland had been, and might very well welcome relief from us. Also, while both countries had a strong Anglo-Norman nobility, in neither country had the old Celtic aristocracy disappeared. King Robert's Norman ancestry had nothing at all to do with his being king. It was his Celtic heritage, traceable back to the high nobility of ancient Scotland and Ireland, that mattered. It was noted that an invasion should have the backing of the prominent Irish clans. We would send an army, but only if the Irish clans wanted it. It was decided then to send an embassy to Ireland, offering the help of Scotland.

I knew, of course, that there was another reason for the Irish campaign. The king's brother, Sir Edward Bruce, was becoming troublesome. He believed, as I have related earlier, that he was at least as capable as his older brother, but knew there was only a slim possibility of his becoming King of Scots. I had come to believe that King Robert had decided to try to make Sir Edward king of Ireland. This would be a suitable honour and responsibility for his brother. Not only would an Irish uprising force the English to fight on another front, it would also give the Bruce family the beginning of a Celtic empire. Perhaps Wales would be next, followed by Cornwall, the Isle of Man, and Brittany. I have already told of how King Robert felt sympathy toward the old pre–Roman Catholic Celtic Church. Perhaps, it was thought, the Bruces could reinstate it and depose the Roman Church throughout the Celtic world. Scotland owed nothing to a faith that had excommunicated it and had opposed Scottish independence continuously.

The embassy was despatched to Ireland. It was hoped that the Irish chiefs, who must have been impressed with what the Bruces had accomplished in Scotland, would see this success as a chance for their own freedom. Partly in the hope that Sir Edward Bruce could be appeased, King Robert had also arranged for his daughter, Marjorie, who had married Sir Walter Stewart, to relinquish her precedence of right to the throne to her uncle. This made Sir Edward Bruce first in succession to the throne if the king died without a legitimate male heir. The crown would thus pass first to Edward, then to his legitimate male heirs, then to Marjorie. The primary purpose of this move was to leave the throne in the hands of an experienced person, but I am sure King Robert hoped also that this arrangement would soothe his headstrong brother, at least somewhat.

The news returning from our Irish embassy could not have been better. The O'Neill family, the aristocrats from the royal line of the north of Ireland, responded enthusiastically. Given that Edward Bruce was of royal Irish ancestry, if he would come with a suitable army for the purpose of liberating Ireland, he might, if successful, be accepted as *Ard Righ*, or high king of the country. This was an important step in King Robert's Celtic empire strategy, and he treated the response with great respect, giving his brother control of several thousand of our best Scottish veterans for the task. Sir Edward was, of course, thrilled at the prospect and spent weeks preparing the expedition. Everyone was in high spirits. The invading army left Scotland when the weather became good and landed at Larne in the province of Ulster in late May 1315.

In order to cover the invasion of Ireland, King Robert laid siege to Carlisle in July, and I was involved in this action. The idea was to give the English two fronts to worry about, and I suppose it had some limited impact. Actually, however, the siege was not very effective. Our men were not able to mount a successful attack, and eventually we withdrew. But our invasion of Ireland had made an impression on the Welsh. They began, in turn, to rise against the English in the hope that Edward Bruce would assist them. This forced our enemy to confront them, and made our borders safer. The Welsh had thus supplied us with the second front, that our siege of Carlisle had failed to do.

The news from Ireland was also encouraging. The Scottish army under Sir Edward Bruce had won several battles, and Irishmen had joined the cause. Our situation was now rather stable, except that our old foe John of Lorne, still on the English side, was back in action in the west. Therefore, when the boats from our invasion fleet returned from Ireland, King Robert decided to go to the western isles to confront the Macdougall chief. We sailed up the great Loch Fyne until we came to a place on the long Kintyre peninsula called in the Gaelic *tairbeart*. I don't know if we have a Scots word to match it, but it means a very narrow piece of land between two seas; in this case, between Loch Fyne and the great waters to the west. It would have been normal to sail around the entire peninsula, but to save time the king ordered that we cut trees and lay down planks so that we could drag the boats across the *tairbeart*. This we did, and hoisted our sails as well to catch any following breeze. Within a very short time all the boats had been "sailed" from one sea to the other to the delight of all of the onlookers. The sight of boats sailing, as it were, across land, brought out memories of an *ald prophesy that he that suld ger schippis betuix the seis with salis suld vyn the ilis, that nane with strynth suld him withstand*. The people of the isles took the fact that King Robert had fulfilled the prophecy very seriously *and tharfor thai come all to the kyng*. In this way King Robert had become legitimate to the Gaelic-speaking folk of the west, and many enlisted in his cause. None would join John of Lorne, and he was thus beaten before a fight even started and was compelled to retreat to England.

Throughout that year and into the year 1316 we continued our raiding of northern England, levying blackmail and driving cattle north. In March we were all saddened by the news of the death of the king's beloved daughter who was thrown from her horse and killed. Marjorie was near to term with child. Quickly, she was cut open so that her male child was taken alive from her dead body. Her husband, Sir Walter Stewart, named the motherless bairn Robert after the boy's grandfather. Little Robert Stewart was guarded closely, as he was now in the line of succession to the throne of Scotland. King Robert was inconsolable at the death of his beloved daughter, and for days would talk to no one.

Several months later we heard that Edward Bruce was

in control of the north of Ireland and had been crowned *Ard Rìgh*, the high king of the country. Sir Edward sent a message to King Robert that he should come to Ireland in force to complete the conquest. The king was ecstatic at this news and immediately prepared an army to go to Ireland. I asked him if I could go and his reply was, "Of course, Davie. You wouldn't want to miss it, would ye?"

It was a very exciting prospect, you may be sure. I hadn't ever seen another country, unless you count barren Rathlin. This would be the real Ireland, with the king and his brother fighting for its freedom. It took several months to gather volunteers, and once again we were off to adventure. Thomas Randolph would come with us. The Kingdom of Scotland would be left in the trusty hands of Sir Walter Stewart and Sir James Douglas. Secretly, I hoped that my friend Sir James would be included in our Irish venture, but I could understand that King Robert would want to leave the country in his capable control. While we were preparing this expedition, we were saddened to learn that our venerable supporter, Robert Wishart, the Bishop of Glasgow, had died, ill and blind. He was one of the true heroes of our Scottish revolution.

Once again we marched toward the western isles, where boats were waiting to take us to Ireland. This time we set sail from Loch Ryan, where we all remembered that King Robert's two brilliant younger brothers, Thomas and my dear friend Alexander, had perished a decade before. Before we put out to sea, the king insisted that we observe a moment of silence out of respect for these two brave young men. The king also requested a remembrance for Bishop Wishart and for Marjorie. Then he became silent as the boat moved out into the channel. There were so many to mourn in those days. I think it helped his mood that our passage was easy and in only a few hours we had landed at Carrickfergus.

It was a beautifully clear but cold day. The town was dominated by a great grey stone castle that had been built by the Normans a century or two before. The land all around was flat and very green. We stayed in the castle at Carrickfergus for several days, arranging provisions and making plans, and then began to march southward. The whole assembly had a festive air. King Edward Bruce was making his royal progress through his countryside. It was similar to that which we had made throughout Scotland years before. I noticed that our Gaelic speakers, which included various Campbells and Macdonalds, as well as the Bruce brothers, were quite able to converse with the Irish. The language was the same. Our Irish comrades were fine, noble people, and we made steady progress through the emerald countryside without encountering much opposition. By February 1317, we had laid waste to Slane, and soon after were at Castleknock, very near to Dublin. The people inside that city were wary of us and hastened to rebuild their defences. We heard even that the Earl of Ulster, King Robert's father-in-law, had been arrested within the city. Since his own daughter, our Queen Elizabeth, was married to King Robert, he was suspected of being in league with us.

One of the Irish chiefs, Brian Ban O'Brian, told King Robert that if we should go to the south where his strength lay, we would provoke an uprising in our favour. Thus, we decided to pass by Dublin, and by March we had reached Cashel, meeting little opposition. But we didn't realise that there was significant hidden opposition, very similar to that which we faced when we began to take over Scotland. There are always traitors who are not up to the patriotic cause. They just hadn't shown themselves as yet.

By April we were near Limerick in the far southwest of the country, but the promised rising didn't occur because another O'Brian chief opposed it. It seemed that some of the clans were more interested in their own feuds than in driving the English out and freeing the country, just as we had found in Scotland. Our enemies began to appear to harass us and we ran very short of provisions, there being a famine in Ireland at that time.

Accordingly, we organised a retreat. But just as we were ready to begin the long march, the scream of a woman was heard. King Robert inquired as to what her trouble was, and when he was informed that she was in childbirth he insisted that the army wait while shelter could be erected, and several women found to assist her. The entire army waited for the baby to be born, and only then did we proceed, taking the babe and its mother with us. This is but one of many such tales that could be told which show the kind of man our king was.

Our army proceeded north in our retreat through the winter, attacked occasionally by our enemies. In May of 1317 we had reached Ulster, and better weather, where we found forage for our horses and food for our soldiers. We might have continued in Ireland, but King Robert was becoming concerned that he had left his kingdom for too long, and he decided to take some of his army and return. When we were ready to launch our boats, the king bade his brother good-bye and Godspeed. I will never forget the emotion, the real love expressed by these two very different but very great brothers at their parting, which, I am sure, each might have thought was their last. They embraced heartily, and we embarked for Scotland.

CHAPTER SEVENTEEN

A Declaration of Independence

We left Ireland in different boats, assigned as to where we were going, for the king had decided to give us a furlough of several months. My boat headed for the Solway Firth in southwest Scotland. We were seven in that craft, all bound for either the mouth of the Dee in Kirkcudbright or, as in my case, for the mouth of the River Nith, close to Dumfries and my family. It was bright and windy as the castle of Carrickfergus receded behind us, its dark grey stones surrounded by the grassy green carpet of Ireland. The water was rough and some of the men were ill. I did not so suffer this time. In fact, during our three-day voyage, I had time to think on things. I had been a soldier for more than a decade and had not a scratch on me. I considered all the men on both sides and how many had been killed or maimed. Even King Robert had suffered from that old wound next to his left eye. We had been in the thick of battle at Methven, Loudon Hill, the Bannock Burn, and other parts, but often the enemy avoided us, and we didn't have to fight much to achieve our goals. Fighting wasn't even risky for us after our victory at the Bannock Burn; our enemies were afraid of us. In our numerous raids on England, and even in Ireland, there wasn't much resistance to our movement. We had developed an aura about ourselves, our warrior king, and his brilliant captains, Douglas, Randolph, and Edward Bruce.

It was a calm sunny day in May 1317 when I sailed up the River Nith to Dumfries and home. Men and boys were fishing all along the banks. Birds were singing their thanks to the bright spring day. Robins hopped. A pair of serene swans glided on the water. The earth was wet, bringing forth life. Its deep scent was carried all the way out to the boat. It felt great to be home!

My family was overjoyed to see me. Is there a man anywhere who can experience anything better than a joyous homecoming? There was a bit more grey in my mother's hair, but I could see that she was in good health and spirits. Màiri was as darkly beautiful as ever. Seumas, now eight, and Ishbel, three, had grown considerably and were jumping up and down with the energy of their youth. Since they were bilingual, they had a hard time guessing which language to use with me, but soon figured out that it would be better to use Scots. I couldn't keep the tears from my eyes. I hadn't seen them in more than a year, and only for a few brief weeks in almost three years.

We passed that summer in a state of bliss. I took my

children fishing, boating, and swimming. We attended a country fair. I looked after my property and improved it. We had animals now, cows among them. We operated a dairy, which my mother supervised. Our cheese fetched a good price at the market in Dumfries. We bred horses and sold the ones we didn't need. We taught the children to ride, and they loved it. We built an extra room onto the house just for Ishbel. She and Seumas were delighted to have their own spaces. The countryside was beautiful, and we were free and happy—rich, too.

It was a beautiful time. Màiri and I would make love when the darkness came, and then we would lie there in our bed and talk of what we would do with our lives when I could be retired after Scotland's independence had been secured. We would fall asleep, sometimes holding hands, and only awake when our noisy rooster decided it was time to be up and alive, as the cool breeze of the morning blew over us. All too soon, the days became shorter. It was time for me to return to duty, and we made the usual tearful good-byes. I took my favourite horse and, loaded with full arms and armour, rode away to be at the side of the great King Robert.

There wasn't much to do that autumn. There was no war and no raiding. Since the king's court was now well financed, thanks to the spoils taken at the battle of the Bannock Burn, he had numerous people working for him—pages, if you will. My services as a page had long expired. I was now treated as an honoured veteran soldier, but also still a confidant of the king, someone who could be trusted to carry out a special task as well as know all the secrets and keep my mouth tightly closed. For this reason I was invited to the audience that the king granted, or should I say almost granted, to two envoys, highly ranked in the church and very close to the pope, John XXII at Avignon.

These papal emissaries had travelled on the usual safe-conduct passes, but despite this had been treated rudely by people in northern England, even being robbed at one point. They proceeded peacefully, however, through Scotland. The king welcomed them and asked what their business was. They started to explain in Latin, but the king halted them and asked them if they would speak in French, as he would better understand. This they did. They said that the pope was desirous of peace between England and Scotland, and suggested a truce of two years between the opposing countries. The king smiled and said that he had been trying for years to arrange such a peace, but that the English had steadfastly refused to recognise the independence of his kingdom, and without that recognition he couldn't make peace.

Then came a dramatic moment. One of the envoys presented a sealed letter from the pope. The king looked at it, then passed it to me unopened, and motioned for me to pass it on to the others. Although my Latin was shaky, I could see right away why he wanted us all to see it. The letter was addressed jointly to Edward II, King of England, and the noble Robert Bruce, *regnum Scotiae gubernantem*. I didn't need to know the exact meaning of those words, but it was obvious that Edward was being addressed as king and King Robert as something much less, a sort of acting governor. The room grew silent while the document was passed round; finally it came back to King Robert. All was quiet, and no one knew what he would do next. Then the king smiled and handed the letter back to the emissary, still unopened. Every one of us excommunicates knew that the king was not afraid of the great pope, and now we sensed what he would say. "We notice that this letter is not addressed to Robert Bruce, King of Scots. Those are our names and title. There are other men in this country called Robert Bruce who are not king. We cannot accept or open this document, as it appears it is not addressed to us. It must be for someone else, and we would never open the letter of another man. The person you seek is not here. You will have to find him elsewhere."

The delegates began to talk to each other in Latin, then addressed the king in French, as he had requested. "It seems that there is a dispute here between you and the King of England, sir, as to what title you should have. Please know that the Holy Father cannot take sides in such a dispute."

Then the king's eyes hardened a little and his smile narrowed. I still remember even now exactly what he said. "*Mais c'est exactement ce qu'il a fait!* But that is exactly what he has done! The Holy Father has addressed one of us as king and the other as something much less. We are recognised as king throughout our realm, and are addressed as king by the monarchs of other countries. The Holy Father has played the side of the English."

For some time the emissaries pleaded with King Robert to accept the letter in the interests of peace and harmony in Christendom, but he steadfastly refused. "If you bring us a letter from the pope addressed to Robert Bruce, King of Scots, we will accept it."

One of the cardinals then complained that the king was treating them unfairly. "Unfairly, you think? We are sure that if you brought a letter addressed like that to another king, you might find that you were treated *worse* than unfairly. You might be lucky to escape severe punishment!"

At this some of our people began to chuckle, and the churchmen began to retreat in confusion. "I warn you, you may be excommunicated," one said rather timidly. Almost in a chorus, our men yelled, "We are already excommunicated! You can't harm us again." The two envoys then left us, to loud jeering. I must say that I felt a little sorry for them. They had just done their duty. I hoped that they would not lose their safe-conduct passes.

Although the pope was insisting on a truce, we paid no attention to his demand. Immediately King Robert and his captains started to plan the recapture of our most important port, Berwick, the most significant place in Scotland still occupied by the English. We had some important help in this enterprise from one Syme Spalding, an Englishman living at Berwick and married to a Scottish woman who was a close relative of the Marshall of Scotland, Sir Robert Keith. The English army unit holding the town was suspicious of Spalding's marriage, and he thought there might be trouble for him. Spalding decided to preempt such mischief, and sent a message to Keith offering assistance. On a certain night he would leave a particular entrance to the town open, and the Scots could enter and try to take the place. King Robert, of course, thought of the possibility of a trap, but but Sir Robert Keith urged him to trust Spalding. The king decided to send his two best men, Thomas Randolph and James Douglas, to test the plan. I was part of the Douglas crew.

On the night of the first of April in the year 1318 our two detachments came near to Berwick, left our horses in a wooded area, and marched to the prearranged place with our ladders. Spalding was waiting for us as agreed, and we were able to climb the walls in the darkness without being seen. When dawn came our men, with greed in their eyes and without orders, began to sack the town, and the whole place came awake. The English fought well and hard against us, and if it had not been for the heroism and leadership of Douglas and Randolph, I think we should have been repelled. But *than Errl Thomas that wes worthy, and als the gude lord of Douglas met thame stoutly with wapnys* and we were able to rally the men and prevail. King Robert soon arrived with his army and established control over what we had won. Within a short time, all the English surrendered. A Flemish engineer, John Crab, was put in charge of building suitable war machines to defend the walls of the town. The king made an exception to his policy of destroying castles. That he *vald nocht brek doune the vall, bot castell and the toune with-all stuff weill with men and vittaill*. King Robert meant to defend this place as it was our most significant port and was important to the Scottish economy. He ordered a year's supplies for Berwick and put his son-in-law, Sir Walter Stewart, in charge.

Then our entire army, led by King Robert, went raiding

in the north of England. It was the same as before. We would levy blackmail against a town, and if they could not pay, we would give them time to raise money and take hostages to guarantee their promise. We met no opposition.

In June, Pope John XXII excommunicated all of us involved with King Robert, and in effect, all of Scotland. It had become an old story to us, and had no significance upon us whatsoever.

II

It was also in the year 1318 that King Robert learned of the death of his friend and ally Lady Christian of Carrick. How this news reached him I do not know, but one day he did not make himself available to the many people who came to see him. Instead he called for me and told me what he had heard.

"Are you sure it is true, sir?" I asked.

"I am quite sure, Davie, and I am greatly saddened. Will you have a drink with me in remembrance?"

"Of course I will, sir. I am saddened as well as you. How could I ever forget the aid we received from her and the hospitality she showed us? It all seems so long ago, and it *was* a very long time ago."

"Aye, Davie, those were times, weren't they? There was so much more at stake then. We were in constant peril. We were really alive, taking whatever pleasure was afforded. Sometimes now there is so much to do that I lose touch with my friends. You have been a true one, Davie, and I don't even see you much now. There are too many people who want to talk to me, to ask me for something. How is your family, Davie?" The king poured me a silver goblet of red wine. I could tell he had had a few already.

"They are fine, sir. We have prospered greatly, as have most of the people in my district."

"Good, good, very good, Davie. I want so much for our people to prosper."

"They are, my lord. I believe this is the best time in the history of our land."

The king and I drank to the memory of Lady Christian, and I left him to whatever he had to do for the rest of the day.

Weeks later even worse tidings arrived. Our man Cuthbert had returned from Ireland with the news that the Scottish/Irish forces under Sir Edward Bruce had been defeated at Fochart, near Dundalk, and Sir Edward had been killed. This time the mourning was public. All his captains rallied round the king to listen to Cuthbert tell the story.

"Sir, your brother died in a fashion that suited him, if I may say so. He died very bravely and very foolishly."

Everyone looked at King Robert to see if he had any reaction to this, but the grave expression on his face didn't change, and Cuthbert continued. "Your brother had put together an army of Scots and Irish with a view to taking Dundalk. He had the backing of the O'Neills, who, I am sure you know, are of the same royal stock as are you and your late brother. Sir Edward, however, faced a much greater force that was ready to do battle with him. Sir John Stewart begged your brother to wait, as *his* brother would soon be arriving with a large unit of reinforcements. But when Sir Edward heard of this, he became very angry, and questioned the loyalty of his captains. It is said that he was emboldened by a jug or two of wine. He was very agitated and insisted that they attack their opponents without delay. At this, many of the Irish supporters said that they would not fight so large an army without those reinforcements. Sir Edward then became so angry that he told them they could stay behind as cowards if they wished, but that he was going to fight immediately. What he said then came out as a little couplet that I believe, my lord, will be remembered as long as there is a Scotland. Sir Edward Bruce said, 'God scheld that ony suld us blame, that we defoull our nobill name!' This was certainly in keeping with your brother's character, sir. He had an enormous sense of honour. Yet passion led him into a battle he could not win, and the result was a catastrophe, sir. A great many were killed, and of those Scottish soldiers who survived many have given up, deprived as they now are of their captain. They have lost their gifted leader and are coming home. The rebellion in Ireland, my lord, is failed. Personally, my lord, I very much regret the death of your brother. He was a great soldier, and a great patriot."

There were many in the room, including King Robert and myself, whose eyes were moist. We had all known Sir Edward Bruce. We had fought alongside him. We had been his comrades. Who could forget his leading our little army's daring charge to begin the battle now called Bannockburn against the astonished English defenders? It was his optimism and flair that gave the enemy pause. Sir

Edward Bruce had set the tone with that brave charge, and the English never recovered from the shock. The news of his death made for a sad day for us all. Sir Edward was a great soldier, a happy warrior, and an unsurpassed fighter. Only his rashness prevented his being a great general.

From that day on, King Robert seldom mentioned Ireland. He said nothing about our soldiers coming home. He still dreamed of a Celtic empire, but it had lost importance to him. If Sir Edward Bruce had lived, there might have been a Bruce dynasty throughout the Celtic world; without him there was small hope of such a thing ever coming about. Nevertheless, the Bruces had changed Ireland forever. The old aristocracy had been roused. Many Irishmen now became certain that the Anglo-Norman way was not theirs. They returned to speaking Irish to their fellow natives rather than French or English. They were turning back to their Brehon Laws, electing democratically by tanistry, and away from Norman primogeniture, in which the eldest always inherited all. Ireland had been reborn in its ancient traditions, and never after that, at least in my lifetime, would the native Irish accept the proposition that their emerald land was no more than a colonial province of another nation.

I stayed with King Robert for the rest of that year. He continued to suffer from his ailment, and at times was confined to bed, too weak even to speak. His complexion had turned dark, and he complained of muscle pains. He had decided to hold a parliament at Scone in December, and after it was summoned I tried to make him well enough to attend. He was depressed and wouldn't eat. He was losing weight. In truth, the king was dying. The news of his disability spread around the land, and his sickness was much discussed. One day an old woman arrived and asked to speak to me. She said she had heard of the king's symptoms and possessed a remedy that would cure him. I told her to come back the next day. In the meantime I inquired as to her reputation. One man told me he thought she was a witch, but others said she was known as a healer. When she appeared the next day, I made a judgment and decided to ask her what she proposed.

"Just this," she said, and produced a small covered bowl.

"What is it?" I asked.

"Fine soup," was her answer. "I believe it will restore the king's health."

I tasted the bitter soup to make sure that it wasn't poisoned. It was horrible stuff, made of vegetables, but after a while I was able to eat a goodly portion of it and was none the worse for having done so. I thought I had little to lose in trying the medicine on my patient.

"Very well then, mistress. Let us go to meet your king."

At this the old woman brightened, almost disbelieving it. I waved the guards away and we entered the king's chamber. He appeared to be asleep.

"King Robert," I said softly, but there was no response. I said louder, "King Robert, there is someone to see you who thinks you can be cured with a potion of soup."

The king raised himself with great effort and looked with questioning eyes at the old woman, who curtsied broadly, practically overcome with joy at meeting the greatest man in Scotland. Then he fell back down on his bed, exhausted by the effort. I motioned to the woman to serve him, and this she did. She gave the king a small drink, and he spit some out, but also drank some. I could see that his opinion of the soup was not high.

"What is this, Davie?" he wailed as if in desperation.

"I drank some, my lord. It is not poison, and may restore you. I think you should drink the bowl, and hope that it will."

King Robert took my advice, although he grimaced and gasped for breath once or twice. Soon the bowl was finished and the king was back asleep. I left with the woman and told her to come back on the next morning. I reasoned that if the king was worse she would be punished, and if he had improved she would bring more of the unsavoury soup.

The next morning I could see that the king's health had improved. It was like a miracle. He was sitting up, giving orders, his condition much better than the day before. The old woman came every day and brought the soup for which she was well paid. Every day the king improved until he was almost completely recovered. Even his depression seemed to have vanished. After some days I dismissed the old woman and gave her a generous tip. When I told the king, he said, "Thank God, Davie. I don't think I could have taken one more bowl of that dreadful stuff."

The Scone parliament opened on schedule in December 1318. As usual, the atmosphere was festive. The weather was cold, but the spirits of the people were not. There was an abundance of musicians and jugglers, and plenty of food for sale. The people danced and gawked at the king and all the nobles in their colourful clothes.

There were many things accomplished at this parliament. The question of the royal succession had become important with Sir Edward Bruce's death, leaving no legitimate heirs. It was decided and ratified that if the king died without having produced a male legitimate heir, the crown should go to his infant grandson, Robert Stewart, whose mother was the king's daughter, the late Marjorie Bruce.

Since we had been warned that the English were planning another attack on our country, certain civil-defence measures were passed in keeping with what we could afford. The English were now used to using paid soldiers, but we could not afford that. Therefore a law was passed that every man worth ten pounds would have to provide himself with suitable armour such as a padded leather jacket, a helmet, and gloves of metal. Everyone either possessing a cow or its equivalent would have to have a spear or a bow with two dozen arrows in a quiver. There was to be a yearly *wapinschaw* at Easter, where everyone's preparedness was to be inspected by the local sheriff. Disobedience would result in confiscation of property.

It was important also that the Scone parliament reinstated some of the old laws that had fallen into disuse under the English domination. Conservation measures were reinstated. For instance, fish traps on salmon streams were permitted but had to have spaces large enough so as to allow the smaller fish to escape. The people, both rich and poor, were to have the benefits of Scots law. The nobles were prohibited from mistreating any of the ordinary people, and if they were so injured, the king promised compensation. The king hoped that all of the people would be bound together in friendship. Throughout Scotland, the Bruce was being referred to as "Good King Robert."

III

Early in 1319 I received another furlough, and went home to my beloved family. My children had grown and had become quite accomplished. Màiri had employed a tutor and they were being taught their sums and to read and write. I began to speak to them in French, and to my surprise they took quite smartly to the language. I had heard that if one learns two languages when very young it was easy to acquire a third, and my children seemed to prove this. The weather that spring was not good; the earth was sodden from constant rain, and I feared for our crops. Nonetheless, I had a marvellous time with my family. They were all quite healthy and happy. But at the beginning of summer my furlough expired, and back I went to the army. Our man Cuthbert had brought news from England that our occupation of Berwick was considered to be a threat to the international standing of King Edward II and his country, and that the town would have to be recaptured at all costs. Cuthbert said that the English army being mustered was very large, with many thousands of men; not as great as the one we had confronted at Bannockburn, but very menacing nonetheless. Sir Walter Stewart, who was still in charge of the castle at Berwick, would need reinforcements.

A month later Cuthbert returned with the news that

Berwick had indeed been attacked. "King Edward is himself at Berwick, sir, having left Queen Isabella at York. He
is anxious to regain the port and assaulted the town on
September seventh in great numbers. Sir Walter Stewart
and his men fought bravely, throwing all sorts of rocks and
other implements from the tops of the walls. This was very
effective. The English also tried to attack by boat, but the
Scots repelled these also. By the end of the day the English
retired to plan anew. The Scots heard nothing of them for
several days, and then the enemy attacked again. This time
they had constructed an enormous vehicle made of wood
and mounted on wheels. It looked like a gigantic sow, sir,
and would hold many armed men. They intended to
breach a gate with the vehicle and after they had done so
their soldiers would come out and fight. But the Scots
ordered their Flemish engineer, John Crab, to design a
weapon that would protect them. Crab soon built a great
catapult and was ordered to kill the sow, as it were, sir. He
did just this, sir. His first two shots missed, but the third
scored a direct hit, breaking the top and sides of the
machine. When the English soldiers ran out of it, the Scots
jeered at the English, yelling that 'The sow had farrowed'
and throwing more rocks over the side of the walls. John
Crab had also prepared bundles of sticks dipped in pitch,
and these were set on fire and rained down on the sow,
which was consumed in flames within a few minutes. That
is all that I can tell, sir. I do not know if the English can
prevail, but I do know there are far too many of them there
for you to attack. They are there in the thousands."

Cuthbert was dismissed, and King Robert called on his captains to consult.

"I have a plan," said the king. "We will trust in what Cuthbert has said. He has never failed us all these years. If he says that there are too many of the enemy at Berwick for us to handle, I believe him. Even if we could distract them by our presence, it would be at the risk of fighting so many again in a pitched battle. But Cuthbert says also that King Edward's queen is at York, which place cannot be well defended with most of the available English troops stationed at Berwick. We will try to capture the queen at York. If we do, her ransom will be the end to all of this warfare and a complete acceptance of our independence."

Everyone agreed this was the right response. Two small armies were established, one led by Sir James Douglas, which I would join, and the other under Sir Thomas Randolph. We proceeded immediately toward York. When we reached the town of Myton, near to York, we were surprised to see an army approaching us. We suspected we had been betrayed, but there was nothing to do but fight. When the enemy grew close, we could see it was not really an army, but a ragtag band of brave citizens led by the Archbishop of York himself. They were just ordinary Englishmen carrying homemade weapons and banners. They came upon us and we advanced on them, shouting war cries. This caused them to break such ranks as they had established, and we made a wholesale slaughter of almost all of them. We soon found we had indeed been betrayed, and Queen Isabella had been spirited away to another place.

During our war we would come close to capturing both the king of England and his queen on several occasions, but each time we failed by a hair. If any one of these attempts had succeeded, the war would have been over. It was like a game of chess—take the important pieces and you win. This time, having missed the chance to capture the queen, we ravaged as much of northern England as we could.

There was a positive result of this Chapter of Myton, as the battle is now called—referring, I suppose, to the religious leaders on the English side. King Edward and his advisors, realising there was a threat to York and that we were harassing dozens of towns and driving off cattle, had to abandon the assault on Berwick in order to deal with us. They were unsuccessful. We eluded them, as usual, and in a short time we were back over the border with our spoils. King Edward's army was disbanded shortly thereafter. Berwick was still Scottish. We had won another great victory.

King Robert was not about to ease up on the English. To keep the pressure on, he sent Sir James Douglas to northwestern England in November of that year. I was along on this raid, and I must say it was a particularly brutal one on our part. We tried not to kill or hurt people, but we destroyed a lot of property in Cumberland and Westmoreland. The harvest had just been gathered and neatly stacked or otherwise stored, and we put a great part of it to the torch. We so demoralised the people that King Edward was forced to send envoys to us to propose a two-year truce, which we granted. King Edward could have had a final peace right there, but he still refused to recognise the independence of Scotland.

When the new year of 1320 came in our two countries were, at last, in a kind of tentative peace, but King Edward would still try by other means to subdue us. He got the pope to summon our king and our church leaders to Avignon. This time the letter was addressed to "Robert Bruce, governing the kingdom of Scotland." This could have been read as an improvement over the previous mode of address, but it still failed to recognise the Bruce as king. Of course, the summons was ignored by King Robert, our nobles, and the Scottish clergy. Soon all were excommunicated once again.

The pope's attitude now became more of a concern to us than ever before. We had continued to demonstrate that we were a separate country, ruled by our own king, yet the pope continued to support the position of the king of England, that he was our proper ruler. King Robert decided on a national response to show the pope what he had so far been unable or unwilling to see. Perhaps we could present facts in our case that would sway him in our direction. A goodly number of the leaders of Scotland would send a letter explaining that our nation was very old, had always been ruled by our own unbroken line of royalty, and that we were determined to keep it that way.

Accordingly, many of our best people came to Newbattle near Edinburgh in the spring of 1320 to agree on a document that we hoped would apprise the Holy Father of our right to independence, the reasons for our claim to it, and our determination to keep it. We hoped also that our excommunication would end and that we would be restored as communicants of the Holy Church.

The Chancellor of Scotland, Abbot Bernard of Arbroath, had already prepared a draft of our letter, and for several days it was debated by those assembled. The draft was written in Latin, but not everyone could understand it, so it was read and reread in French, Scots, and Gaelic as well. When we heard the draft read for the first time, all of us were stunned, even overwhelmed by the noble, majestic language. After several days, with all changes made and agreed upon, we were ready to send our petition for justice to the pope at Avignon. Many of our nobility signed the document, affixing their seals to it. Then Abbot Bernard took the document back to Arbroath to gather more signatures from men in the northeast of the country who had not been at Newbattle. Then the document was sent off to the pope.

Before the signing at Newbattle, the document was made available for all of us to study. We realised what a broad sweep it contained. I decided to copy and translate the few parts of it I could understand so that I could show them to others, particularly in my own family. At times, I enlisted the aid of a clergyman who helped me.

The letter subsequently sent from Arbroath begins by listing the signatories, including my best friend *Jacobus Dominus de Duglas*. Others mentioned with whom I was quite familiar included *Thomas Ranulphi Comes Morauie; Duncanus Comes de Fyf; Malcolmus Comes de Leuenax; Gilbertus de Haya Constabularius Scocie; Willelmus Comes de*

Ross; *Magnus Comes Cathanie et Orkadie; Walterus Senescallus Scocie; Robertus de Keth Marescallus Scocie,* and *Douenaldus Cambell.* Most important, after naming all the signatories, the document claimed to speak for the whole Community of the Realm of Scotland—*tota Communitas Regni Scocie.* I noticed something else. King Robert had long been trying to pull together the Scottish nation, which was, after all, of diverse origin. Significantly, as spelled out in the declaration, all the signatories claimed to be of the old Scottish stock, descended from the royalty of Ireland. But their family names, of course, were of not only Gaelic, but also of French, Anglish, and Scandinavian origin. King Robert had succeeded. All the signatories now considered themselves Scots.

The declaration begins by being extremely polite to the pope. Then it tells of how the ancient kingdom of the Scots traces its origins back to Scythia in eastern Europe, whence it passed to the Mediterranean Sea, through the Pillars of Hercules to Spain, where it sojourned for a time, maintaining its independence even when attacked by barbarous tribes. For some reason I don't know, it doesn't mention that we were next in Ireland, and at last had come from there to Scotland. But it says quite definitely that twelve hundred years after the Exodus of the Israelites, *mille et ducentos annos a transitu populi israelitici,* we became established in the land we now occupy, after having expelled the Britons and the Picts. Further, that although we have been attacked by Norwegians, Danes, and English, we have always maintained our independence through

Regno Centum et Tresdecim Reges de ipsorum Regali prosapia nullo alienigena interueniente—a hundred thirteen kings of our own blood, with no stranger intervening.

Then the letter speaks of *Princeps Magnificus Rex Anglorum Edwardus*, the mighty king of England, Edward, and tells the awful tale of how he has harassed us with *violencias, predaciones, incendia, prelatorum incarceraciones, monasteriorum combustiones*, deeds of violence, plunderings, burnings, imprisonment of prelates, burning of monasteries, *nulli parcens etati aut sexui*, sparing no age or sex. The declaration next tells about how King Robert has rescued our country from the English, and how he is governing it according to our own laws and customs, *leges et Consuetudines*, and is reigning with the due consent of us all, *omnium Consensus*. The Community of the Realm was telling the Holy Father that the people of Scotland had the final say in deciding who should reign, and that King Robert was governing with our consent. All who signed the document believed it was a new step for monarchies. The governors must now have the consent of the governed.

The Community of the Realm of Scotland went farther. The document also said *Quem si ab inceptis desisteret Regi Anglorum aut Anglicis nos aut Regnum nostrum volens subicere tanquam Inimicum nostrum et sui, nostrique Juris subuersorem statim expellere niteremur et alium Regem nostrum qui ad defensionem nostram sufficeret faceremus*. With the help of one of the clerics I was able to translate this. It refers to our wonderful King Robert. "But if he were to desist from what he has begun, and wished to subject us or our kingdom to the English king or to the English, then we

would expel him at once just like an enemy as the sub-
verter of our rights and his, and make another our king
who would be able to defend us." Then came a sentence
that I really liked best. William Wallace would have liked
it, too. *Quia quamdiu Centum viui remanserint nuncquam
Anglorum dominio aliquatenus volumus subiugari. Non enim
propter gloriam diuicias aut honores pugnamus set propter liber-
tatum solummodo quam Nemo bonus nisi simul cum vita amit-
tit.* "For as long as one hundred remain alive, we will never
be subject to the dominion of the English. Since not for
glory, riches, or honour we fight, but for liberty alone,
which no good man loses but with his life."

The letter also asks the Pope not to discriminate against
us in favour of the English, because in the sight of God all
are created equal, and since the pope is His representative
on earth, he can make no *distinccio Judei et greci, Scoti aut
Anglici*—no distinction among Jew and Greek, Scot or English. The tone of the letter becomes I think, a little impu-
dent, but what do excommunicates have to lose? It implies
that we will aid in papal causes, but only if the Holy Father
puts pressure on the English to leave us in peace. It says
that England should be more than sufficient for the English king, and that he should let alone *nos Scotos in exili
degentes Scocia ultra quam habitacio non est*—we Scots living
in poor little Scotland beyond which there is no human
dwelling.

I hoped that the letter to the pope would be well
received and the long war would end. But even if not, I was
very proud of the document that we sent to the Holy
Father. It was an expression and explanation of everything

that we had been fighting for these fourteen years. I hope that as the centuries go by the declaration Scotland sent from Arbroath in 1320 will inspire others as it did me. I believe, as it expresses, that in the sight of the Creator the worthiness of all the various ethnic groups of the world are created equal; that the whole people are the legitimate source of political power; that governments must be consented to by the governed; that the people have the right to alter or abolish malicious governments and institute new ones; and that liberty must be defended with life even if there are only one hundred men left to fight for it.

CHAPTER EIGHTEEN

A Mission to the Pope

Treason struck, quickly staining the feeling of unity that had been brought about by the sending of our letter to the pope. In the latter part of 1320, there was a conspiracy to kill King Robert and usurp the throne of Scotland for Sir William de Soules. *The lord of Sowlis, schir vilzame had mast defame, for principall thereof wes he.* Many in the conspiracy were still bound by blood or political ties to the old Comyn party, which, we had believed in error, was finished. Fortunately, one of the plotters confessed and the entirety of the scheme was discovered. Several hundred usurpers, including de Soules, were captured at Berwick. In August a parliament was convened at Scone for the purpose of trying them. It is still called the Black Parliament. De Soules admitted everything and was given life imprisonment. Several were acquitted and some were found guilty, received the sentence of death, and were executed. Others fled the country.

For a while, the letter we sent from Arbroath to Pope John XXII at Avignon seemed to have a good effect. The Holy Father was influenced, I supposed, by the sincere tone of the letter, and he urged King Edward II to make peace with us. There were numerous meetings and negotiations, but nothing had really changed. England would not concede our independence and we would not relinquish it. The pope still sided with our enemies. As we marked time, I was able to spend almost six months with my family. I was very happy being a country laird.

King Robert was exasperated, of course, by the lack of progress, the English stubbornness, and the pope's unfairness. The two-year truce between England and Scotland expired at the end of 1321, and on the very first day of the year 1322 King Robert sent a huge force south to the north of England led by all of his best captains, Douglas, Randolph, and Stewart. We burned at will and levied blackmail as we pleased, taking hostages as security for payment. I felt sorry for the English people we were harming, but what could we do? This was war and we were fighting for our lives. Our depredations did not go unnoticed by the English. King Edward decided to launch a campaign against us with quantities of soldiers and provisions even greater than those employed at Bannockburn, or so some said.

In military leadership, however, King Edward II was no match for King Robert, who acted swiftly when told of the English king's plans. First, the Bruce burned the entire southeast of Scotland, evacuated all the people, and took all the cattle and put them in hiding elsewhere. Then he stationed his army north of the Firth of Forth at Culross. To get at King Robert's army, the English would have to march for days through a veritable desert with no forage for their horses and no food for their troops. Thus, when the English invaded, their army found the southern part of our country completely bare. They had sent supply ships, but these were blocked by contrary winds. They sent out foraging parties far and wide, but found little but a single lame bull. When this was brought in, the Earl of Warren is said to have remarked, *"I dar say this is the derrest beiff that I saw euir yeit, for sekirly it cost ane thousand pund and mar."* The English army was starving. There was nothing for it to do but retreat, and back it went over the border to the northeast of England, where the harvest was just coming in. The English farmers had to pay again—this time to their own army.

It was now time for us to react, and King Robert was ready. He moved our army south from Culross to the northwestern part of England. All along we burned and extorted. We were not opposed in any way. Then, one night, our chief scout, none other than our man Cuthbert, came to see King Robert. "Sir, I have knowledge that King Edward and his queen are lodged near Byland." Without delay our entire army marched toward Byland, but found that it lay beyond a pass and that the pass was protected by a very large English host apparently ready to defend it. Sir James Douglas volunteered to take some men and go to the top of the pass and force the English onto open ground. I went with him, of course, and we were followed by Thomas Randolph and others. The English saw us and advanced. We began to fight. The English came on bravely, and then King Robert sent his Highlanders and isle men to our assistance, and before long we had overcome them, taking many prisoners.

We now moved the short distance to capture the king and queen of England, whose ransom would surely end the war and bring about the recognition of our freedom. But King Edward had been warned and had fled on horseback. Sir Walter Stewart pursued him as far as York, but its gates were barred, and once again the king of England barely escaped capture. As before, however, he had left behind a large treasure, as well as the Great Seal of England. When Sir Walter returned, King Robert supervised the portioning of the treasure left behind by the English. Everyone prospered. We made our way back to Scotland without the English king but with a great deal of spoils. We plundered along the way and reached our own country in November 1322.

Gradually, certain Englishmen became weary of the Scottish obsession of their king. Most of them didn't care anything about Scotland and were content that it should be left alone. Decades of warfare had produced nothing but destruction and loss of men and silver. Early in 1323 one Englishman, Andrew Harclay, the magistrate at Carlisle, made his own treaty with Scotland, but when he was found out, King Edward had him hanged, drawn, and quartered. King Edward and his policies were becoming overbearing, and his nobles were putting great pressure on him to halt the warfare. Heedful of this dissent, Edward agreed to a truce of thirteen years, but without giving up his claim to an overlordship of Scotland. The Bruce insisted on ratifying the treaty by styling himself as king, as he certainly should have. Thus, by accepting the truce in this form, King Edward was pushed a little closer to the reality of accepting our independence.

In the latter part of that year I was summoned to the king's presence. The only other person in attendance was Thomas Randolph, the Earl of Moray. King Robert addressed me: "Davie, I have given a very important mission to my nephew here. You know each other well, and both of us have discussed your assisting him in this venture. We think you are the logical choice. You can take care of yourself if any trouble arises. You are completely trustworthy. You are an excellent horseman, and there will be a great deal of riding to do. You speak French well, better than my nephew here, who prefers Scots or English. What do you say, will you do it?"

Of course I would do anything the king asked of me, but I hadn't any idea what it was about, except the clue about speaking French. "How long would the mission last, sir?"

Thomas Randolph said, "The better part of a year, Davie. We are going to France. I can't say more. No one is to know any details except the king and myself."

"It will be hard on my family, certainly," was my reply, "but I am honoured to be chosen. Of course I will go on the mission. It is my duty." It was also an exciting prospect. I had never thought I would ever see the great and powerful country to the south.

"Good," said the king. "It's all arranged, then. You will go home to your family for a month, then return here, ready to go. Shall we have a bit of food to celebrate the mission? Come with me. I believe that something has been prepared."

The three of us walked into the next room, where the queen and several of her ladies were seated at table. I was introduced, and a splendid meal of roasted and stuffed peacock began. A waiter poured the best wine obtainable from the port of Bordeaux, most likely recently taken as booty from the English. A musician played a lute softly in the background. It was a glorious banquet, and it made me remember those days seventeen or so years before when the king and I were close friends only because of circumstance. He maintained some distance from me now. He had to run a kingdom, and couldn't sustain any closeness with some of his old associates such as myself. Still, he was very polite toward me, even seeing to it that my goblet was filled. I remembered that night in the cave so long ago, where he and I had been, at least at that moment, almost equals. It would never be like that again, but he had picked me out for a major assignment. I could be proud of that.

I hadn't spent much time around Queen Elizabeth, but I was able to observe her quite well at that meal. She looked sad, resigned to her fading beauty. The king was in his social mode that day, telling witty stories and jesting with the ladies. The queen only gave a modest response to these pleasantries. She had had a hard life. The daughter of an English king's best friend, she had found herself married to the archenemy of that king. After the disaster at

Methven, she had been captured and imprisoned in one English house after another for eight years, deprived of her husband, and in harsh conditions. In recent years she had been reunited with King Robert, and that must have been very difficult after so long a time. They would have been almost strangers to each other. Worst of all, the country needed a male heir and she had not been able to conceive one after years of trying. I am sure that she felt a great deal of pressure. It was a fine meal we had that day, though, and I was sorry when it came to an end. I bid separate good-byes to the ladies, the king, and his nephew, and rode out for Dumfries and home.

It was another of those blessed months when I could be with the ones I loved most. Seumas was now fourteen, the same age I was when I joined King Robert's quest. He had become quite a young man, taking charge of the estate in my absence, although he was younger than any men he employed. Ishbel was now nine, and an absolute delight to me and to her mother. She had a beautiful voice and at night would sing some of the Gaelic songs Màiri had taught her. My favourite was *Mo nighean donn bhòidheach*, which means in Gaelic "my beautiful brown-haired girl," a lively tune that I think will last as long as the Highlands. During the days, Seumas and I would be off fishing or into the woods to cut fuel for the winter. My mother was becoming frail, but still helped out with the chores and the cooking. At night my wife and I would wait until everyone was asleep, and then I would draw her to me and feel the softness of her and embrace all of her. When at last I told my family I would not be seeing them for a long time, there were protests, of course, but by then they were used to it. It was part of our life that I would be gone for periods, some-times long ones. I consoled them by telling them that where I was going there might be magical and important presents that I could buy for them, and that I would return with something for each of them.

There were tears all around on the wet morning when I rode away. A day later I met up with Randolph, and we prepared to depart.

"Ready, Davie?"

"Ready to go when you give the order, sir."

We rode all day to the port of Leith, where Randolph and I and two other men who were to serve us, embarked.

"Have we safe-conduct passes?"

"We do, but they are probably not necessary for this trip, Davie. The recent truce with England allows us to visit the pope and beseech him to lift the bans on us. That should cover us against any English interference, although we must be careful as the English are in control of the southwestern part of France and cannot be trusted. Once we cross the water we will be in France, our strongest ally, so we should expect no trouble there. Caution is necessary, though, as some parts of France are not under government control. I know what you are getting at, but, believe me, we have taken precautions. You and I are bound for Hon-fleur, a port in Normandy, but no one, not even our cap-tain, knows that. We are going to Avignon, a great city in the south of France. No one save King Robert knows our probable route to that city. In addition, yesterday another man carrying papers identifying him as Thomas Randolph,

Earl of Moray, left Berwick on a ship bound elsewhere. He is, in fact, a merchant pretending for the moment to be me. The captain of our boat here doesn't know my name."

It was a well-designed plan. We sailed several days in very rough seas. One of the seamen looked at my face which must have had a greenish cast. "It's always like this, sir," he said, smiling at me. As we arrived on the French coast the winds didn't favour us, and we couldn't make port at night. But as the dawn came the next morning we could see Honfleur and its fortifications. The gently rolling land behind it extended far into the distance. It was raining. It was France! It wasn't since that morning in Bannockburn, nine years ago, that I had felt so excited.

We docked in the harbour, a sort of square-shaped inlet bordered with heavy stone dikes to protect it from the mighty Atlantic storms. All around the square fronting the quay were houses of commerce, some of them reaching several stories, and all topped with grey slate roofs. The quay was crowded with men rolling barrels of freight, lifting things on board a boat or unloading them from another. Orders were shouted. A cheese auction was in progress on the quay in front of one of the buildings. The place was alive with the sounds of commerce. The flags on the various boats bore the colours of several nations. Vendors sold food from stalls, and a juggler performed in hopes of receiving small coins.

We left our boat behind with the two men who had been aboard to protect us in case we had run into some hostile shipping on our way, and Thomas gave them some money. With our luggage, we made our way to an inn and ordered a room for the night. Since we were very hungry, Thomas suggested we take one of the tables on the quay in front of our hotel. It was still raining, but not hard enough to deter us. When a young serving woman arrived, she told us she had fresh sole cooked in cream and butter, along with some dark bread. I asked her if we could have a jug of wine; she replied that she had none, but recommended the local apple cider. She brought the fish and the bread and two large bowls of cider, which we tasted immediately.

"*Aimez-vous le cidre?*" she asked.

"*Je l'aime beaucoup,*" I answered. I had never tasted cider before.

The whole dinner was absolutely delicious. I had never eaten food anything like it. Our food in Scotland was very plain by comparison. The sun appeared and the harbour warmed. Bold seagulls argued over scraps, and wasps tried to take the cider from us by intimidation. We waved them off and ordered refills, and the earl began discussing our plans.

"First of all, Davie, we have to talk about protocol; we can't cross an entire country being different. This is what we will do. When we are alone, I prefer that you call me Thomas. We are comrades on this trip, after all. When we are with others, you should refer to me as the earl and address me as 'my lord.' Is that understood?"

I nodded, unable yet to say "Thomas" and positively ordered not to say "yes, my lord."

"Our mission," he continued, "is nothing less than a visit to the pope himself, the result of which should be his recognition of Scottish independence and the lifting of our excommunication. It will not be easy, of course. It will be a long trip to Avignon, more than six hundred miles, I have been advised. But we shall have an adventure, right?"

"Indeed we will," I said. "Why is the pope in Avignon? Shouldn't he be in Rome?"

"Davie, I don't know the answer to that. There is a disagreement of some kind, I suppose. It's all politics. I have heard that the move will be permanent, and that a great papal palace is being built in Avignon. Say, you look a bit tired. Why don't you go to the room and rest up a bit?"

He was right. The cider and the long boat voyage had made me drowsy. Besides, the numerous wasps were becoming more than an annoyance. I decided to leave the little things the dregs of my bowl and retire. I slept all the rest of that day and all night. When I awoke I found the earl not in his bed, so after visiting the privy out back, I went down to the quay and saw him sitting at the same table where we had eaten the fish and cider.

"Glad you're up and about, Davie. We need to find passage on a boat for Paris. We must be on our way. Fellow over there told me there are boats for hire on down the quay. Are you ready? I need your advice with these boats."

"Quite ready," said I.

Within an hour we had paid off our boatmen, who looked like they had nearly drowned in cider the night before, and sent them home to Scotland. We hired a French *bateau* to take us to Paris, paid for our room, bought provisions, and were on our way up the Seine on a flood tide. We moved along rather smartly for a while, but then the current began to reverse and our progress was very much slower. The Seine winds and bends through the flat country of Normandy and it took us two days to reach the town of Rouen, but what a country it was! Everywhere on both sides of the river were great farms. France looked soft to my eyes, not hard like Scotland. The land was rich, supporting diverse crops. There were oceans of grain and many orchards. Cows were everywhere. I had not expected such wealth, which was in quite a contrast to our poor Scotland. Yet as different as it was from our country, both Thomas and I felt somewhat at home. Most of us Scots had, after all, some Norman ancestors. This is where Scottish names like Bruce, Hay, Fraser, Menzies, Montgomery, Sinclair, and Grant originated. When we got to Rouen it was dark, and Thomas didn't want to spend much time there. We bought bread, some wine, and some cheese, and were on our way in the darkness without even looking at the great cathedral that I knew was there.

In another two days we had reached the Château Gaillard, which stands high on a cliff above the Seine. Thomas recognised it immediately.

"Magnificent, isn't it? It was built about a hundred years ago by King Richard I of England, Davie. They called him *Coeur-de-Lion*, Lion Heart. He was tough, trying to keep Normandy for England, and he was successful for a time largely because of that fort."

"Isn't that the King Richard who had the miserable brother King John?"

"The very same. I'm surprised you know it."

"We had many people interested in history around Dumfries," I said, a bit defensively.

"Well, anyway, you are right. That is the King John who was forced to sign the Great Charter by the nobility of England."

We sailed right by the fort and toward Paris. The weather was mostly beautiful, and we had good wine and cheese. I was beginning to like Thomas, and had got up enough nerve to call him by his Christian name. It was an easy trip, and I realised he was the perfect man to send to the pope. King Robert knew his men well. Thomas Randolph was brilliant, capable, and very knowledgeable. You could just tell it.

At last we reached Paris and paid off our French boatmen. They had done a good job but were not very friendly. Perhaps they were not used to foreigners. We suffered a disappointment; the great city of Paris, about which all have heard, was a mess. The place was full of dirty mud streets and unbelievably crowded. Many incomprehensible languages were spoken, including an ugly tongue called Frankish. It sounded something like the Flemish of my two soldiering companions. The town had a great brooding cathedral, and everything was exciting, but it was just too much for me. The houses were mostly mean, except for a few old remnants from Roman days. We had no such metropolis in Scotland, and I wasn't used to it. One couldn't walk ten paces without being jostled by someone coming from another direction. Merchants called out their songs. Fires cooked meat and heated metal, and their smoke was omnipresent. Garbage was everywhere. Pigs and chickens ran in the streets. I had seen all this before, but not on such a staggering scale. Thomas had the same reaction to the place as I, and as soon as we could we left it. We never even saw the cathedral, except at a distance.

Thomas bought us three horses for a very great sum, and we loaded our bags on one and rode out to the south on the other two past a church called Saint Germain des Prés. It was a huge place with a large church and great gardens running along down to the river. To our surprise, several of the clerics of Saint Germain were Scots, and we were greeted warmly. They were happy to find us a place to sleep, and a very good supper as well. The Scots were eager to hear stories of King Robert, and they kept us up late answering questions about the war. Thomas told them we had been soldiers in the war but were now merchants trading to the south.

The next morning, Thomas asked for directions to Chartres, where the greatest building in the world stands. It was finished less than a century ago, and Thomas said we must see it, though it was a bit out of our way. Accordingly, we bought provisions again and set out to the southeast with our three steeds. The first day we made it about halfway from Paris to Chartres, and we stopped at an inn, where we were very well treated. The next morning we made an early start and by noon could see the twin spires of the cathedral beginning to appear in the distance over the flat fields, which were thick with grain ready for the harvest. It was a memorable sight, I can assure you, and as we approached the town more and more of the great church became visible. At last we arrived and found an inn, whose keeper agreed to take care of our horses. Then it was time to see the cathedral.

I doubt anyone could be prepared for Chartres. It is simply overwhelming. I had heard all of the stories that it was constructed on high ground hallowed even before the Christian era. It had been built once and consumed by fire, then rebuilt by people who came from all over Europe to help. Noblemen had dragged stones beside peasants. Women of high rank had brought food for the workers. Thousands contributed their labour. It seemed that many of them were in attendance that day, as pilgrims speaking many languages were everywhere. But despite their numbers there was a sort of reverential quiet about the place. People talked in whispers. For Thomas and myself, I can only say that we stood transfixed at the front portal. The stone carvings are glorious; I should say perhaps miraculous. There are men and women represented as pillars, and they have the most serene faces I could ever imagine being carved in stone. They are the faces of kind, wise people, some of whom smile down upon the pilgrim.

But however moved he may be by the outside of the cathedral, the pilgrim passing into it is struck dumb. In my case the hair on the back of my neck stood up. The place is immense and gloomy in parts, and is large, almost incomprehensibly so. We were told we were in the largest enclosed space in Europe. The incredibly high roof seems to be floating far above the floor.

On the sides are stained glass windows of overpowering beauty. The visitor is surrounded by multicoloured light. I have seen stained glass in Scotland, but nothing like the glass at Chartres. There are several shades of light green and purple, and blues from deep to light. There are penetrating reds and golden yellows. Animals are portrayed, and knights in white glass. There are three huge windows shaped like roses, and each contains what must be thousands of pieces of glass. The cathedral is awash in light. Thomas and I stayed for a long time in the place, making our devotions and inspecting as much as we could. We were especially impressed to see the tunic, a relic of the Virgin Mary, to whom the church is dedicated.

In the evening we returned to the inn. I made sure that the horses had been taken care of and that our kit was safe. We had each packed a suit of fine clothes for what we hoped would be our audience with His Holiness, and it wouldn't do to lose those. Thomas and I sat down to our evening's meal at a great communal table. There were many languages spoken there, but we could find no one conversing in Scots or English, so that we were left to speak to each other. The meal was a great bowl of delicious beef and onion soup, with heavy loaves of dark bread. The wine was good and included free with the cost of the night's stay. Wine was cheap in France. The man next to me had been speaking to his companion in Latin, but I heard him say a few French words, and realised that I might be able to speak to him. I asked him in French for directions to the south, and he told me that the safest way was to go by way of Orleans and then through Burgundy to the Rhône River. From there, he said it would be an easy and safe journey to Avignon. He warned me that between

Orleans and Burgundy some roads were unsafe, merely trails in some cases, and that highwaymen were a constant problem. I was glad Thomas had decided we would both carry a sword and shield in view of this disclosure.

After dinner, Thomas bought another jug of the best red wine in the house. He and I sat on a terrace outside the inn, where there were others doing the same. It was cool and very dark on the terrace, but we had our heavy cloaks and didn't mind at all. Many women came by us offering services I wouldn't have thought appropriate for such a religious place, but I suppose that what they offered was, in a way, as necessary for men travelling as were food, drink, and lodging. It reminded me of my days as a soldier and of the great rabble that always accompanied us, particularly at our victory at Bannockburn.

When I awoke the next morning I found Thomas already buying our provisions. I brought up the three horses and gave them food and water. With one great long last look at the cathedral, we were off for Orleans. It was a hard ride with wind and a cold rain in our faces most of the time. It was long after dark when we decided to stop, for we could not see the road in front of us. I watered the horses by a stream and tied them to a tree. We and they fell asleep almost immediately beside the road there. It was miserable throughout the night. When dawn came we could see a town in the distance, and we rode to it without delay.

Orleans, situated on the beautiful Loire River, seemed rather large, like a capital city. There were many crowded streets and, I am sure, much to do. But Thomas was insistent that we ride as soon as possible for the south. While he bought provisions, I went to an inn and bought a bowl of wine. I began to speak to two other men at the bar. Since they looked fairly respectable, I bought them each a bowl and inquired as to the best way to Burgundy. They both agreed that we should follow the Loire upstream to the port of Nevers, which was three days' journey ahead. I had never heard of the place and said so, but this only made them laugh. Nevers, they explained, had been a port since the days of the Romans. They told me also that from Nevers to the interior of Burgundy was very rough country. "*Gardez-vous des voleurs,*" they admonished me, one of them wagging a gnarled finger. "*Il y a beaucoup de voleurs dans les environs.*" I must say I was a little taken aback by this pronouncement. During our time in France so far we had seen no sign of crime, but we were travelling alone in a strange country. To think that we might be attacked by robbers was unsettling. I was glad again we were carrying arms.

The instructions I received at the bar turned out to be almost perfect. We rode for two days up the Loire without incident. There were inns to stay in, and no *voleurs*. On the third day, however, as we were approaching Nevers, we stopped at an inn and the people advised us not to proceed in that direction any farther. They told us that the route to Nevers was blocked by bandits, and that we should proceed instead to the northeast to the town of Vézelay. From there we would find the Saône River at a place called Chalon, and this would connect to the Rhône River at the great trading city of Lyon. From there, it would all be downstream to Avignon. One man offered to be our guide to Vézelay, but Thomas didn't want the responsibility of another in our party. Anyway, he could be leading us into a trap. We thanked him, and bought a jug of wine that we shared with our new companions, and hoped that we didn't look too prosperous.

We considered this new situation and retired to sleep for the night. Thomas told me that he would keep watch for a while and then waken me so that he could sleep. During the night we changed shifts twice each, so that by the time the first light came we slipped out as quietly as possible and proceeded to the trail we hoped would lead us, as promised, to Vézelay. It was a clear morning, and we looked back on the inn to see if we were being followed. We saw nothing. The inn was still asleep.

We travelled over rough country and slept on the ground in shifts that first night. When we awoke, it was back to the trail, when suddenly we saw them, three men on horseback, armed and looking very evil. We halted our horses perhaps fifty paces away, and Thomas asked me to feel them out and ask for directions. *"Bonjour, mes amis,"* I called. *"Pouvez-vous nous donner directions pour Vézelay?"*

"Par ici, monsieur," was the reply, delivered with a wicked grin. The answer "This way, sir" was a dare as well. This grim person and his two henchmen were blocking the way.

"Do nothing," said Thomas to me. "Let's see if they come at us. They may think better of it." Then their leader spoke. *"Vous devez nous payer pour directions, dans cette campagne. C'est normal ici. C'est notre tradition."* I translated for Thomas, "He says that we must give them money for directions. He says it is the custom here."

"Right," said Thomas. "They have shown us who they are. Now they will find out who we are. They think we are weak, pilgrims or something, I suppose. Let them come, and say nothing."

The three riders approached us, their leader in front. "Just what I hoped," said Thomas. "He is so arrogant that he comes first, and he will be the first to go. Then each of us will take one of the others. Ready, Davie?"

"Ready," said I.

"Then on them!"

At that moment we spurred our horses toward the first bandit, swords drawn. Thomas was a yard or so ahead of me, and his sword pierced the leader in the chest. When I got there the highwayman was drowning in his own blood, which bubbled in his throat and out of his mouth. His head was back as he gasped for air. While Thomas pulled his sword out of the bandit's chest, I severed his head from his body. Then we spurred on again, each of us taking one of the others. It was quite easy for us. It was dangerous, of course, since one couldn't ever tell what might go wrong, but we had done it so many times over the years that it had become routine. We searched the bodies and found a good deal of silver, but we decided to leave it; we might be accused of stealing it ourselves if we were questioned. I whipped their horses to let them go free wherever they wanted, and we mounted our own and continued toward Vézelay. "Thanks for the directions," said Thomas, looking at the bodies.

At night we arrived at Vézelay. We found a room and

retired immediately. We were physically exhausted, and as soon as I had fed and watered the horses, we went to the main room and inquired after food and drink. It was too late, supper was over, but we were provided with some good bread, cheese, and wine. We ate ravenously, and were soon asleep. We were too tired to change shifts, so we both got a deep rest.

In the morning I awoke first and went for a walk in the town. I was surprised to find myself at the bottom of a great hill. As far as I could see a street ran far up the rise. Being curious, I decided to climb it. It was a beautiful clear morning, and there wasn't a soul to be seen in the town. The street was lined with well-built houses and some had pretty flowers in the windows. Ivy covered some of the walls. As I drew near to the top the street curved, revealing a large cathedral. There it was in front of me, not perhaps as grand as Chartres, but of a different, softer architecture. The face of the building was impressively covered with many carved figures, but the true glory of the place was its interior. I stepped into the abbey church and was greeted by a room of breathtaking beauty. There was no one there but me. The morning sunlight streamed through the windows, as if heaven were illuminating the place. The roof was very high, featuring stonework in an alternating pattern of white and brown. It was a defining moment in my life, and thereafter I resolved to look for beauty wherever and whenever I could find it, but I doubt I have ever seen anything to equal that morning.

I ran back down the hill and found Thomas eating

breakfast. He was ready to start off again, but I insisted that he come with me to the abbey church. He was doubtful, but when he had seen the glorious room with its vaulted ceiling, he too was captivated by the sight. Later we found relics of Mary Magdelene, *Sainte Marie Madeleine* in French, to whom the church is dedicated. Thomas made his devotion, and we stood quietly, reverently for a short time. Outside, we walked around the monastery to a terrace and saw the best view either of us had ever sighted stretching out for at least fifty miles in front of us. Before us, basking in golden sunlight and far below, lay the richness of Burgundy.

As we left the Basilique de la Madeleine and began to descend the long hill back down through the town, we were both very quiet, struck by the place. After some time Thomas said, reverently, I thought, "Some say that she was the wife of the Savior."

II

The two-day ride from Vézelay to the town of Beaune was uneventful but quite miserable. The weather had grown colder and very wet. At times the rain turned to sleet. We and our horses were worn out when we came down from the hills to the great vineyards of Burgundy, running in orderly rows up the western slopes. Once admitted through the town gate of Beaune, we found the place quite hospitable. I remember that night in particular, because we were treated to a chicken dinner and the best wine I have ever tasted. It was so good I couldn't have imagined it. The white wine had a great flinty taste of the soil, and the red wine—well, you would have to taste it to believe it. It was earthy, and deeply rich, almost like syrup. It had a deep earthy after-taste, and smelled deeply of fruit—was it cherries I imagined? It was quite wonderful, and for the first time on our journey, Thomas and I let down our guard and got rather drunk. We drank the best wines the house could offer. After all, we were travelling on the business of a king, certainly not the richest king, but a king nonetheless. We made several toasts to Scotland throughout the evening, as well as to the pretty French girls who served us.

My memories of how that night ended are vague, but when I awoke the next morning, I was in a bed, and across the room was one of the lovely serving girls, combing her hair. She smiled at me as I awoke. I didn't know what to make of it, so I said simply, *"Bonjour, mademoiselle."* She didn't reply, but smiled again. I gave her a silver piece and thanked her, ambiguously, for her service of the previous evening.

I found Thomas at the communal table, eating eggs and cheese and drinking a great bowl of red wine. I noticed that the other guests were doing the same, and I was served this also. The eggs were rich and the cheese was creamy. Thomas paid our bill, and we mounted our horses for the half-day ride to Chalon on the River Saône. We were both so groggy that we struggled on in near silence, reaching the port in the afternoon.

Chalon was a busy place with a grand quay. Commerce was everywhere, and it was very noisy. We sold our horses and bought a *bateau* for about the same price, and added provisions for several days. Wearily we loaded our gear and without any hesitation shoved off into the current that would eventually, and without much effort, take us to Avignon. Thomas soon fell asleep, so that I had to guide the boat for several hours. It was easy, really. The weather was pleasant, and there was nothing to do but relax and let the current take us southward. The hardest part of our embassy to the pope was now over.

In a long day we came to the confluence of the Saône and Rhône rivers, where the grand city of Lyon stands. This is a true metropolis, even cosmopolis, with traders from many lands exchanging their goods and silver. I heard Italian and Greek spoken for the first time. There is an island in the middle of the two rivers and this place was thronged with traders. There is a great hill on the western side, and one can see a Roman amphitheatre near the summit. But Thomas was anxious to leave and we spent less than an hour in the city before boarding our flat-bottomed *bateau* again and heading down the great river.

It was getting late in the year of 1323 as we lay back on our cushions and enjoyed the slow easy ride toward the south. Despite the season, we could see all along the way that there were still flowers blooming in the villages. The weather was quite mild by our northern standards. The water lapped at the sides of our vessel, rocking it gently, and we became drowsy and took turns sleeping from time to time. We had bought bread, hard-cooked eggs, cheese, fruit, and the local wine, all of which were good, so that this last leg of our journey was more of a party than an ordeal. Thomas was in good spirits and began to tell rude stories that made us both laugh. We had been without the steadying company of women now for some time, and I think men always become rough in all-male situations. Women, after all, civilise the beast. Nevertheless, Thomas had an endless stock of stories and we laughed greatly. One evening we sang some of the rough ballads of our country. It was great fun, and I am sure it drew us closer.

As day turned to night and back to day we passed Vienne, and then Valence among other cities, until at last the Rhône brought us to the city of Orange. Thomas decided we were close enough to Avignon that we should debark and find a way to make ourselves presentable on arrival. Orange is a bit off the river, so we paid a man to watch our boat and hired another to take us to a public bath. I had never seen such a place before, but I must say the steam and the hot soapy water felt good, and we emerged refreshed. We donned clean clothes and threw the others in a sack; some laundress in Avignon would put them back in order. There was a beautiful Roman arch in the centre of Orange, but that was not the city's main attraction. That was the enormous Roman amphitheatre. I walked the wall of this stupendous structure and found it to be about a hundred paces in length. It looked like it was at least a third that distance in height. The wall was behind the stage, and stone rows for seating were arranged in a semicircle running up a hill, which could have accommodated, I judged, several thousand people. I climbed up a few rows in the immense emptiness of the place and was fascinated. At the top of the wall behind the stage was a niche with a statue in it. It was, I suppose, one of the caesars. I imagined that the theatre was more than a thousand years old. I would have loved to have attended a performance, but Thomas would have none of it. He was eager to return to the boat and get on to the last short part of our journey. We floated easily down the broad, peaceful Rhône. It was early evening when we saw the great walls and the famous bridge, the pont d'Avignon.

The large city was quite busy when we landed. We made arrangements to store our boat and proceeded on foot to the centre of the town. It was dark and the streets were crowded when we came to what I took to be the main square. Here there were tables set up and lit by candles. Looming in the darkness was the hulk of the huge papal palace, which was still under construction. We found a room, stowed our luggage, and went back out to the tables. The square was crowded and a man was playing a stringed instrument, softly, and people were giving him small coins. We found a table and ordered wine and excellent fresh fish. Several men sat down next to us, and one, hearing my accent, asked me where I had come from. "*Je suis Écossais,*" I told him, and then he inquired about our purpose in France. He was a large man, rather unsavoury, I would say. He seemed to be suspicious and I didn't want him to know how important we were. "*Nous sommes pèlerins,*" I responded, hoping he would be content that we were merely pilgrims on our way to some shrine. I poured him a drink, and that seemed to placate him; he returned to talk with his companions. We had to be careful. How could we know what he was up to? Better just leave him alone. Later in the evening he tried to engage me again, but I apologised for my poor French and pretended not to understand him. Eventually, he went away with his friends. Thomas and I became tired and returned to our room.

We awoke early and put on the fine garments we had been saving. We must have looked rather conspicuous as we strolled to the mansion that was serving as a papal headquarters until the great palace was ready. Both of us were extremely nervous. Our journey was over, but its purpose remained. The two of us were responsible for the souls of the Scottish people, to say nothing about the independence of our country and the legitimacy of its king. We could not fail at this court, the supreme court of Christendom, and yet I realised that the pressure was not on me but rather upon Thomas. It was he who would have to be the brilliant diplomat, and neither of us could guess at the outcome. We presented our credentials at the door and hoped for an audience that day with His Holiness. An expensively dressed fop of a doorman gave us seats in an anteroom, and we waited for the call. It never came that day. Others were taken in to see the pope, but we were not. No one explained to us what was happening, and when the evening came, we were told that His Holiness was busy and that we should try another day. There was nothing to do but retreat. Perhaps our credentials were not enough; it seemed that we were not welcome. Scotland was a problem for the pope, and he wanted nothing to do with it. That evening Thomas and I sat at our table in the square, our cloaks buttoned against a cool wind, drinking red wine. It was New Year's Eve. When the church bells rang we retired. It was first hour of the year 1324.

We waited in the anteroom four hours the next day, when Thomas became angry and asked for paper. I helped him compose a note in French and he demanded that it be taken inside. The paper said that he was Thomas, Earl of Moray, second in rank only to his uncle, Robert, King of Scots, and that he had urgent business to present to the pope on behalf of the king. After another hour two huge guards came out to get us. They were heavily armed with swords and spears. Each of them took hold of one of our arms and led us into the room as if we were prisoners. I must confess that I wondered if indeed we were.

The room itself was richly decorated with tapestries. The pope himself, sitting on his throne, was so elaborately wrapped in beautiful gowns that it was impossible to decide if he was fat or thin, tall or short. Surrounding the Holy Father were several cardinals as well as other men. One of them I recognised as Henry de Sully, a French knight who had been in the service of England when we captured him at Byland. He had been treated so well by King Robert that he had actually helped to arrange this audience. The room was heady with the smell of incense. The guards conducted us forward to the holy presence, and we knelt before it. As we expected, the pope extended his hand and we kissed, in turn, the heavy, brilliant ring. He did not invite us to stand or sit, so that we were forced to stay on our knees. I realised that the earl and I were being deliberately humiliated, and I hoped that Thomas would be able to contain his temper and remain diplomatic, or our mission would be ruined.

The pope spoke to Thomas. *"Vous avez des affaires avec nous?"* Thomas looked at me, and I said, "He wants to know if you have business here."

Thomas looked at me in disbelief. Then he said, "Your Holiness, we are here on business of the King of Scots." The pope looked around the room. He had not understood the Scots words and he searched the other faces, but no one offered to translate, not even de Sully, who, like the others, spoke no Scots or English. The pope looked at Thomas, and Thomas looked at me again.

I didn't know how to address the pope in French, so I began, "Most Holy Father, *nous avons des affaires très importantes. Nous avons été envoyés ici par Robert, Roi d'Écosse.*" This was, of course, just formality. The pope knew exactly who Thomas was and that he had been sent by King Robert.

I knew it was difficult for Thomas to be speaking through a translator, but that was the way the entire interview went. The pope began by saying he had been disappointed by the Scots, who had been difficult in their relations with England. When I translated this to Thomas, I could see his eyes narrow ever so slightly, but he kept his composure. Thomas then answered, through me, that it was the wish of the King of Scots that there should be peace between England and Scotland, and that the king fervently hoped that the pope's excommunication of Scots would be lifted. The pope answered that he should not even deal with excommunicated people and seemed to be becoming impatient, perhaps ready to end the audience.

He reminded Thomas that he had sent letters to our king demanding that violence between the two countries be ended. In his opinion, Scotland had an obligation to make peace with England, as he had insisted in the letters.

This gave Thomas a route to a diplomatic triumph, and he didn't waste it. He smiled at the pope and said that the King of Scots was well aware of his obligations to the church, but that clerical errors (which I translated as *erreurs cléricaux*) had resulted in improper addresses on the pope's letters that had prevented their reaching our king. Thomas, still smiling, suggested that all the problems between the Holy Father and the King of Scots could be surmounted if the pope would just make sure that his aides would address his letters to our ruler with his proper title of "king."

This speech, I thought, was brilliant. The pope already knew why his letters had been returned unopened, but it was clear that he, with his desire to end the seemingly endless dispute and perhaps see his treasury increased by its resolution, had been given a face-saving way out of the impasse. It was his aides, according to Thomas, who had made the *erreurs cléricaux*, and the pope could "make sure" that this was corrected.

Thomas then asked if there was a letter he could take back to his king, and if there was anything that he could do to end the excommunication. With his expressionless face the pope said that if we would appear tomorrow in the afternoon he would have a letter for King Robert. Then he refused to end the excommunication. "*Je ne peut pas encore,*" he said. It was definite.

The Way to Holyrood

We left the audience with a good feeling. We had failed to end our alienation from Christendom, but thought we had achieved our main goal: the recognition of the independence of Scotland. We worried all that night, wondering whether or not the letter would be properly addressed. We picked it up the next afternoon. It was addressed to *Robertus Brus Rex Scotorum*, that is, Robert Bruce, King of Scots. We were both ecstatic. That evening the weather had moderated, and the square in Avignon was alive with festivities. People were there from many countries. Avignon was, at that time, like a world capital. Thomas and I joined in the dancing and even learned to sing a few new songs. I already knew the one about the city's bridge.

Sous le pont, d'Avignon
On y danse, on y danse

III

The next morning I made purchases of gifts from some of the local merchants. I bought jewels and fine formal clothes for my family. Then we sold our boat in exchange for horses and rode out of Avignon to the southwest. We had been told that there were enterprising people in the port of Narbonne who could book us passage around Spain toward home. Thomas felt that to return the way we had come was too risky; the flow of the Rhône would retard us.

It was now becoming winter even in the south and the farther north we went it would be too cold to travel by land. So we progressed through the great walls of Avignon out into the country on a beautiful day. It wasn't long before we passed by a truly wondrous sight. The Pont du Gard is a great aqueduct built by the Romans. It is enormous, made of massive stones fitted together perfectly. The small stream of the Gard is dwarfed by this construction. Thomas and I were awestruck in the presence of the bridge. That our ancestors had the ability, the power, and the diligence to build this work so long ago seemed to us astounding.

On our way to the sea we passed through another Roman city, Nîmes. There is a beautiful pre-Christian temple there. It was quite an experience to enter that temple and feel nothing but cold. The place was barren, empty; just walls. It was not at all like the reverent feeling I felt at Chartres or the absolute bliss of Vézelay. There is also in Nîmes a beautiful Roman arena. It was empty the day we saw it but it wasn't hard to imagine a Roman audience cheering at some event in the distant past.

Our trip continued along the coast to Montpelier and Beziers. When we reached Narbonne, we were surprised to find the city not exactly a port. There had been a great storm several years before and the harbour was entirely silted up. We faced a discouraging prospect. As night had come we went to a convenient tavern, stood at the bar, and ordered wine and food. The natives asked us who we were, and we told them that we were Scots who needed to find a way home. Some of the men laughed at this and some, more sober, explained about the storm and the silt and said that the great port, the oldest in southwestern France, was closed. No one knew of any boats that were sailing from elsewhere. We were anxious then, and only the excellent house *ragoût* and the heavy southern wine kept us from depression. When these pleasant things wore off, we looked at each other, not knowing what to do next. Then a man at a table in a dark corner beckoned to us to come and sit. This we did.

"I have heard what you request," he said in English. "I believe I can help you."

"Who are you?" I queried.

"I am Jacob *dit le Juif*."

"You are a Jew?" I asked this in all seriousness. "How is it that you speak English?"

Jacob the Jew answered, "I am a Jew by descent only. I speak many languages, and I have traded in many lands. In early times this city was largely occupied by my people. It was one of the most prosperous cities in the world, until the reign of Philip the Fair." As if to punctuate his naming of the former king, Jacob spit into the dirt floor and added, "May he rot in hell." He continued, "King Philip expelled all of the Jews over two hundred years ago and the city has never recovered, nor will it, in my opinion, even if the harbour were to be dredged. I am one of the few Jews to return. Now let us talk about your passage to Scotland. There is another harbour not far down the coast. It is late in the season, but if you hurry there I think there is a good chance you will find someone trading to the north."

"You know that we cannot land in England," said Thomas.

"Of course I know, and I know about your Robert de Bruce as well. He is gaining a good reputation in many places." Thomas nodded with a slight smile. "I have in mind a colleague who was to set out for Denmark near this time. It may be that he has not yet departed. Can you afford the passage?"

Thomas was tempted to say that he was the nephew of the king and on the king's business, but that would have been too dangerous. He answered instead, "I am sure I have the silver required, and also I can trade three fine horses."

"Then we should leave as soon as the first light. It is not far."

We agreed to meet him at our stable and, with some hope, retired. When the light came, Jacob was at the stable waiting for us. The three of us rode slowly out of Narbonne and down the coast. It wasn't far at all, and there were several ships at anchor in what was more of a small cove than a port.

"You are in luck," said Jacob. "I can see my friend's ship."

It wasn't long before we were introduced to the captain, also called Jacob and also of the Jewish race. His ship was loading the last barrels of wine for the north and he was leaving the next day. Jacob spoke to him in what sounded to me like Spanish. Silver changed hands between the captain and Jacob, and between Thomas and the captain. It was all arranged very quickly, and we left the next morning.

Our captain had been well paid to go out of his way to take us to Scotland. He was very generous with his wine, perhaps because he was carrying so much of it. He was a quiet man, but because of language differences we couldn't speak much in any case. We used a sort of broken French to communicate what little was necessary. He was polite, and I wondered why his people were sometimes poorly spoken of.

The trip was arduous in the extreme. About the only thing I remember was sailing past the great rock at the southern tip of Spain. After that we turned north into the winter. The air was cold and the sea stormy much of the time. The farther northward we sailed the worse the weather became. The crew were surly but plodded through their work. Thomas and I said very little, as the food became foul and we became sick for long periods. Both of us were losing weight and stank as well, not having bathed for a very long time.

It was tense when we sailed the narrow water between France and England, but we saw no English ships. We saw very few ships of any nation. Perhaps most had decided to wait for spring. It was stormy in the German Ocean and we decided to put in at Leith. What a glorious feeling we had when we saw the Firth of Forth, yet poor winds kept us from landing for two days. It was frustrating just sitting there, looking upon Edinburgh on top of the great hill and not being able to reach it. But a sudden turn of the weather allowed us into port on the third day. Thomas and I fairly ran down the gangplank to the quay. It was exhilarating. We were home at last. The voices on the quay were Scottish. We had completed a successful mission for Scotland—*gud ald* Scotland!

Chapter Nineteen

A Just Peace

It seemed miraculous that we were back. My memories of France and our long voyage were already hazy, like a faded dream. Thomas went immediately to the captain of the guard at Leith and, showing his credentials, demanded to know where the king was staying at that time. He was told that the court was at Lochmaben at the moment, and I was overjoyed to hear this, since Lochmaben was close to home and my family. We immediately bought three horses and set out for the southwest. It was a beautiful trip, just Thomas and myself, comrades now, riding slowly through the clear breezes, with the sweet smell of the spring season in the air, the rich soil of the countryside damp and ready for plant-ing, and the thrushes and wrens singing us on.

We reached Lochmaben late one morning and found

King Robert busy, as usual, listening to complaints and disputes and no doubt making decisions in his fair style. When we were announced, there was a great stir of excitement, and I confess that we were startled by it. The king interrupted his meeting and rose to greet us. We found ourselves standing in front of many of the most prominent men of Scotland. It was intimidating.

"Well, well," said King Robert. "We have here our ambassadors to the pope, the Earl of Moray and the esteemed laird David Crawford. What news have you, gentlemen? We are very anxious to hear."

"Sir," Thomas began nervously. "I have some poor news and some good news. I will tell of the bad first. It is, simply, that His Holiness has not lifted the excommunication from Scotland. We are still out of communion with the Church."

At this I could see the looks of everyone fall. They had expected a perfect score from us, I suppose, and were disappointed.

"Very well," said the king. "I had hoped that you would fare better in this regard, but I will admit you had a very hard tree to cut and only a blunted saw for a tool. Go on, Thomas. We await the good news."

"Thank you, my lord. I hope you will think this news was worthy of the great expense our journey has occasioned. I have here a letter of greetings from the pope addressed to you."

Thomas, his hand shaking, handed the letter to King Robert, whose eyes had only to see its address: *Robertus Brus Rex Scotorum*. Immediately the king's face broke into a broad grin, and he passed the letter unopened to one of the nobles standing with him. It was passed again and again, and soon everyone was cheering and yelling, coming around Thomas and myself and slapping us on the back. Wine was demanded and produced and the king read the letter. Everyone wanted to know what was in it but the king assured them all that the pope was only giving us vague pleasantries, and encouraging us to make peace with the English.

"There is nothing new or of any import in the letter," said the king. "It is what is on the outside that matters, and also on the inside at the beginning of the letter. It says, 'To the most illustrious Robert Bruce, king of Scotland.'"

At that everyone had another bowl, and someone started a chant that was taken up by almost everyone in the room. "Robert Bruce, King of Scots! Robert Bruce, King of Scots! Robert Bruce, King of Scots!"

"Nobles and gentlemen," the king addressed us, holding up his hand for silence. "This is truly a remarkable achievement. In a way it is actually better that the pope has not lifted his excommunication, because it shows that despite the fact that we have in his holy eyes misbehaved, we are nevertheless an independent kingdom, and that the pope will deal with us as such."

Then King Robert came forward to embrace first his nephew and then me. It was quite a moment, especially in front of all of those great men.

"Thomas, Davie," he said simply, looking each of us directly in our eyes. "What a show. Our nation will ever be in your debt. Now, both of you, get to your homes. Your work is done for a while. Someone will let you know when we need you again."

We were standing outside the court at Lochmaben, readying our horses, when of a sudden there came a great roar from inside. We tethered our horses and ran back in, wondering what had happened. Was the king in danger? But my fear was easily overcome. Queen Elizabeth had gone into labour in an adjacent building and was about to give birth. We joined in the anxious vigil. Within two hours the king had a male heir, to be called, eventually, King David II. I thought the choice of the name David was excellent inasmuch as it had been King David I who had invited the Bruces to Scotland some two centuries before. I wouldn't have dared to believe that my own name had anything to do with it.

This event provoked a party such as, I believe, Lochmaben had never before seen. It lasted almost a week and people came from all over the country to see the new prince. It was an easy distance for me to go home to Dumfries to pick up my family. I hadn't seen them in so long. Seumas was now a strapping lad of fifteen, and Ishbel was ten. They were, I thought, very good-looking, like their mother. I was so happy to see Màiri, I was brought to tears. She was older but as beautiful as ever. Seumas and Ishbel had obeyed their mother and their grandmother, helping out with the work of the place.

I had brought everyone in my family presents from France. The women got bracelets and jewels. Everyone got new outfits of clothes, the very best that the purse of the king's ambassador could purchase, and better than anything available in Scotland. There were all pleased, trying them on and prancing about like nobility.

My mother was ill and couldn't attend the festivities at Lochmaben, but the king made a great show towards the rest of my family when we arrived in our new clothes. He talked to us and introduced us to some of the most important people in the land. It was a wonderful time for Scotland, and for the family of the esteemed laird, me, David Crawford.

When the birthday party was over I returned to my little estate in Dumfries. It would be good to get some rest and be with my family. I was thirty-two years old, but I think I felt much older. For most of eighteen years I had been a soldier, and a soldier in an army that seldom had enough for its men to eat and couldn't properly clothe and shelter them. The service had abused my body. I had a few scars, but more important I had pains in my joints, which I think exposure to the elements over a long period of time had brought about. But there was nothing to do about that. It was time to enjoy what I could, and to be kind to the family I had not been able properly to serve. I had been a good provider for my children, but hardly a reliable husband or parent. Seumas was a big strong young man now, itching to get into the service, eager to fight for his country. He was a year older than I had been that cold night when the future king swept me up on his horse. Ishbel was lovely, almost a woman. Her hair was dark like her mother's and swept back close to her head. She smiled often, and loved to play tricks on me in what was left of her childhood. Both my children had been educated; their mother took care of that. They could read and write Scots, and had studied French and Latin. The spoke Gaelic fluently, but, like their mother, could not read or write it. My wife was, well, the best thing that ever happened to me. All of that summer of 1324 we used to wait for everyone to go to sleep, and then we would lie back on our soft down bed and talk, just as we had for years. I was often tired and sometimes I would fall asleep. But quite often we would make love in the darkness, just like we had in the old days. I remember one night in particular when the warm air was still, and a nearly full moon softly entered our chamber, a nightingale serenaded us and I thought to myself, Davie, whatever you do, this is what it is all about. This cannot be exceeded. Màiri was asleep, but I jostled her a bit and said to her, "Just promise me one thing. That whatever happens, you will remember this night. This is the night that I will always remember." She said nothing, but smiled at me in the moonlight and squeezed my hand.

II

In the spring of 1325 a summons came from King Robert. I was invited to join him at a reunion of his soldiers at his new home at Cardross, near the great double rock fortress of Dumbarton, *Dun Breatunn* in Gaelic, meaning the fort of the Britons. Why the king chose this place, close to an ancient stronghold of our Welsh-speaking ancestors, I do not know. It was a beautiful location overlooking the Firth of Clyde, and in an area that was then mostly Gaelic-speaking. One would have thought the king would have preferred a palace or perhaps one of his castles in the southwest, yet here he was, far from all the places he had frequented before. Perhaps it was a continuation of the Irish strategy, which he had not forgot. The water route down the firth made contact with Ireland easy.

The house itself was still under construction, not really ready for habitation, and it certainly wasn't fancy. It was really more of a summer house, a very large cottage, if you will. The beginnings of a garden were distinguished by the presence of the king's pet lion, secure in an iron cage. There was also a place for hawks, since falconry was one of King Robert's favourite sports.

It was wonderful to see the old comrades again. James Douglas and I hugged each other enthusiastically, and he inquired as to the health and progress of his godson and namesake, Seumas. Thomas Randolph and I greeted each other similarly. It had always been a pleasure and privilege to have been associated with these great men. Thomas told me that he was worried about the king's health, and that the new house was a place for him to spend what he thought would be his last years. This saddened me, of course, but when the king made his appearance, I noticed a change in his demeanour. I had seen him look worse, at times, when he was sick in the field, but this was different. He was not camping out in a cold field. He was living with no lack of material comfort. Yet he looked poorly. Thomas told me that some of his teeth had fallen out. I could see for myself that his complexion had gone sallow and his eyes seemed to have sunk in his face.

The Great Scot

King Robert greeted each of us, his veterans, warmly, spending a few minutes with each, asking about his family and circumstances. Despite his obvious ailment, he still had his rough good looks and magnetic personality, and I noticed that Queen Elizabeth wasn't present for this occasion while the former Countess of Buchan was. How long it had been since I had seen her! I made my way to her seat, which was somewhat apart from the rest, and she gave me one of those sweet kisses she had bestowed on a fourteen-year-old so long before. She was still as beautiful to me as she had been then, and very cheerful. I wondered how often she'd been in touch with the king, but I didn't find out. They were very discreet about their relationship, I suppose. She had been invited to Cardross as a heroine of the War of Independence, and had every right to that title, but I also sensed it was partly pretence to allow Isabel and the king to appear in public together.

The king announced he had news. He was going to build a castle at the narrow point of the Kintyre peninsula, at the place that is called in Gaelic *Tairbeart*. This seemed to confirm that his idea of bringing Ireland under his control to promote his Celtic empire was still very much alive in his mind. A castle at *Tairbeart* would control the sea route to Ireland. The king also outlined a French strategy. He was sending Thomas Randolph at the head of a delegation to France to renew the *Alliance Ancienne* between our two countries. It was hoped the treaty would guarantee that, if either France or Scotland were to be attacked by England, the other country would fight against the English. Further, it was to be proposed that Frenchmen and

Scots were to have automatic citizenship in each other's lands. This was an astonishing idea, and I think Thomas thought it would be unique in the history of Europe. In addition, King Robert was going to propose that a Scots College be erected for Scottish scholars at the University of Paris. Scotland was too poor, he said, to construct its own independent place of learning, but Paris was the centre of the civilised world and would do nicely until funds could be found for a college at home. It was obvious, also, that an official Scottish presence in the French capital would solidify the alliance between France and Scotland.

I was disappointed that I was not appointed to go with Thomas on this adventure. I wanted to be chosen, and not overlooked. I felt a little hurt, but I could not deny I was not the best person for the job, and anyway, I would be able to spend that time with my family. It was all right. I hadn't liked Paris much, anyway.

The king provided a celebration with wine, music, dancing, and roast venison for one and all, but there were not enough accommodations at the new house at Cardross. Most of us left that night to return to our own homes, but well satisfied that our country was making progress in the world. Perhaps that is why we heard nothing from England.

In the next year, 1326, the king called a parliament in July at Cambuskenneth Abbey. As I could have predicted, Thomas Randolph had returned with the French treaty that had been signed at a place in France called Corbeil. Thomas was competent in whatever he worked on. His treaty made us allies of the greatest power in Christendom. The English would be upset. There was also news that

Charles the Fair, king of France, had agreed to the founding of the *Collège des Écossais* at Paris, and had presented property to David, Bishop of Moray, for the purpose. At last our remote Scotland was joining the civilised world.

There was much else attended to at the parliament. Land forfeited by those who had opposed us was given to those who had supported us. Donations were provided to churches, and, as usual, those establishments honouring ancient Celtic saints such as St. Fillan were treated fairly. Most important, perhaps, it was agreed that the succession to the throne should go to the king's son, David Bruce, and his heirs, and failing any such heirs, to Robert Stewart, the son of the king's daughter, Marjorie Bruce, and his heirs.

King Robert also asked that his subjects use either Scots or Gaelic for their daily business, putting aside French, Flemish, Welsh, and other tongues still current in the country that were not in his opinion "Scottish." The king was still consolidating his subjects into the Scottish nation.

All was going well in Scotland. The country was secure and prosperous under the man now almost universally referred to as Good King Robert. He ruled with grace. He was, as the French would say, *de bon air*.

III

These times of good feeling were soon to come to a close. The year 1327 began ominously, with a king's messenger arriving at my home bearing a command from King Robert. Christiana Macruarie, Lady Christiana of the Isles, had died and my presence at a memorial service a week hence was requested. I was saddened, remembering that this fine woman had introduced me to my wife. The service was held at Glasgow Cathedral, and although it wasn't a great distance from Dumfries, it was a difficult journey. The weather had turned bitter cold and snow fell most of the time in near-gale winds blocking out the slate sky. Nonetheless, much of Scotland turned out to give honour to this heroine of our independence. It gave me a strange sensation to remember those first days with the king, almost twenty-one years before, and to remember old Bishop Wishart as we met him in the cathedral in 1306. He had meant so much to us when we had little support save that of the Scottish Church. King Robert was visibly moved by the tribute paid to Lady Christiana. I wondered if I was the only person present who knew they had been lovers.

After the service the church remained almost full and various people had audiences with the king, who was recovering from another of his sick spells. After some time the gathering was interrupted by the appearance of a dishevelled old man wearing dirty clothes covered with snow. He limped forward until barred by guards from approaching the king. He was arguing with them in a corner, and I thought I had better try to see what was going on. When I got close I realised it was Cuthbert, our spy.

"What have you, Cuthbert?" I asked.

"I have important news for the king."

"What is its nature?"

"I will tell it only to the king."

"Very well," I said to the sentry. "Put him in my custody," I answered. "I am David Crawford."

At the mention of my name, the guards gave way, and I proceeded toward the king with Cuthbert, the snow melting in puddles below his cloak. King Robert recognised him at once and interrupted his interview.

"Sir," the old man said. "I have important news from England."

The king said, "Then let everyone hear it."

Cuthbert looked surprised, but the king motioned him toward the pulpit and addressed the throng, who quieted almost instantly when he raised his hand. "This is our messenger, Cuthbert, who has served us well these many years. He has news for us from England. Proceed, Cuthbert."

The church remained quiet as all strained to hear the weak voice of the messenger.

"The news is that King Edward II is dead."

Even though we were in a holy place, there was immediate and loud cheering that continued for some time. Then King Robert held up his hand again and once more there was immediate quiet. "How did the king die, Cuthbert?"

"Most think it was of natural causes, sir, but I know well that it was murder."

"Murder, Cuthbert? Tell us more."

"Well sir, there was a conspiracy involving the queen and her lover. You may have heard that King Edward was captured, and proclaimed incompetent, and a revolutionary parliament chose his son to be crowned Edward III. Still, a living king existed, inconvenient to their plans, my lord. The conspirators tried to kill the king in several ways, and always they wanted to make it look as if he had died of natural causes, but they failed. Finally they conceived a clever answer to the problem. They rammed a hollow marrow bone up his arse, sir, and pushed red-hot pokers through it into his entrails, cooking them well, which killed him properly without a trace of his pain or even a scar. That is the true story, sir. King Edward II died in utmost agony, he who claims to be the Prince of Wales has been crowned as Edward III, and mighty England is in the hands of a criminal government."

King Robert let everyone digest this grisly story for a few minutes. There was murmuring throughout the church, and then the king raised his hand silencing the crowd as before. "Have you anything else to tell, Cuthbert?"

"Yes, sir, just this. King Edward III is very young and headstrong. He wants Scotland, sir, just as did his father and grandfather, and the criminals supporting him will use him against you, sir, very soon, if I am not mistaken."

"Cuthbert, we cannot take actions on mistaken opinions. What do you know?"

"Sir, the English are coming again, soon, I believe."

So there it was. The peaceful time was over. It was war again.

IV

King Robert began to move swiftly against this new threat. He himself was well enough to travel to Ireland with a force that would prove to be sufficient to render that country unable to aid England. Before he left he commissioned Sir James Douglas and Thomas Randolph, Earl of Moray, to make a preemptive raid on northern England. We were all given a one-month furlough to visit and provide for our families, then we mustered in southern Scotland to attack northeast England. By June our forces were burning the county of Durham and in general creating havoc throughout the area. As we had been told, the English under their young king had moved to York ready to take Scotland with a truly formidable army, including mercenaries from the Low Countries. By July our armies were situated close together near the River Wear. The English sought to attack us, but Thomas Randolph was more than cunning and our army was, compared with England's, very mobile. Not only were we able to move out of the way of England's best, we were able, under James Douglas, to attack their camp at night, and very nearly succeeded in capturing the boy king Edward III. His personal guard saved him and we had to return in the darkness to our camp without a royal hostage.

It was a season of much rain, and the English army, lumbering with its heavy baggage train, became demoralised trying to lure us into battle. As a final blow to the pride of England, we won another victory. As our two armies were encamped close together, we lit fires at night and made much commotion, as if to be ready for battle on the morrow. But by morning we had moved many miles toward Scotland and the English, standing in the countryside that we had wasted, were starving and could not pursue us. There was nothing for them to do but return to

York and disband the army. The young king of England was brought to tears, we heard later.

King Robert, just returned from Ireland, received us back home with great joy. As a result of his campaign, England could expect no help from her Irish allies, and with the disbanding of the English army, it now appeared that England's ambitions in Scotland were at an all-time low. To apply even more pressure, our king, in better health than in several years, led a Scottish army into Northumberland. We all knew there would be no opposition, so we stole and burned and ravaged the countryside at a leisurely pace, taking time out for ball games among the troops. The king even did some hawking, and everywhere we went we received tribute from the people and let it be known that we were about to annex the north of England to the Kingdom of Scotland.

The English parliament was impressed. It refused even to consider any more money for a war against Scotland. It had already lost a huge amount of treasure, and was losing prestige among the nations of Europe as well. Now it appeared that they might lose the fifth part of England itself. Early in October 1327, a delegation appeared in the English town of Norham to ask King Robert for a lasting peace. This time, for the first time, England really meant to give us what we wanted—freedom.

King Robert, at Berwick, dictated his conditions for negotiation: England's absolute acceptance of the independence of Scotland and recognition of his legitimacy as its king. It was a high moment for King Robert to be able to do this, but as it is with life, there was sadness along with the happiness. Queen Elizabeth died that same month. She was not our most popular queen, to be sure, and her marriage to King Robert was, as I have said, not perfectly harmonious. Nevertheless, she was our queen, the mother of the heir to our throne, and the entire country was plunged into mourning. For some days the Bruce made no public appearances whatsoever.

Several months later, in the early part of 1328, I received a summons from the king and travelled to Cardross to see him. There he received me alone.

"Davie, how have you been?" He seemed quite sincere. Perhaps he was recognising that we who had been so close had not seen each other in private for years.

"I am fine, sir. What service may I perform for you?"

"You look well, Davie. As you can see, I am not. My time on this earth is now very limited."

"Say it is not so, sir," I pleaded, but I could see from his dark complexion and hollowed-out eyes that it was.

"Davie, you have served me and your country so well. I have an important request of you, and I doubt that I will have many more. Please journey to the place where Isabel, the former Countess of Buchan, resides. You know it well. You established it for her at my request. Do you remember?"

"Of course I do, sir."

"Then you will go to her as soon as possible. Tell her in my name of my desire for her to come here to live with me for the last days of my life. If she rejects me, then tell her that I hope she is in God's grace and that I wish her well and farewell. If she accepts, then bring her to me. Tell her that she will have a separate apartment, and everything of the best that can be had."

"I will do as you say, sir."

"Good, Davie. Thank you for your service. One thing more, Davie." His voice was weaker. "Tell the former countess that I love her, and that I have always loved her."

I made my apologies, and left the king immediately for the west country. Seeing the great man in such a weakened state brought me near to tears. After several days of riding, I came upon the lodging of the former countess. She invited me in at once and called for some wine and cheese. We sat at her table. She looked beautiful still, and was slim as always. Her golden hair had become snow-white a little too soon as is in the nature of our people.

"I come with news of King Robert," I started.

"How is he?"

"Not well, Isabel, not well at all. His illness has returned, and he is very weak."

"You give me ominous news then, Davie?" She looked worried.

"He does not think he will be blessed with long life." This brought tears to the lady's cheeks. "He asked me to tell you that he loves you and has always loved you."

Now the lady began to sob. "Forgive me, Davie. I'm sorry. I should be braver."

I walked across the table and put my arm around her shoulder as she was drying her eyes. Then I spoke. "The king asks you to come and live with him at Cardross for his last days. Will you come?"

"Oh, Davie, of course I would come. Do you think that he is sincere in his invitation?"

"My lady, we have both known King Robert for many years. I do not recall his ever being insincere, do you?"

"No, of course not," she said. "I just couldn't stand his pity, if that's all it is. But you are right; he is always true to his words. I shouldn't have asked the question. We will leave tomorrow, after I have packed some of my belongings."

Within a few days I had successfully installed the lady at Cardross, but the king was not there. He had been carried in a special litter all the way to Edinburgh, where the English peace delegation was busy negotiating with our committee. I bid the lady good-bye and left her in the hands of the servants, who had been told to expect her. Then I continued on to Edinburgh.

The city was alive with activity. There were great crowds in the streets and the innkeepers were kept busy. People had come from all parts of the kingdom. There were earls and small freeholders, bishops and ordinary citizens. Most prominent were all the old heroes of the war: Sir James Douglas and Thomas Randolph, as well as Robert Keith, the Marischal of Scotland, and Gilbert de la Haye, the Lord High Constable. They had come to witness what I regard as the second most important event, after Bannockburn, in the history of Scotland. It was to be the end of a long and painful struggle. We had won, and no one could question it. The date June 23, 1314 now had a counterpart: March 17, 1328.

Under the treaty, composed and approved at Holyrood

Abbey, the English king renounced all claims of sovereignty over Scotland and acknowledged King Robert and his heirs as our rightful sovereigns. A marriage was arranged with Joan, the sister of King Edward III, to David Bruce, the heir of King Robert, both of whom were small children. There was created an alliance between England and Scotland, with the English acknowledging that the Franco-Scottish Treaty of Corbeil of 1326 had precedence. The Scots agreed to pay £20,000 indemnity to England, perhaps to make up for some of the blackmail we had levied on the hapless population of northern England for so many years. While this was a lot of silver for our poor country, it seemed a small price for our freedom. In addition, the English agreed to use their best efforts and influence with the pope to end the excommunication of our country. It was hard to believe that, after all the hatred we had shared, King Edward III agreed to sign the document referring to our king as "the lord Robert, by God's grace illustrious king of Scots, our ally and very dear friend."

Throughout this great triumph, King Robert took little part. He lay in his sickbed in the abbey, rousing only to make sure that his conditions were met.

Following the signing there was a great party that spilled out of the abbey and into the streets of Edinburgh. The members of the English negotiating team took as great a part in it as did the Scots. There was a wondrous good feeling to that day. The Englishmen present were having such a good time, they seemed to have forgot, or perhaps didn't care, that Scotland had won this long struggle. There was a genuine relief among all that justice had been done and that war had ended. The Scots were in a mood to be magnanimous and made sure that all English drinking bowls were filled. One Englishman raised his glass to the sun and shouted, "Long live Scotland! Long live King Robert!" There were great cheers at this, and one Scot yelled, "Long live England! No more war!"

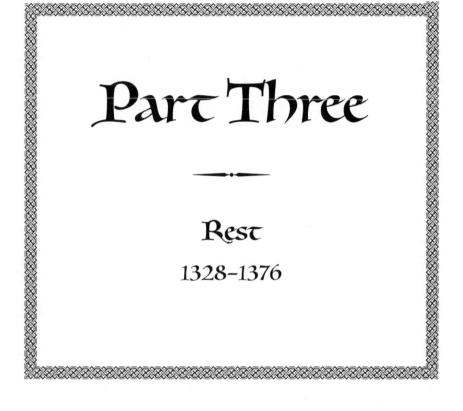

Part Three

Rest

1328–1376

CHAPTER TWENTY

Passage to Dunfermline

The celebration was beginning to die down when Sir James Douglas found me in the crowd. "Davie, great show, isn't it?" he asked, embracing me. I nodded. "Davie, the king is asking for you. You had better go to him."

I wasted no time and went directly back into the abbey, where I found the great man. He was lying in bed, almost too weak to talk.

"Davie, Davie," he whispered. "Isn't it wonderful? All that we have gone through, but it was worth it, Davie, was it not?"

"Aye, sir, worth every minute."

"Davie, we have not been close for these many years. There were so many people to deal with; the English kings and their nobles; our own nobles, the bishops; the pope. I didn't have time for you. I didn't have need of your service. But you have been happy with your family, is it not so?"

"I am fortunate, sir."

"Good, I am glad for you. You deserve everything you have. Davie, in the old days you served me as a special confidant. I need your service again. The government now operates without my efforts, or nearly so. I need not help in this regard. My nephew Thomas is quite capable. Now I need personal help to see me through my last days. You were very good at that type of work in the old days, Davie. Will you serve me again, Davie? I need you."

"Of course I will, sir," I said quietly while looking directly at him. "It will be a great honour."

I agreed to meet King Robert at Cardross a month hence, and meanwhile set out for my estate in Dumfries. All was well there. My son and daughter were advancing well and Màiri was as lovely as ever. The freshened air of April was all around us, filling us with the smell of the new blossoms, and the birds were gay. Every day I wondered how I had come from so far to deserve all this. My house was solid. There was plenty to eat. Fish were in the stream. Deer were in the forest. Occasionally we used a bow and arrow to shoot a grouse. We had at least a year's supply of oats, and cheese and butter and cream galore in the lower pantry. The cellar was full of good wine, and it was on the table every day. Seumas and Ishbel were becoming accustomed to its pleasures. Màiri was an excellent cook, and I had brought her a special collection of recipes back from France.

It was a wonderful time we were having. No one was

sick. My mother was happy to see me again. She was now quite frail, but she still cooked and helped out around the place. I played with my children. We went to Dumfries town and people doffed their hats as we walked by. We spent many happy, quiet moments together, and Màiri was upset when I told her I would be leaving soon again in the king's service. I assured her that the king himself knew that his end was near, and that I would soon return to her. In any case, I couldn't refuse the summons of my king.

At last it was time to go, and I rode off for Cardross, arriving in the morning a few days later. To my astonishment, King Robert was busy tending his orchard, walking about his trees, examining them. He looked a little feeble, but he had recovered so much that it was hard to believe.

I ventured, "You are in good health, sir. You have improved."

"Thank you so much for coming, Davie. Yes, I am recovered somewhat, but I'm afraid it is only temporary. Sometimes I am better, sometimes not. I know not why. But I grow steadily worse, Davie, you must know that. I am indeed well enough to make a pilgrimage to the shrine of Saint Ninian at Whithorn, however, and I shall be going there ere long. It was a great victory we won at Saint Ninian's Kirk the day before the Battle of Bannockburn. I am going to pay my respects to the saint. I am hoping you will accompany me."

"Of course I will, sir. I am at your service."

"Have you heard the news, Davie? Bishop Lamberton has died, may God rest his soul. He was such a help to the cause."

"Indeed he was, sir. I am sorrowed to hear of his death."

"Davie, my son David is to marry at Berwick next month, as has been arranged in the treaty. I will not attend. It would be too much of a strain on me, or at least that is what I will tell people. Since he had to capitulate to us in the war, King Edward III is too ashamed to come and will not attend the wedding. His absence is an insult, a snub to me, and therefore I will not attend, either. I have changed my plans. I am going instead to Ireland, to make sure that Carrickfergus continues to be an influence in Irish affairs through my late queen's de Burgh relatives in Ulster. I want at all times to have good relations between Ireland and Scotland. One reason I chose this place to retire is that it allows for easy access there. I will not need your services until I return."

"But, sir, will you be well enough to carry out this mission?"

"I am well enough now, Davie, and while I am away I hope that you will attend the royal wedding. Please bring your family."

I bade the king good-bye and rode back to Dumfries. My family was surprised to see me, and when I told my wife and children where they were going and what they would experience, they grew very excited. My mother's health was too delicate for her to make the trip, and she agreed to stay behind if we all told her the tales of the wedding when we returned.

My family was arrayed in their fine French satin and linen. Màiri wore a beautiful red gown, trimmed with jewels, that complimented her dark hair. New shoes for all had

been purchased from the best souter in Dumfries. No one
would say the Crawfords did not belong at a royal wedding!
We proceeded across the country to Berwick, the border
town chosen as a symbol of the two independent countries.
Yes, after all, independent!

The little city was packed with the gentry of both Scotland and England. Everyone seemed to be in a festive
mood, and I doubt there were many there who weren't
glad the long war was over, and that this royal marriage
would seal our agreement to live in peace with each other.
There were so many people trying to get a view of the proceedings that my family was nervous they would not be
allowed to view the ceremony, but I knew that if I could
find either James Douglas or Thomas Randolph, a place
would be made for us. In fact, I found them both together,
and soon learned that the king had directed we be given
seats with the nobility. My wife fairly swooned when she
heard it. I introduced her to Thomas, who was very polite
to her, and her eyes sparkled. She had already met James.

In a way, the proceedings were dominated by the English dowager queen, Isabella, the mother of the little
bride Joan. I didn't hear anyone mention her except to
compliment her. But it was on my mind, and the minds of
everyone else there: Was this a murderess who had plotted
the death of her husband, King Edward II, in order to put
her son, Edward III, on the throne? Or was this the charming, sophisticated mother of the new king's dear little sister? Could she really be both? Who could tell? Given the
importance of the occasion, I'm not sure if anyone cared.
It was a festive time; I had never seen so much colour in

one place. The bright colourful arms of the greatest families of both England and Scotland were everywhere to be seen, blurred and blended as in a rainbow. The men and ladies were dressed in their finest.

By the time the service began, the church was full to bursting. A hush fell over the congregation as the two small children, about to be united in matrimony, were brought forward to the altar holding hands, announced by splendid English trumpeters. I don't believe that either bride or groom was yet eight years old. They delighted the assembly as the holy words were said, and when the priest pronounced them man and wife and motioned for the boy groom to kiss his bride, I don't believe that there were any dry eyes in the place. Not only were the two so beautiful and innocent-looking, but it was also what they symbolised; that two old adversary nations had made peace, and there was hope for a better future for everyone.

That night there were parties all over Berwick. The old streets were lit up with bonfires, and there was music and dancing everywhere. Scots and English celebrated together. The alleys of the town, which not so long ago had been slippery with blood, were now glazed with spilled wine.

II

After I had returned my family to Dumfries, I had several months to be with them and to enjoy them. We had a wonderful time and it seemed that everyone in the town visited us to hear about the royal wedding. They rode or walked to our place, in awe that we had really been in such august company. We were the pride of Dumfries. The fact that the Crawfords had been guests of the king, and seated with the nobility, added immensely to our social standing.

When the leaves turned colour and the wind had an icy snap to it, I told my family I had to be off again in the king's service. They accepted this with their usual good humour and a few tears.

It was winter when I returned to Cardross. The days were short, and the king was feeling worse. But he was eager to tell me the news:

"Davie, Davie. Have you heard? The pope has finally lifted his excommunication of us. We are all Christians in good standing again. I was afraid I would never live to see it."

Even this welcome news couldn't keep up King Robert's spirits for long. He felt, I could tell, very poorly, and his health grew worse. Yet he didn't stop making visits to his caged lion, which he had named Adam, after an early Norman Bruce ancestor. He still sailed on the River Clyde while I accompanied him as a bodyguard. The irony of it: Here was one of the greatest warriors ever, the man who had taught me how to fight, and now I was guarding him. This is how age changes everything. Some of the intimacy of what Robert Bruce and young Davie Crawford had experienced began to come back. The king taught me about how to use falcons. We went fishing, and hunting, and we talked of the old days.

As the Christmas season approached, Thomas Randolph and James Douglas came to Cardross with the newly married David and Joan. They had escorted the English Queen Isabella to the border, then made a leisurely progress toward Cardross, showing off the royal couple to as many people as possible. A parliament was called, and it affirmed that, should the king's son, David Bruce, not have any male heirs, Robert Stewart, whose mother was the king's late daughter Marjorie, would succeed to the throne. Upon the death of King Robert, his son and heir, Prince David, would reign as King David II under the joint regency of Thomas Randolph, Earl of Moray, and Sir James Douglas. All of the nobles swore to and attested to this agreement, and then, with great ceremony, King David II was crowned, with his beautiful little queen beside him. A marvellous celebration followed. The king provided entertainment for all, and there were many parties, but my spirit was not festive that time of Hogmanay. I missed my family; there were times when I could see that Isabel, the former countess, was worried about the health of the king. She didn't want to stand out in any way and kept to her quarters when others, especially children, were around. One time, she took me aside.

"Davie, I don't understand these changes. Sometimes he is well, and sometimes so weak he cannot stand. He seems to get better when he eats kale soup, and worse when he doesn't. He absolutely hates kale, and will usually not eat it even if I plead. Do you think it possible that kale can cure disease?"

"I don't know, my lady, but I remember that years ago an old woman made him better with such a soup."

"I think it possible, Davie, that the kale acts as a kind of cure for him, but he will eat none of it at times, and I fear, anyway, that it may be too late to help him. Despite his brief recoveries, the disease progresses. Each trough is deeper than the one before."

When February came, the king announced he was feeling stronger and that he and I were going on his long-planned pilgrimage to Withorn. Isabel told me in private that for several weeks she had forced more kale soup into him. He had spat out some of it in disgust, but had managed to get a good quantity down. We packed our gear and left in the king's boat on the next morning's tide. Our boatmen were happily chanting a song; I noted that it wasn't one of the sad Gaelic rowing songs for which the west was famous. Soon the breeze freshened, the current was with us, the sails filled, and rowing was unnecessary. The sun danced on the bright waters of the Firth of Clyde.

Gradually, I became aware that the boatmen were giving me quick glances, and then one of them broke into a broad grin and the other began laughing, it seemed, at me. And then I knew. They were the Graham brothers, who had helped us rescue Lady Isabel from her cage in Berwick all those years ago. The king had remembered their ability, courage, and discretion when he had told them he was "Hob." He had hired them to be his boatmen on a generous pension. They had moved across the country to accept this position. When they saw I had caught on, the brothers and the king as well had a good laugh at my expense.

When my embarrassment died down, a small cask was opened and passed around and we relived one of the great adventures of our lives.

But the passage was rough, and the rolling and pitching of the boat as we reached deeper waters was too much for the frail king. Accordingly we made for land, where we had a litter constructed and engaged bearers to take the king farther south. Even this was difficult, and we had to stop and rest in Ayrshire for several weeks. At last, in April 1329, we arrived at Withorn, where Saint Ninian had first brought Christianity to Scotland almost a thousand years before. King Robert chose this place especially. It was not that he had no regard for the Roman Church; he had always respected the authority of the pope. But it was at the shrine of a Celtic saint that he had chosen to make his last confession. I think, also, that King Robert believed that Saint Ninian had blessed us at Bannockburn, and was for that reason doing homage to him.

We stayed at Withorn for several days, where the king prayed to be forgiven for his sins. I think he would have stayed longer, but he became exhausted. He realised that his time on earth was coming to an end and that he had better return to Cardross to die. Our journey home to Cardross went well, and all our spirits were buoyed when we passed those places where we had won glory. We marched through the king's beloved Carrick and passed by his birthplace at Turnberry and near such places of glorious victory as Loudon Hill and Glen Trool.

I walked along with King Robert as he was borne on his

litter northward, and we talked about the old days. We spoke of the defeat at Methven and of our exile to barren Rathlin. We remembered the cave and the spider that had encouraged us against the almost impossible odds we faced. We laughed at Cuthbert, our English spy, who always looked terrible but had played an important part for us. We talked of Campbells, Keiths, Stewarts, Boyds, Hays, and all the others who helped our cause, such as Tom Dickson. We mentioned our enemies, too, the Comyns, John of Lorne, the Macdoualls, and, of course, the Hammer of the Scots, King Edward I, as well as his son and grandson. The king brought up his lovely relations with the women who had helped us, Lady Christian of Carrick and Lady Christiana of the Isles. He became quiet after he mentioned his brothers, Thomas, Alexander, Nigel, and Edward. They were all gone now. Then he mentioned his daughter Marjorie, and tears began to come into his eyes. "She was my pride," he said, "and I scarcely got to see her as she grew up, Davie. I had not time to properly mourn her death. Oh, if I had it to do over again."

"We would all like a second chance at something, sir. Please don't make it hard on yourself."

"Och, Davie. I do have regrets. My actions are responsible for many deaths. Look what I did to my poor queen. I was not the proper husband for her. There is also the murder, Davie, when we first met. It never goes away. My brother Edward tried to excuse it as an act of war, but it was murder plain and simple."

"You will be forgiven, sir. I am sure of it."

"Forgiven, I hope, Davie, by God. But not forgiven by myself."

III

All the important men of Scotland were summoned to the bedside in Cardross of the hero king, who appointed me doorkeeper. He was now so frail that he could only see a few people a day, and then only for a few minutes each. At length came an order.

"Davie, I must talk to the twenty best men. Please select them and bring them to my presence that I may address them for the last time."

This was a difficult task, but eventually I wrote the names of twenty on a piece of paper and read them out to the king: Randolph, Douglas, de la Haye, Keith, Boyd, Macdonald, Fraser, Stewart, and the others, right through to the end.

"You have chosen well, Davie. Call them in now."

I stood at the door and pronounced the names, and they filed in until the room was full. Then the king addressed them, saying that he must die bravely, as all men should. *"Lordingus, it is gane with me that thar is nocht bot ane, that is the ded withouten dreid."* He then asked that his heart be sent to the Holy Land, and that the assembled twenty should choose one knight among them to do so. *"I wald the hert were thidder sent, that ye amang yow cheiss me ane, ane nobill knycht that be honest wiss and wycht."*

Almost immediately James Douglas was nominated and

unanimously approved for the task. At this Douglas knelt at the deathbed, weeping as no one who had ever seen this brave man do before. *"For yow schir will I blithly mak this travell gif god will me gif space so lange till liff."*

After this speech, most of the twenty cried openly. After they all left the room, I approached the king.

"Sir, is there any other thing I may do?" He didn't answer right away, and I feared he might have died, but with one finger he beckoned me to come closer.

"Send for Isabel," he said.

I immediately went to the anteroom, where I knew she would be.

"He wants to see you," I said taking her gently by the arm, guiding her to the bed.

The king's face brightened at the sight of her. She walked gracefully into the room, tall and radiantly beautiful, dressed in a long blue gown that set off her azure eyes and snow-white hair. She took hold of his hand.

"I have always loved you," he said in a soft voice. Then suddenly his sallow complexion changed to a chalky white. The life had gone out of him. Robert the Bruce was dead.

IV

It was, I am sure, the largest funeral ever seen in Scotland. The king's body was embalmed, his ribcage sawn open, and his brave heart extracted. His body was escorted by the flower of the Scottish nobility and carried across the country from Cardross to Dunfermline Abbey for burial with

other kings and queens of the realm. The journey took
days, and all along the way the people turned out to pay
their respect to the greatest man their country had yet produced. He had given us freedom, the most important thing
there is, as our letter from Arbroath to the pope had proclaimed. Freedom, it said, which no good man loses but
with his life.

CHAPTER TWENTY-ONE

Highlander

Just a few days before King Robert's death, he gave me a document, signed and sealed by himself, granting me a small estate in Argyllshire. I think he had made some sort of arrangement with one of the Campbells in order to get me this property. He said it was a gift for the recent service I had performed, and he asked me, in consideration, if I would convey Lady Isabel to her estate. Of course I agreed. The lady had not attended the funeral, so when I returned to Cardross she was ready to go. We took three horses, two to ride and one for her baggage.

It was a journey of only a few days, and when we arrived I realised that my new land was actually quite near to hers; only a few miles separated the two estates. I was anxious to get to my family in Dumfries, so we said good-bye, and she thanked me for all the services I had performed for her over the years.

"I am particularly grateful, Davie, for the grace of your presence during difficult situations."

I considered this to be one of the greatest compliments ever paid to me. Then she gave me another of those kisses, the soft touch that had stunned me as a youth when I had first met her.

A few days later I was back in Dumfries, and I lived in peace with my family there for several years. Late in that year of 1329 my mother died of some pestilence that the rest of the family escaped. I mourned her deeply, and realised that I had always taken her for granted. I missed her, and wondered why it is that people don't see what they have before it is too late to say "Thank you for all you have done" in a proper way. At least I got the words out, or something like them, while she lay dying.

At the end of the next year I was sickened to receive the news that Sir James Douglas had been killed in a battle in Spain en route to the Holy Land. Sir James had died wearing a leaden case around his neck, which held the heart of our brave king. Most of the Scottish party was killed, but Sir William Keith survived to bring King Robert's heart back to Scotland. It was buried, reverently, in Melrose Abbey. I was greatly sorrowed, of course. Next to King Robert, James Douglas was the best man I ever met.

In 1332, Thomas Randolph, Earl of Moray and Regent of Scotland, died—of poison, it was said. Thus, both the regents appointed for little King David II were now gone. This was a calamity for Scotland, and the vultures began circling. There were all sorts of conspiracies to wrest the throne from the boy King David. It was very depressing. Worse was to come. In the summer of 1333, King Edward III repudiated the treaty we had done so much to obtain and came north with a large army. My son Seumas was now twenty-four and demanded to join the Scottish army. What could I say? I tried to dissuade him, but it was useless. He wanted to imitate me and help to preserve the freedom of the realm of Scotland. I gave him a horse, some weapons, and armour that had served me well, and sent him off. I never saw him again. There was a great battle, nay, massacre of our forces at Halidon Hill near Berwick. Most of the Scots were killed. King David tried hard to emulate his father and fought bravely, but he was only a shadow of Robert the Bruce. King David was able to escape the battlefield, and the king of France gave him asylum at the Château Gaillard on the Seine, which Thomas Randolph and I had seen on our visit to the pope so long ago.

So it was now that I, David Crawford, was to have no male heir. I couldn't stand Dumfries then. It held too many bitter memories, so I moved Màiri and our daughter, Ishbel, to the new place in Argyll, and left the Dumfries estate in charge of my tenant.

Our life in the Highlands was fine, but Scotland was in turmoil again, and the glorious life I had been privileged to live eventually fell apart. In 1352 Màiri died. She is buried nearby, and for years I visited her grave every day. She had taken a fever, but I don't know if that is all of it. She had never got over the death of Seumas. I hadn't, either, but somehow I think that women suffer more than do men in such a situation. It was after Màiri's death that I began to think about writing this memoir, and I started to recall information, note it, and put it in order. Writing implements were not always easy to find in Argyll, and there were years when I would write nothing. But I kept after it, and it began to take shape.

My daughter Ishbel married and left to live in Edinburgh, so that I was all alone in Argyll. Alone, except for the presence, nearby, of the former Countess of Buchan. We took to seeing each other, and even to staying in each other's houses. Often we slept together. We were both terribly alone, and nights when the weather was foul and the rain hit hard on the roof, sharing a fireplace, a meal, a jug, and the warmth of a bed were marvellous tonics for us both.

I showed Isabel the beginnings of my manuscript and she read it avidly, and made suggestions. Her favourable opinion inspired me and I had made progress on it by 1371, when King David II died childless. There would be no Bruce dynasty. Robert Stewart, the grandson of King Robert the Bruce, was made King Robert II. I wondered if those Stewarts would ever have a lasting dynasty. I wasn't sure they were cut out for it. But then I realised that no one was really worthy to follow in the line of the Bruce.

King Robert was a warrior unparalleled, I believe, in history. When he started on his course, that cold night in Dumfries, he had many powerful enemies, almost no resources, and only a handful of friends. Scotland was heavily garrisoned and occupied by thousands of English soldiers. The odds against him were overwhelming, yet he freed Scotland by his iron will and unusual intelligence. He regained or even in some cases won the high standing in the world that Scotland now enjoys. Throughout the course of his life he insisted on the concept of a Scottish nation, which he carefully melded into being out of the country's diverse ethnic origins. King Robert always believed that all are Scots, whether our names are French, Scandinavian, Gaelic, Welsh, Flemish, or Anglian in origin. As an administrator of law and justice, he became Good King Robert in the minds of most of us. He was always fair and held few grudges, making himself a prime example of magnanimity. During his rule, Scotland prospered as never before.

Most of all, King Robert taught us that tyranny must be opposed at any and all cost; that there is no price too high to pay for freedom. These are lessons that, I believe, will be remembered forever.

My daughter visited me for the Hogmanay season in 1374. She, too, expressed interest in my manuscript, and cautioned me to protect it.

"Father," she said to me, "I am proud of the life you have lived and of your close relationship with King Robert. Your manuscript is our family legacy, but when the history books are written, you will not be mentioned. You have no title, you were captain of no troops. Yet you were a trusted servant of the king and of great importance to the cause of Scottish liberty. By your writing, people will forever know what you did. Even more important, perhaps, is that you write as an eyewitness to so many events. You can testify to episodes that otherwise would remain hidden forever from other historians. You must finish the book, Father, and you must protect it. Have you tried to find someone to copy it and preserve it?"

"I have tried, daughter, to interest someone, the government, the Church, anyone to preserve the work, but have not been successful. Someone in Aberdeen, Barbour I think his name is, is already completing a story of the Bruce and the War of Independence in poetry, and is about to have it put forth. Here in rural Argyll I haven't much chance."

I told my daughter I agreed with her, however, and that I would bring the story to as swift a conclusion as I could manage. Implicit in her concern was my age and the fact that I lived alone. When I died, which could be soon, my work might be destroyed by vandals or otherwise just lost as a result of the neglect of whoever found it. Perhaps it would make good kindling for someone's hearth.

As a result of these conversations, I resolved to write the rest of the book as soon as possible. I thought my daughter could then take it with her to Edinburgh, where she would eventually find someone interested in it. But she would not stay, saying she would have to return to her husband in a few days.

"Very well, then," I said to her. "When it is complete I will bury the book in the ground, so that when I die you will be able to come here and retrieve it. I will bury it in a leaden box near my stone dyke." I showed her the spot exactly. A week later she left for Edinburgh, urging me to finish the work and promising to keep it safe for posterity.

Rest

In early 1375 Isabel, the former countess, died. It was very sad for me; I was after that completely alone in the world. To the end she had been dignified, and remained beautiful. I cannot forget her, nor, of course, my beautiful Màiri, the love of my life. Men need women, if only to remember.

It is now late in 1376 as I complete this work. My daughter has not returned to visit me. I can only wonder why and hope she is very busy in the city and safe from misfortune. I see no one except an occasional hunter or traveller for whom I always provide the Highland hospitality, which is expected in these parts. I have forgot a great deal of the Scots language, and have had few occasions to speak anything but Gaelic these past years. I am old now, having passed my eighty-fourth year, and much afflicted by pains in my joints. It is harder each year to walk, and I feel also some discomfort in my chest, and have difficulty breathing, which makes me think that my heart is beginning to fail me. I have already exceeded the three score and ten years promised in Scripture. It is time to end this discussion. It is Saint Andrew's Day morning, and I have decided to bury this manuscript before the sun falls today. I worry that my daughter will not come soon to retrieve the work. I realise, sadly, that she may never come. I am forced to admit she may be dead, in which case it may be years or even centuries before this book is discovered. By that time it may be difficult to read. I know that languages change over time and that the Scots, French, and Gaelic herein may have to be translated. If so, I hope someone will find the work to be worthy of the effort.

The Great Scot

Argyll is a beautiful place. The reflection of the low green hills in the blue loch below my house is lovely, but in winter Argyll can be cruel. A cold November wind finds its way through the cracks in the walls of my dwelling. Seated alone before my hearth, the peat fire dances and casts shadows on the floor, and I think of what might have been. I wish I could have been more educated like my friend Alexander Bruce, King Robert's brother. Had I been younger, I might have been a candidate for admission to the Scots College in Paris. But no man can have everything he wishes, and I do not complain. I was a warrior in a great and successful cause, and was neither killed nor maimed. I became rich. I had a beautiful family. I was on close terms with several brilliant and famous men and women. I was privileged to have known and served one of the greatest men in history. There will never be another like Robert Bruce.

At night, before I go to sleep, I can still hear the clash of swords, the heavy breathing of the horses, the cries of men in combat. I can smell the blood and I can exult in the thrill of victory. You can read your historians, but I was there.

DAVID CRAWFORD

ARDNABREAC, ARGYLL

NOVEMBER 30, 1376

Acknowledgments

I would like to thank several people who long ago assisted me in becoming a writer: my mother, Marian Bruce, who taught me to read before I went to school, and my father, A. Duncan Bruce, who instilled in me his love of words and literature. Teachers who encouraged me include Elizabeth Miller and Elizabeth McClure, and two instructors at the University of Pennsylvania who I remember only as Mr. Rosenberry and Mr. Biswanger. I also thank my wife, Tamara, for her constant support. She read early drafts and made suggestions, as did my daughter Elizabeth. Thanks also to my daughter Jennifer, who insisted for several years that I write this book. If she hadn't it wouldn't exist. Thanks also for her corrections. Thanks to Lord Elgin for helpful suggestions and comments. Adam Bruce answered questions about the Bruces. Bill Eakins was generous in

Acknowledgments

lending his time and knowledge in correcting my Gaelic. Dr. David H. Caldwell of the National Museums of Scotland provided helpful period information. Bernard Adnet taught me about fencing and the French language. Martha Jaeckle and Bob Crawford were, as usual, supportive. My editor, Truman Talley, and St. Martin's Press made the book possible.

Bibliography

There are many sources for the subject of Robert Bruce and the Scottish War of Independence. The most important is *The Bruce*, by John Barbour, written in 1375. In quoting I have relied on my 1870 copy printed in London. In 1997 a new version of *The Bruce*, with an excellent translation, was produced by A.A.M. Duncan in Scotland. There are other old works such as Walter Bower's *Scotichronicon* and the *Chronicle of Lanercost*, the latter presenting the English (not at all favourable) view of the events. Also interesting are Thomas Gray's *Scalacronica*, and *Orygynale Cronykil of Scotland* of Andrew of Wyntoun.

In the last third of the twentieth century two really excellent books based on deep scholarship of most materials available were produced. The first, *Robert Bruce and the*

Bibliography

Community of the Realm of Scotland, by Geoffrey W. S. Barrow, is the more comprehensive. *Robert the Bruce King of Scots,* by Ronald McNair Scott, is easy to read and adheres to the chronology of events.

Also helpful are *Robert the Bruce,* by Eric Linklater, *The Battle of Banockburn,* by W. M. Mackenzie, and *Bannockburn,* by Peter Reese. *The Wars of the Bruces,* by Colm McNamee, is good for the campaigns in Ireland and England. *On the Trail of Robert the Bruce,* by David R. Ross, is excellent for geographical perspective. The story of the Declaration of Arbroath is well told in *'For Freedom Alone,'* by Edward J. Cowan.